UNDYING HUNGER

A Novel of the Enclave

JESSICA LEE

Entangled Publishing, LLC
2614 South Timberline Road
Suite 109
Fort Collins, CO 80525
Visit our website at www.entangledpublishing.com.

Select Otherworld is an imprint of Entangled Publishing, LLC.

Edited by Erin Molta
Cover design by L.J. Anderson of Mayhem Cover Creations
Cover art by iStock

Manufactured in the United States of America

First Edition June 2015

For my husband and son, who are my world and my inspiration. You make everything sweeter.

Chapter One

Being a third wheel sucked big hairy balls.

Alexandria Stevens plastered another *I'm having a great time* smile on her face and glanced over at Eve Devonshire. With Guerin Lombardi's arm wrapped possessively around her, the tall brunette walked quietly next to Alex along the sidewalks of Elizabeth Bay, South Carolina's bustling nightlife district. Yet Alex hadn't missed the numerous heated looks between the two. Or the occasional caress against the side of Eve's breast when Guerin's hand accidentally slipped from his mate's shoulder—actions that telegraphed loud and clear they wished to be alone but were too polite to get rid of her.

Dear God, remind me why I let Eve talk me into going out for a solid meal and shopping with them? Vampires don't even have to eat!

"I'm glad you decided to join us," Eve said. "I know the walls of the Enclave mansion must get claustrophobic for you sometimes."

"You have no idea," Alex groaned, swinging the sack containing her purchase from one of those twenty-four-hour superstores. "But I know you two don't get many nights out as a couple. It's either you or Kenric and Arran on constant patrol rotation." With the Enclave having lost two of its male warriors, only three of them were left to protect humans from the vampires who couldn't control their blood lust, thus they became mindless beasts addicted to Death Euphoria or DEAD. That meant they always killed when they fed. Now, at least, they had Eve to help in that fight. Even though Kenric, Eve's father and master of the Enclave, as well as Guerin hated the idea of putting Eve at risk on the streets. But good luck with trying to keep her friend from doing something she was determined to do. Like the shopping trip she'd insisted Alex tag along on tonight. Alex lifted the red-and-white bag for reference. "You know this could have waited."

"Maybe," Guerin interjected, surprising Alex. He slowed their pace, pinning her with his dark gaze. "But you shouldn't have to."

Alex's chest tightened at his kind words, and she swung her attention to the traffic buzzing past them.

A year ago, going out wouldn't have been a big event. But that had been before the blinders shielding her from the real world had been brutally ripped away. Before she'd learned the truth about the monsters lurking in the dark.

Before she'd been turned into one of them.

The warmth of Eve's palm brushed Alex's arm, drawing her back. "Living among a bunch of overbearing alpha men can be a bit oppressive sometimes."

"Really?" Guerin rumbled. "Overbearing?"

Eve rolled her eyes, but her expression contained a humorous grin. "Yes." She propped a hand on her leather-clad hip. "But I know how to handle you."

A growl rolled off the dark-eyed male vampire right before he cupped Eve's nape, placing them face-to-face, hip to hip. "Later, you and I will have to discuss *how* you 'handle' me."

"I look forward to it," Eve whispered, yet thanks to Alex's heightened hearing, she didn't miss the lust infused in her friend's reply to her mate.

Christ, this night couldn't end soon enough.

"You're still very young, Alex," Eve said, returning to their previous topic. "And not at your full strength."

"I know. I know." Alex waved a dismissive hand. "My sister and I have had this discussion more times than you can imagine. *I'm only trying to protect you, Alex. Make sure you don't screw up and reveal yourself by accident, or get caught out here with a bunch of DEADs who might want to use you for target practice.*" God, it was ridiculous that she could quote Elle verbatim by now. She sighed. "I understand. I do." Alex came to a stop and faced them. "I'm just so sick of being the proverbial damsel-in-distress." She rolled her eyes. "You have to understand, before all this happened, I had a life of my own and a career. I was an aesthetician and had a nice job at a day spa back in Fairfield. I was an independent woman with hopes and dreams." She shook her head. "It boggles my mind how someone's life can be irrecoverably changed so quickly by one simple, seemingly innocent choice."

"Believe me," Eve said. "I get where you're coming

from." She stepped in and wrapped her arms around Alex, giving her a slight squeeze. "I really do."

"I envy you," Alex whispered, fighting the sudden wave of melancholy threatening to drag her under.

Eve pulled away, tucking a fallen strand of hair behind her ear. "I wouldn't wish my life, before Guerin and the Enclave, on anyone." She scoffed. "On the run and hidden from the world since the day I took my first breath. Why in the world would you envy me?"

"Because you've made peace with what you are," Alex said. "You're strong and confident, and go after what you want without apologies." She could barely recall what it felt like to be comfortable in her own skin.

"You have to remember how old I am, hon." Eve smiled, and the warmth spread to her eyes. She leaned in, her voice lowering. "Growing up not quite human, yet not completely a vampire, at times it's been hell. But I've had three centuries to come to terms with what I am…but please don't share those numbers with my mate." She smirked. "I wouldn't want him getting the idea I'm an old woman."

Laughter bubbled up from Alex. She couldn't help it. Eve had a way of making her feel better.

"Hey, old lady," Guerin called out. "We should probably be getting back."

"Watch it, Lombardi." Eve spun around and clasped her mate beneath his chin in a move no other male or female would dare attempt with the Enclave's second-in-command. Badass rolled off the six-foot-plus vampire in waves. "Look who's calling whom old. I do believe you've got a few years on me."

Guerin laughed. When it came to Eve, she seemed to

get away with just about anything with him. They were so in sync.

Perfect together.

A connection Alex couldn't imagine ever having with a man. The thought of allowing a male to get that close and under her skin…

Memories of a dark-haired vampire with eyes the color of brewing storm clouds flashed across her mind's eye. Unbidden, the scent of chocolate and cinnamon invaded her nostrils, as if his flesh was once more pressed against hers, his essence filling her mouth, warming her veins. The hairs on her arms and legs stood on end, and her sex swelled to the point she literally ached with need.

Markus.

A tremor rolled over her. Alex's fists clenched, fighting her growing arousal. Closing her eyes, she willed the images to fade with every ounce of strength she could summon.

"Alex…? Are you okay?" Eve's fingers wrapped around her arm, yanking Alex back into the present.

Alex blinked. "Yeah. I'm fine." She did her best to laugh it off. "Just got lost in thought for a minute there."

"That must have been some daydream." Eve grinned. "Where were you?"

Swallowing hard at the lump of panic swelling at the back of her throat, Alex scrambled for something—anything—other than the truth about where her thoughts had gone. Because how was she supposed to reveal the fact that she'd been fantasizing about a male whom she should hate with every fiber of her being? The one who'd turned her into a vampire and held her prisoner. The male who'd betrayed the entire Enclave by hooking up with their enemy, Marguerite

Devonshire. And what was worse…the daydream about Markus hadn't been her first.

How could she explain feelings she didn't understand herself? Was it only lust? Or had something deeper been formed during her time with him? Mentally she shook herself. Stockholm syndrome. That had to be it. Her "attachment" to the male had to be a result of her captivity. Nothing more.

"*Uhm…*" Alex licked her lips, her mouth suddenly dry. "Just reminiscing about the past. That's all."

The past. She nearly choked on the ridiculousness of her explanation. There was so much she couldn't even remember about the weeks she'd spent as Markus's captive in Marguerite's stronghold last year. Marguerite, the insanely powerful female vampire who centuries ago had tortured and sired Kenric St. James—the leader of their band of warriors—had miraculously given birth to Eve. She still found it hard to wrap her mind around the fact that such an evil creature had been her friend's mother.

Large gaping holes of just…nothing taunted her.

And the black emptiness of those nights gnawed away at her insides like blank pages in a book screaming to be filled. She was the author suffering from writer's block.

Yet every time she tried to convey to her sister how much she needed answers, Elle insisted maybe it was for the best that she never remembered and that she should consider her amnesia as some kind of psychological grace. Sort of like the mercy bestowed by the mind when waking and not remembering a nightmare. Because no doubt, that's what she'd endured. A nightmare.

But she wanted to know. She had to know. Markus

was the man who'd turned her, held her against her will for weeks, but he was also the same man who, she'd been told, had killed Marguerite to save Alex. How had someone who'd done something so cruel to her turn around and be her savior, too? Markus was the personification of the term antihero.

She shook her head.

But Elle was probably right. Alex needed to let him go.

Move forward. Don't look back and all that shit. Easy, right?

"Alex, are you sure you're okay?" Eve's gaze narrowed on her.

"Hold up." Guerin came to a dead halt, his palm against Eve's back. "Do you hear that?"

No. Alex hadn't heard anything beyond the beating of her heart. But she thanked God for the interruption and the distraction.

Eve cocked her head, then nodded. "Yeah. I do." She glanced up at her mate. "Damn."

"What's going on?" Alex scanned their surroundings. Based on the sudden spike in tension between the duo, something was going down.

"Alex, stay close to Eve," Guerin said, sliding his hand inside his knee-length leather coat where the warriors stashed their weapons. "But let us handle this."

He brushed past her and Eve followed, hooking her arm with Alex's and tugging her along.

"If you listen closely," Eve whispered. "You'll hear what sounds like muffled cries."

"DEADs?" Alex's pulse surged at the thought.

Eve nodded. "That's what we're going to find out."

Shit. Alex quickly sifted through the roar of the traffic and the chatter of the crowd passing by for what Eve and Guerin had detected. One by one, she compartmentalized the noises, checking them off and dismissing what she didn't need until finally Alex heard what she'd been seeking. In the distance, the distressed sound of panic—terror.

"Oh God," Alex muttered as her gut twisted. Images of the night she'd been herded into the basement of the nightclub Wicked Ways flashed across her mind like the flickering faces on a deck of cards. She may not remember everything that had happened to her afterward, but what she'd seen there, what she'd experienced in that room—residual talons of fear dug into her abdomen and nausea swelled—she'd never forget.

At the next alley, they ducked inside and the whimpering sounds became louder, clearer. Guerin picked up his pace as if he'd homed in on his target's exact location. From the back of her waistband, Eve withdrew a dagger. She palmed the hilt and twirled the blade before finally allowing it to settle into her grip.

"Stay behind me," Eve ordered, releasing her hold on Alex and closing in on her mate.

With Guerin and Eve leading the way, they reached the end of the corridor and came to a halt. Guerin nodded and pointed left. Alex glanced in the direction he'd indicated, and her stomach roiled. In the narrow path that ran behind the row of businesses, two feasting vampires—DEADs— had a couple of humans on the ground near a Dumpster. Growls and sucking sounds filled Alex's ears. Bile surged to the back of her throat.

"Time to say good-night, boys," Guerin called out and

marched forward, the blade in his hand glinting beneath the pale yellow glow of the streetlight. "Permanently."

Their heads jerked up in unison, a pissed-off hiss spewing from between their teeth.

"Fuck off," the DEAD on the left, with long, stringy black hair, spat.

"Not going to happen," Guerin replied. "But we'll gladly fuck you up."

Unfortunately, based on the amount of blood covering the DEADs' faces and clothes and pooling beneath their prey, it was too late for the humans. But Alex understood, as well as Guerin and Eve, that these monsters couldn't be allowed to continue terrorizing the people of Elizabeth Bay.

Guerin leaped into the air toward the one dark-haired DEAD. With his fangs bared, blood and saliva dripping from his chin, the creature lunged at the warrior. They slammed into each other with a solid *thud*, Guerin's blade slicing across the male's chest before they crashed back to earth. A crimson stream sprayed from the addict's torso.

Oh shit! Alex watched, her back plastered against the wooden slates of the fence as the other DEAD charged toward Eve, his claws extended. But Eve didn't flinch. Dressed in body-hugging leather, she stood her ground, a silver-plated dagger tight in her grip, her obsidian tresses lifting behind her like a dark veil. The female was stunning. Lethal. It was no wonder that Guerin was completely in love with her.

The DEAD roared, took flight, aiming straight for Eve's head. In a move born straight out of *The Matrix*, the female warrior jumped, spun, and like a blender on high, carved the descending DEAD's midsection open.

Oh yeah. Eve kicked ass.

The injured vampire fell to the concrete, a putrid smoke rising from his wounds due to the reaction of his flesh to Eve's silver blade. Alex covered her nose with the back of her hand in an attempt to block the nasty smell from her nasal passages.

"Well, hello, beautiful," a deep male voice said, coming out of nowhere and catching her off guard.

Alex jerked her head away from the carnage and looked toward the newcomer. A few feet away stood a man wearing a dark leather jacket that stopped at his hips. Long hair that nearly matched the cowhide skimmed his slim shoulders, and skin the color of decadent chocolate gleamed in the dimly lit alley. He sauntered a little closer, his midnight eyes boring into hers. Unease crawled under her skin. The kind that said she'd be better off anywhere but here.

"Who are you?" Judging by his lack of surprise at the macabre scene playing out before them, he had to be a vampire. "What do you want?"

The stranger cocked his head as if puzzled, then a corner of his mouth lifted, forming a sly grin. One that revealed the sharp point of a fang.

"What the hell!" Guerin called out from behind her.

Glancing over her shoulder, Alex glimpsed the Enclave's second-in-command as he yanked his dagger from the heart of the deceased addict, his glare pinned on their new arrival. The corpse sizzled and smoke billowed from the chest. Then it bloated, seconds before imploding, leaving nothing but dust. Alex blinked. Damn, she'd heard about the effects of silver driven straight into the heart, but this was the first time she'd witnessed the rapid decomposition.

"Enrique, you son of a bitch," Guerin spat, his boots

eating up the concrete between them. "Get away from her!"

"Enrique," Alex mumbled, her blood running cold at the sound of a name she hadn't heard since — since...

"Tell Markus he should keep a tighter hold on what's his," Enrique whispered, his voice closer than before, drawing her attention back to him as if she were a fish snagged on his line. He reached out, his fingers coming within a hairbreadth of her cheek before reflex had her knocking his hand away. "Or he just might lose it."

Guerin slammed into the male with a hard *thud*. Enrique stumbled back, laughter rolling from him.

Eve rushed to her mate's side, her weapon bloodied from her battle with the DEAD, but ready in her palm. "Who the hell is this?"

Enrique sobered and straightened, his focus narrowing on Eve. "Well, well... Who do we have here? A female Enclave warrior?"

"Marguerite's former commander," Guerin said. "Enrique — "

"Enrique Mateo," the other male interrupted, and bowed. "And you are?" He tilted his head.

"She's no one to you," Guerin barked.

"Ah, of course." Enrique chuckled. "Protective, are we?" He shook his head. "There is nothing to fear from me. I was just...passing through." He shrugged. "Alexandria..."

Alex tensed, but nailed him with a hard glare.

"Please tell Markus I said hello, and remind him of what I said." His lips puckered, and he kissed the air in her direction right before his form shimmered. He was gone.

A shiver raced up Alex's spine as if death itself had brushed her soul. Flashes of images assaulted her mind.

Her, in a small room, sitting on the edge of a bed. Markus standing in front of her, angry…so angry. His words clipped, heated, ricocheting off her skull like a mallet. But his bitter venom wasn't aimed at her. *No.* Someone else hovered at the edge of her vision.

A male.

There, by the door… *Enrique.*

Markus's rage was directed at him.

Oh God, she was in Marguerite's den. Her heart raced with desperation. The primal urge to run singed her veins. *Get out!* her mind screamed. But she couldn't move.

Trapped.

Dear God. I'm trapped here.

"Alex." Guerin clasped her arm, yanking her back to the present. Her breath hitched, and her head swam. If not for the hold Guerin had on her, she would have stumbled. Alex blinked, forcing herself to comprehend what Guerin was saying.

"I'm sorry," she murmured. "What?"

"I said, what the hell was Enrique talking about?"

That was an excellent question. She shuffled through the confusing array of memories once more. They were like pieces of a puzzle, but she didn't have the picture to help decipher how to put them all together.

There was only one way to fill the voids in her memories and discover what Enrique was getting at. She couldn't escape Markus's presence in her daydreams, and now the traitor's dangerous past was bleeding into her conscious reality.

Alex looked up at Guerin. "I want to see Markus." And God help her, she wouldn't leave his cell without answers.

Chapter Two

The mental compulsion holding his head in place and forcing his throat to convulse on the thick liquid pulsing into his mouth finally eased.

Markus Santini jerked away from Kenric St. James's wrist. "Get the fuck away from me!"

The master vampire's essence lingered inside his mouth and on his taste buds like sour milk. Markus lowered his head and spat, the putrid substance splattering the white tiled floor with specks of crimson near the other male's boots. For more than a century, the lust for blood had fueled a hunger so fierce the pain of its absence had taken him to his knees until he had obeyed its call. Yet now...

Death held a more decadent allure than what his former master offered from his wrist.

"I don't know why I keep this up—keep coming back, attempting to will my blood down your throat." Kenric shook his head. "If you're too much of a coward to live, I should just toss your sorry ass into the sun."

"Sounds like a plan to me," Markus drawled before lying back on his cot, rolling over toward the wall and closing his eyes. He didn't get why Kenric kept coming back either. Markus, for damn sure, would have given up on someone like him after a couple of weeks, never mind almost a year later. The master was relentless with his insane idea and hope that Markus might one day return to the Enclave.

Fucking crazy.

The rest of the Enclave's warriors would never trust him again or welcome his return to the fold. And with good reason.

He'd betrayed them. He was a traitor, and they weren't idiots. Hell, if the right situation presented itself, who was to say he wouldn't turn on them again? After the number Marguerite had done on his head... He didn't recognize the male staring back at him from the mirror. Yet Kenric, even with all his power, couldn't seem to comprehend the depth of the stain on Markus's soul.

Markus sighed, and for a moment, he was mentally transported back to Fairfield. Silver bars had held him there as well, imprisoned by his fellow warriors after Arran and Elle had tracked him and Marguerite there during Elle's search for her sister, Alexandria. That cage was just like the one that contained him now, in the basement of the Enclave headquarters/mansion. Except his current residence possessed three solid walls with the latticework of the poisonous metal hidden within the drywall to prevent his escape by phasing. Not a good idea, unless he wanted to materialize on the other side looking like a waffle fry.

Inhaling through his nostrils, Markus recalled that

pivotal night, the moment Kenric had offered his "deal."

"But there is another choice—a deal—one I'd be willing to make for Elle. For one of my former Enclave warriors."

Kenric stood with one arm wrapped around his mate. Markus spun on his heels, facing them.

"A deal..." What the hell? And based on the shocked look plastered on the face of Guerin, his commander, whatever he'd cooked up wasn't something that had been part of their little plan.

"I understand the physical pain involved in walking away from Marguerite, from her ancient blood. But mine, a master's blood, is as potent as an ancient's, if not more so."

"Your point?" Markus stated, edging forward.

"I offer this: give us Alexandria back, and I will help you escape Marguerite's hold."

Rolling onto his back, Markus opened his eyes and stared at the drop ceiling's tiles.

Alexandria.

His heart jerked behind his sternum at the sound of her name pinging off the inside of his cranium. *Dammit!* How many months—years—would it take? How long would ever be long enough to truly let her go? As hard as he'd fought against it, the dark-haired vixen had gotten under his skin. Made him feel something more than rage. He despised what Marguerite had aroused inside him, but he'd never regret the night he met Alexandria.

Fisting the thin cotton of his shirt over his breastbone, he twisted the material, his nails scoring the flesh beneath. If only he had the balls to shove his clawed fingers through, rip the defiant muscle from its hiding place, and be done with it. Be done with his fucked-up excuse for a life.

Physically, Markus had let Alexandria go as he'd promised. Released her mind from his psychological control, and had erased most of her memories of their time together. He hadn't initially planned it, to take her memories. The mental hold on her mind had been enough of an assault on someone as strong-willed as Alexandria. But after everything she'd been through during her time with him and Marguerite, Alexandria had deserved a fresh start. A chance for at least some semblance of a normal life. And if he were honest with himself, part of the reason he'd wiped her slate clean had been purely selfish. She would already despise the fact that he was her sire, but perhaps she wouldn't detest him—forever—if she didn't know how far he'd gone. He'd not only been the one who'd destroyed her human side, but for a while, he'd also controlled her like a puppeteer. Her mind had been his. But the only reason he'd gone so far—taken her will away—was because if he hadn't gotten control of the spirited female, Marguerite would have destroyed them both. And that was something he had refused to allow.

He hated it—hated himself for what he'd done—but at the time, he couldn't take the chance of Marguerite becoming suspicious that his feelings for Alexandria went beyond a temporary curiosity.

What happened back then needed to stay buried. She'd loathe him even more than she already did if the truth ever came out. Luckily, Alexandria's sister, Elle, had felt exactly the same way. *"Alex is better off never remembering how you manipulated her mind."*

He wasn't the only one keeping secrets from the raven-haired vixen. And he couldn't help but wonder how much destruction that bomb would wreak on Elle's relationship with Alexandria if it ever surfaced.

A grunt that relayed a mix of frustration and disgust came from Kenric, tugging Markus back to the present. "I'm out of here," the master said.

Opening his eyes, Markus listened as the soles of the male's boots thumped off the tile, telegraphing his exit. The cage door clanked shut, and the sound ricocheted off the walls and washed over Markus with a stinging, icy wave. He shivered. From the sound? The hunger? Who the hell knew? It wasn't like it fucking mattered, anyway. Soon he'd cease to exist, to breathe, his brain cells dormant, and Kenric would put him to ground.

He'd be free. Finally free from the demons riding him inside his head.

The exterior door *snick*ed open. "I want to see him," a female said.

Alexandria.

He'd know that voice anywhere. Even from his grave.

Every neuron in Markus's brain fired. What the hell was she doing here in the basement of the Enclave mansion?

"Tell her this isn't a good idea, Kenric." It was Guerin who spoke up. Of course. The bastard hated him.

"What's going on?" Kenric asked. "Why do you need to see him?"

"I just need to talk to him," she said.

"We ran into some DEADs tonight," Guerin said, "and Enrique popped in."

What the fuck?

That dose of info made what blood he had left in his veins surge, laced with adrenaline. Markus rolled over and up onto the side of his bed, his joints rebelling.

"Enrique?" Kenric rumbled. "I had no idea the asshole could function without Marguerite's direction. What in hell did he want?"

"You'll have to ask Alexandria," Guerin replied.

"What does that mean?"

"He mentioned something about Markus to me," she patiently added, but Markus didn't miss the sound of growing frustration in her voice. "I just need to speak to him first. Then if you want, we can talk."

Markus's pulse roared inside his head. *What had Enrique told her?*

Closing his eyes, he drew in a calming breath, his mind returning to the female who stood only a few feet away. It had been at least a year since he'd last seen her. How would Alexandria look? Had she changed? Did the fire still burn in her violet gaze?

"Fine," Kenric said. "I'll take you to him."

"No."

She wanted to see him. Alone. Markus pushed from the mattress, steadying himself on his feet. Anticipation hummed inside his veins.

"I don't think that's a good idea," Kenric said, his tone firm.

"Are you implying he's dangerous—even from the other side of your silver cage?"

A corner of Markus's mouth curled. The little vixen hadn't lost her fire. Alexandria had never taken no for an answer.

Kenric sighed. "It's not that he's dangerous per se. Not in his current state—"

"Then I'd like to speak to him in private," she said. After

a second or two of tension-filled silence, she added, "Please."

"Anyone ever tell you that you're a tad stubborn?" Kenric asked.

"Maybe once or twice," she said. "But I like to think of it as being relentlessly determined. Will you give me some time to speak with Markus…alone?"

"We'll be on the other side of that door," the master vampire said. "Call out, and we'll be in here before you can blink."

"This may take a while. I need some answers from him about a few things, and I'm pretty sure getting him to cooperate won't be something that happens quickly."

"Getting Markus to do anything that isn't his idea is never an easy task," Kenric said.

"Exactly," she said. "Give me a little time, okay? Like you said, he can't hurt me from the other side of the bars."

"I don't like it," Kenric replied. "But if this is something you feel you really need to do, I understand."

"It is."

A moment later, the exterior door thumped shut. And Markus found that the desire for his next breath had vanished. He shoved the thick strands of dark hair partially covering his eyes back, then coiled his fingers into a tight fist at his side. Then she was there.

Alexandria strode in front of the cage's door. She wore her blue-black locks loose, the ends curling, nearly brushing her firm, denim-covered ass. Damn. His cock swelled. Her hips swayed with every step, the heels of her boots clicking off the cement floor. He raked the female with a gaze from the slender curves of her legs and the swell of her calves hidden behind the black leather all the way back up to the narrow belt sitting low on her hip bones. A short black leather jacket covered her arms, but the tail of her purple blouse didn't quite make it to her waistband, leaving a tantalizing peek of smooth, creamy skin for him to obsess over. He flexed his fingers at the sight, the pads itching to stroke her exposed flesh. Would she quiver under his touch?

She stopped, but didn't turn in his direction. Instead, Alexandria continued to stare at the wall, inhaling deeply as if she were building up her nerve to face her maker.

Come on, Vixen. Look at me. Let me see your face.

Slowly, she rotated on her heels, searching the expanse of his room. Searching for him. At last, her head swiveled, and he didn't need his sight to know when she found him. The gasp exiting her lungs told Markus the moment it happened. He glanced down at his arms to where the skin hung loose on his bones. Opening and closing his fist, the knuckles appeared bulbous compared to the frail-looking digits extending outward from the hinges. He had to look like shit. Death-on-a-stick pathetic.

"Markus?" Her voice was hushed as if she were afraid if she spoke too loudly he'd break.

Shit. He wasn't that damn fragile.

"I may not look like you remember, Vixen, but I'm pretty sure I can endure a conversation."

"Vixen?" A perfectly arched brow rose on her heart-shaped face. "Is that what you used to call me?" She scoffed, narrowing her eyes on him like daggers, and assessed his form. If she'd been anyone else, he would've told her to fuck off. But this was Alexandria. If she wanted to throw actual knives, he probably wouldn't even duck.

"I'm not sure what I expected," she continued. "My

memory isn't quite clear on the details of when I was your prisoner." She stepped in closer to the bars, her violet stare unwavering. "That's why I'm here."

"Is that so?" Markus closed more of the distance between them. "And here I thought it was because you missed me."

"Dream on." One small fist curled at her side.

He couldn't help but chuckle at her defiance. Everything had been a battle with Alexandria. She'd never willingly given in to anything he'd wanted of her. And she'd been exhilarating.

"Don't pretend you didn't hear my discussion with Kenric at the door."

"Humor me." Markus shrugged. "Tell me exactly why you're here, Alexandria."

"While I was out with Eve and Guerin tonight, Enrique popped in."

Shoving his fists into the pockets of his loose sweats, Markus steadied himself, doing his best to appear collected, unaffected by the news she'd delivered. Truth was, he was anything but cool knowing that Enrique had come anywhere near her. Steeling his expression, he waited for her to reveal the rest.

"He told me to tell you hello."

"How thoughtful," Markus said, making his way over to his cot. After having a seat, he glanced back up. "Is that all?"

"No." Alexandria eased nearer to his side of the room. "He also wanted me to relay another message." She tucked a loose strand of hair behind her ear. "He said that you should keep a tighter hold on what was yours or you might lose it. What the hell did he mean by that, Markus?"

"Ouch! Such language, Vixen."

"Oh, please." She rolled her eyes. "Like I've offended your delicate sensibilities. From what I've heard about you, I doubt you have any."

Placing a hand over his heart, Markus grimaced. "You wound me."

"Quit playing games and just tell me what I want to know," she snapped.

"You could at least ask nicely." He cocked one brow.

"Oh my God," she muttered, her eyelids lowering. "Why would Enrique insinuate that I was yours?" She opened her eyes. "Please," she bit out from between her teeth.

"I think you're asking about more than what Enrique said tonight." It was happening. A part of him had known that she wouldn't be content with the few paltry memories from that time.

"I can't live like this any longer," she said, studying the floor, her voice ragged. "Whether it's pleasant or not, I have to know what happened to me. What you and Marguerite did to me." Her glare slammed into his once more. "I know you took my memory of that time. For some reason, you don't want me to remember. But I have to. And I will. One way or another, Markus, I'll dig up every detail."

His jaw ached under the pressure from his molars. He inhaled deeply through his nostrils and managed to utter, "Good luck with that, sweetheart." His voice was steady, calm, belying the tension in his body. *Damn, I'm good.*

"It would be a hell of lot easier if you'd just tell me." She crossed her arms under her breasts.

"Then what would be in it for me?" Yeah. He was taunting her. But the path to one's treasure wasn't always a straight line.

Her spine went rigid. "Are you kidding me?" She scoffed. "What's in it for you? Don't you think turning me into a monster like you was enough of a prize?"

He lunged for the bars, stopping short of slamming his palms around the poisonous metal. Alexandria's eyes widened, but she didn't flinch, didn't jump back. She stood, rigid, fire blooming, swirling around her pupils. "You think you're like me? A monster, Vixen?" He curled his upper lip, making sure a long, sharp section of a fang was exposed. "You don't have a damn clue about what I am," he snarled.

"Don't I?" Her brow lifted. "You're a former trusted member of the Enclave who betrayed his fellow warriors to their worst enemy and became second-in-command of Marguerite's minions. You sired not only me but my sister, as well, against her wishes. But now look at you." She raked him with her gaze. "You're a prisoner of the very Enclave you betrayed. You don't scare me, Markus." Her hands went to her hips. "I want answers, and I'm not leaving till I get them."

Markus chuckled. She had balls. "Fine." He shrugged. "I'll give you what you want." He rocked on his heels, then pivoted away from the door. "But under one condition."

"Of course there would be a condition," she mumbled. "Why would you do anything just for the hell of it?"

Alexandria would like his terms about as much as she'd enjoy a raging case of herpes. But there was no other way around it. With Enrique sniffing around, he had no choice. He'd need to keep tabs on her. Besides, as a bonus, he'd have her next to him…

Yeah. He was a selfish motherfucker.

"So what is this 'condition'?"

Markus turned around. "Come to me, Alexandria, of

your own free will. Feed me, and I'll answer your questions."

As if struck by a blow, Alexandria stumbled back, but quickly regained her balance. "You're insane," she breathed.

Stepping forward once more, he added, "You want something from me... I want something from you. It's simple, really." He held his arms out to his sides, palms open.

"Kenric constantly offers to feed you, but I hear you refuse him. So why the hell are you suddenly hungry for my blood?"

He perused her with his gaze. "Do you really have to ask?" It was partly true. He wanted her more than he ever believed possible. With Marguerite, the lust had been driven by the addiction. She'd been alluring, but true chemistry? Primal desire? Neither had been why he'd stayed. "But if it'll make you feel any better, I give you my word it's only what's in your veins that I'm after."

She glanced toward the outer door, chewing her bottom lip.

"What? Are you afraid to be alone with me, Vixen— without the bars between us? I already gave you my word."

"Dammit," she snapped. "Just stop talking."

Such a tough and icy front, yet Markus hadn't missed the hesitant swallow or the twitch in her hands. She was nervous. Smart girl. She should be. He didn't trust himself around her. Not really. Her presence chipped away at his control. Reminded him of cravings that would never be satiated and fantasies of a future that would never be his.

"How am I supposed to even get inside there?" She shoved her hair back behind her ears.

His pulsed leaped and his cock twitched. *Fuck. She was going to do this.* "The key's inside the cabinet on the wall behind you."

Looking over her shoulder, she smoothed a palm over her midsection. "Oh…"

After another quick check of the main door separating them and the rest of the Enclave, Alexandria edged closer to the metal box hanging on the wall.

And each step elevated Markus's heart rate.

Squeezing his fists, he jabbed his nails into the flesh. *Focus on the pain.* He had to rein in the beast, or he'd become a feral animal the moment she stepped across the threshold. *I must not hurt her.*

The metal jingled on the ring in her hand, and she faced him. "Just this once." Her voice was low, steady. "I do this, and you tell me what I want to know. Do we have a deal?" She snagged a glove and stepped forward.

Markus nodded.

The key rattled in the lock, then the door swung open. She stood there as if frozen. And it was all he could do not to charge her, take her to the floor, bury his cock and his fangs inside her. Drink from her until nothing identifiable remained of himself.

Fuck. Me.

What would it feel like to lose himself inside her?

Oblivion. Inside her, the darkness would recede, and he could almost believe there was hope for his heart. His shaft throbbed with each beat of the tainted organ. *Get a grip, vampire. Males like you don't get a chance with a female like this one.*

Lifting his arm, he crooked his index finger in her direction, beckoning her to come in. With her shoulders squared, she stepped inside. A smile lifted a corner of his mouth. She was actually here, inside his four walls, and it wasn't a dream. "There… That wasn't so hard, was it?"

"Spare me," she said. "Where do you want to do this?"

This. Allow him to take from her vein. His gut twisted at the thought, the pain nearly doubling him over. *Dammit.* He'd pushed the hunger back for months now, refusing to succumb to its demand in favor of death. But now… Markus choked back a groan. Nothing had ever sounded so incredibly delicious.

"Here," he said, his voice hoarse. Without a second glance to see if she followed, Markus settled onto the edge of his mattress, then looked up.

She hadn't budged. "Seriously? You want me on your bed?"

"Beside me, Alexandria. Not under me." He hit her with a mocking glare. "Although that could be arranged, if it's what you'd prefer."

"You really are an ass, you know that?" She stomped forward and plopped on the bed beside him.

"So I've been told," he murmured.

She jutted her arm out in front of his face while staring at some distant part of the room. "Get on with it," she demanded with her fist curled tight.

Oh hell no. "What the fuck is this?" he grumbled. "You're not a child about to receive an inoculation."

"Are you truly expecting me to sit here and pretend as if we're lovers?" she spat.

"Not at all." He yanked on her arm, not enough to hurt, but hard enough to bring them shoulder to shoulder. "But I expect you to be here. Watching. I want to feel your eyes on me while I drink you in."

Alexandria jerked her arm back to her side. "The deal

was I feed you." Her eyelids narrowed, and her expression was venomous. "That was it. There wasn't any specification on how to do it."

"It's not like I'm asking you to bare your neck." He grasped her wrist once more. She tugged at his hold, but not enough to break his grip. "You want answers…you do this my way."

Seconds passed, and for a moment, he thought she might bolt. Then she exhaled and allowed him to lift her arm. "Fine," she bit out.

Score two.

He closed his eyes, doing his best to mentally wrap a vise grip around his heart. To tame the monster inside who wanted to tear down the walls around his mind and claim the female at his side.

"Why?" she whispered.

He opened his eyes. "Why, what?"

"Why is it so important that I watch while you do it?"

Because it's the closest I'll ever have you, and for some damn reason it matters that I know you're willingly at my side.

"Because I said so," he said.

"Control freak, much?"

"When necessary."

Lifting her wrist to his mouth, he forced himself to slow down when all he wanted to do was dive in and drown in her essence. But he had to make this last. Savor every delectable drop. Her pulse lifted the delicate flesh just beneath her palm, and he inhaled along the surface. Vanilla laced with honey. So damn sweet. Yet something was different. Gently, he ran the tip of his tongue over her artery. She jerked, but held her place. Glancing up from under his lashes, he rolled the flavor around on his tongue. Ah, that was it. His scent was missing. After he'd turned her, Markus had been the only one to nourish Alexandria. Her blood was now littered with a cocktail of various molecules from whom she'd fed.

Breathing her in once more, anger sparked like a lit fuse on a block of C-4, ready to blow. "Where have you been going to satiate your hunger?" *And how many of them were male?*

"I don't think that's any of your damn business," she said, her tone stern.

His spine stiffened, ready to snap back that everything pertaining to her was his business. Yet a second before he opened his mouth, he glanced up, and the whitewashed walls of his cell reminded him of his current status.

Markus swallowed hard, forcing back his initial rebuke. "You're absolutely correct."

Her wide-eyed expression told him that his response hadn't been the one she'd expected.

"Go ahead." She nodded and captured her lower lip with her teeth once more. "If we're going to do this, let's get it over with," she whispered.

At her words—her permission—a hard cramp seized his stomach. He couldn't deny the pull any longer.

Opening his mouth, his fangs fully extended, Markus sank them into her supple flesh. A gasp sounded from her a half second before the heat of her essence burst into his mouth. Hot, sweet, a decadent flavor he had no right to savor, yet every fiber in his body cried out for more. He swallowed, and a tremor racked his body. *Oh fuck...* His cock surged to life, going rock hard, forcing a groan from his throat.

How in the hell had he thought one taste of her would ever be enough?

Chapter Three

What was I thinking? How could Alex have believed allowing Markus this close would be something she could walk away from unscathed?

The moment he'd wrapped his fingers around her wrist, she'd toed the edge of a cliff. The second his fangs had pierced her flesh she'd toppled over. Flying. Lost to sensation. Spellbound by the male who devoured her.

And Christ help her, she didn't want it to end.

Every pull at her vein resonated across her nerve endings and pooled between her thighs. She moaned, and her head lolled forward. Arousal swelled in her core, making her squirm. *Oh God.*

Markus's hair fell forward, brushing her arm, and the effect hit her like a tidal wave of lust. Her nipples hardened to stiff peaks, and the bundle of nerves at the apex of her sex throbbed, and it took every fiber of her control not to reach down with her free hand and relieve the ache.

What the hell was wrong with her? Arousal came with feeding from or donating to the opposite sex, especially if there was an attraction. That little side effect she understood all too well. She'd been a vampire long enough to have experienced the reaction. Not that she was ready to give in to those urges, the lust. She wasn't in any hurry to confirm her suspicions that sex wasn't going to be any more pleasurable as a vampire than she'd found it as a human. It was enough just trying to keep her leash on the bloodlust.

But this was different.

The need was too strong.

Her desire for the male went beyond enticing. It was mind-altering.

Her pulse raced, hammering inside her head like a bass drum of warning.

"Stop!" she cried out and tugged at his hold. "That's enough!" She couldn't take another second of his mouth on her. Alex yanked hard and Markus's head popped up, but instead of letting her go, he snagged her forearm, growling, and jerked her next to him. Her blood stained his mouth, and his fangs glistened beneath his lip. His pupils filled his eyes, engulfing every visible inch of the white.

Swallowing hard, she attempted to bring some moisture back to her suddenly parched throat. Markus's appearance had altered since his confinement. His hair had grown longer, his signature goatee lost within his unkempt beard, and his weight had plummeted, yet between them—the way she responded to him—nothing had changed. "Let me go," she bit out.

She pulled once more, testing his grip. He didn't budge. Instead, his nostrils flared.

"Is that what you really want?" His voice was barely human.

Was it? A shiver raced over her flesh. Her breasts, her sex, ached with need. Yet...

"Yes," she managed to utter, surprising herself with the conviction in her voice.

She couldn't give in. She could never allow herself to act on the lust burning up her veins.

Not with him.

It had to be the beast inside her responding to the feeding, their history. Because there was no way in hell she actually wanted anything more than answers from Markus Santini.

"Release me," she ordered, her voice hoarse.

Uncurling his fingers, Markus eased back. He repositioned himself on the edge of the bed. A grunt exited his throat with the movement. If he was half as aroused as she'd been—was—she could only imagine the deep shade of blue his balls were now sporting.

Hate it for him. After everything he'd done to her and the Enclave... Aching balls was the least he deserved. This was the deal he'd concocted. Not hers.

She started to stand, but he reached out for her arm once more.

"I haven't healed you yet," he said.

Blood trickled from the open bite, traveling down to her fingertips. She curled her fingers, trying to contain the flow.

"Let me help you," Markus added.

Alex dodged his touch. "I think you've done enough." She darted toward the back of the small room, seeking out his bathroom. Inside the lavatory, she sealed the wounds to her wrists with her tongue, then twisted the faucets and shoved her hands beneath the stream of cool water.

She'd been such an idiot stepping inside his cage and expecting this to be a simple matter of give and take. The giving…well, she'd done more than her share. Now to receive what he'd promised.

Sighing, she plucked the soap container from the porcelain ledge. She pumped the top, dispensing a generous amount of foam onto her trembling fingers. *I need to pull myself together. I can't let him see how much he got to me. He'll smell my weakness to his allure and use it like a weapon. Remember what he did to Kenric, to his own partner, my sister, hell, the whole Enclave.*

"I could have done that for you," Markus said.

Lost in her thoughts, she jumped at the sound. "I can handle washing my hands."

"I'm sure you can," he said, his voice a deep vibration along her spine. "But as the one who sank his fangs into you, I should have at least sealed the wound."

"I would think vampire etiquette would be the least of your worries." Alex grabbed a paper towel and brushed past him.

"Just because I can be an ass doesn't mean I've lost all my manners."

"Well then, Mr. Post, how about fulfilling your end of our agreement." She spun around and faced him. Wearing a loose pair of black sweats and a white T-shirt that had to be at least two sizes too big, Markus stood with his arms crossed. His dark hair hung in thick long strands around his face and brushed his shoulders. The color was a stark contrast against skin that she remembered had once possessed a rich olive tone, but now was a ghostly white. Yet thanks to her feeding, she could already detect a bit of color returning to his cheeks.

Damn, even in his anorexic state he had the power to make her legs wobble. And the ability had nothing to do with his wicked reputation. Unlike any other male, something about him drew her in, as if she were a ship adrift in a dense fog and he was the seductive beacon coaxing her to shore. Except in this case, a part of her would rather crash into the rocks than allow the devil to be her savior.

"What do you want to know?" Markus eased back onto his bed and shoved himself up against the wall, facing her. Bending one of his legs, he draped an arm across his knee, then cocked a brow.

"I want to know what happened to me while you and Marguerite held me captive."

"You were brought in by a few of our DEADs along with several others. Instead of killing you"—he sighed—"I decided to turn you." He waved a dismissive hand, as if he were done.

No way in hell. He was playing with her.

"I remember that much. My memory isn't completely blank. Tell me about the stuff I don't know. All of it," she spat.

"All of what? What more can I tell you?" His upper lip curled. "I stole your life. Your humanity. I destroyed you. At least that's what you would incessantly rant, day after day!" He lunged from the bed and into her face. But Alex held her ground. She'd never been a shrinking violet, and she wasn't about to start now. "Does that bring back a few memories for you?"

"Sounds like me," she quipped. "What else?"

"There's not much more to tell. I fed you when necessary. Kept you safe. Made sure no one could touch you."

"You touched me," she muttered.

"Not like they wanted to. Not like that."

"Did *you* want to?" *Why am I playing cat-and-mouse with this guy?*

His mouth formed a grim line, and he turned, giving her his back. "And then the cavalry came to your rescue," he continued on, as if she'd never asked the question. Thank God. Did she really want to know the answer to that one? "End of story."

"Bullshit."

"Believe what you want, Vixen. That's all I got."

"What about Enrique?" She braced her hands on her hips.

"What about him?"

"Something tells me he has a story to tell. Maybe I'll find him and see if he can fill me in on a few more details." She whipped around toward the exit, but before she could take a step, Markus captured her arm and swung her back around.

"Stay away from Enrique," he commanded.

"You don't get to tell me what to do," she snapped.

Markus's eyes flashed a fiery red. "Listen to me. He's dangerous. Do not seek him out," he said, each word perfectly enunciated.

"What is it you're so afraid I'll find out?"

"That's not what I'm worried about."

"Really? You could have fooled me." What the hell was he keeping from her?

"He was Marguerite's former commander. The one

before me. Let's just say, we were rivals for her attention, and I won." His brows lifted in amusement. "Enrique didn't particularly like the outcome."

"What's that got to do with me?"

"I'm your sire. For that fact alone, he'd like nothing more than to take out one of my fledglings."

"*Uh-huh.*" She nodded. "That's what all this is about… I'm your fledgling so he'd get his kicks from killing me?"

"What more could there be?"

"You're such a damn liar," she snarled. "We made a deal, you bastard. For some reason, *you* wiped my memories. I want them back."

"I don't know what the hell you're talking about." He sauntered away from her and leaned against the wall, crossing his ankles and going all Mr. Nonchalant and shit. "You should be heading upstairs. Dawn is coming soon."

She wasn't buying what he was selling. Anger raced like hot lava in her veins, and her fangs slid into place. He'd played her. Markus had never intended to give her any answers. At least not the ones she wanted to hear.

"Whatever happened in Marguerite's lair didn't wipe out weeks of my life from my mind. This had nothing to do with some kind of traumatic response." She closed the distance between them. "You took them from me. And now it's time to own up to what you did and fill in those blanks. You owe me!"

Markus glared down at her. "I don't owe you a damn thing."

"Tell me why you did this," she bit out, her pulse throbbing at her temples. "What are you hiding?" she shouted and lunged at him with her fists. She couldn't have stopped if she'd wanted to. God help her, she'd beat it out of him. Alex pounded into him, unloading a year's worth of frustration onto his chest.

Yet he wasn't fighting back. Dammit. He wasn't even trying to block her punches.

"Damn you! At least hit me back!" Her vision narrowed, blurred, until all she could see was the white of his shirt. Everything inside her wanted to rip him apart. Hot streams of tears ran down her face, scalding her cheeks. She wanted to hurt him. Destroy him the way he'd destroyed her life. So why the hell was *she* the one crying?

"Alex!" Large hands clamped onto her wrists from behind, stalling her blows. "Alex. What are you doing?"

Dammit. Kenric.

The male yanked her back and into his chest, surrounding her with his arms. "Christ! What the hell are you doing in here?" The Enclave's commander spun her around to face him. "Alex." He stared down at her, confusion narrowing his eyes into a frigid blue glare. "Talk to me."

Her chest heaved from her exertion, with her rage. "I wanted answers. And I know he's holding out on me."

"So you felt the need to put yourself at risk and come inside his cell?"

"I can handle myself," she chewed out. "Besides...look at him." She glanced over her shoulder at the male still propped against the wall. Markus nailed her with a *sticks and stones* kind of look. "What do you really think he can do to me in that state?"

"Still." Kenric moved her toward the door. "You shouldn't be in here. He's contained for a reason. Markus is dangerous. Unpredictable. You, of all people—"

"I'm sorry," she softly said. "It won't happen again."

"You're right. It won't," he said, his expression grim. "I should have never allowed you in here alone in the first place. Elle will want my head for giving you one-on-one time with him."

Kenric was right. She should have never come in there. It had been a stupid, impulsive idea. Markus would never be the answer for anything she needed. "Like I said." She looked once more in the direction of the dark vampire. "It'll never happen again."

Alex made her way out of the containment area, darted upstairs, down the hall, and into the kitchen. And came to a halt. *No, no, no...* She did not need this now. Elle stood with a coffee can in her hand, chatting it up with Kenric's personal assistant, Michael. *Damn. Why did they have to be such social butterflies this morning?*

Michael was also the Enclave's trusted human driver and cook. But that's where his role ended. He didn't serve them as a Calyx, a vessel used for feeding. They respected him, and the feeling was mutual.

The majority of humans didn't realize vampires existed outside of a horror movie. But Michael did, and Kenric trusted him. So for the rest of the Enclave, that was good enough. And from what Alex could tell about the human, Kenric was right. Michael was a good guy.

Alex took a step in reverse. Maybe if she were careful enough, she could make it out of there before her sister ever noticed her presence.

Silently she turned, aiming for a quiet but quick exit.

"Alex!"

A sigh slid from her lungs.

"Hey there, sis." Elle's hand brushed Alex's arm. "I

almost missed you."

"Hey."

"What's going on?"

"I'm fine." Alex shrugged.

"You don't look fine." Elle's brow wrinkled. "Were you downstairs in headquarters?" She nodded in the direction from which Alex had come.

"Why?" Shit. Elle was like a dog with a bone when she had something on her mind.

"I'm surprised to see you coming from that direction of the house. That's all. You never go down there."

"Maybe it's time I do." Alex shrugged once more and sauntered back into the kitchen. "Is there coffee?" No matter how many centuries she lived, Alex couldn't imagine ever outliving her taste for the dark brew. And right now, she really could use a cup.

"Yup. Just finished," Michael replied.

At that moment, Eve strolled into the kitchen wearing a white cotton robe and a pair of flip-flops. "Morning, Michael," she said, pausing behind him to grab a mug and pour a cup.

"Good morning," he said. "You heading outside for your morning swim?"

"Yes, I do enjoy watching the sky brighten as I get in a few laps," Eve said. "A girl's got to keep her shape." She laughed and flexed her free arm.

Watching the sky brighten... How wonderful would it be to experience a sunrise once more? Alex lowered her eyelids, recalling how the horizon would burn with the fiery brush strokes of a South Carolina summer sun. Yet she would never experience that again. Neither she, nor her sister.

However, Eve, being the only born-vampire, could survive in daylight. Having become close friends over the past several months, they had discussed Eve's differences from a typical vampire. She could tolerate sunlight and she could knock out her opponent with a mental pulse. Eve had also shared how she could implant vivid telepathic images in the minds of people and had done so once, to an enemy—crippling him. But it was her ability to walk in the sun that had made her a target in the vampire world back in Europe. Thank God, Guerin and Kenric had located her when they had and brought her back to the States, where she was safe among the Enclave.

"Wish I could join you," Alex said. "I could use the exercise and the distraction."

Eve rounded the counter. "I would love that, too." The softening of her expression telegraphed the sincerity of her words. "I'm sorry. I hope you don't feel as if I am boasting about going outside at this hour?"

"Don't worry about it." Alex smiled. "I didn't take it that way." Eve had been nothing but kind to her ever since they'd met. There wasn't a cruel bone in her body, despite who her mother had been.

"Neither did I, Eve," Elle added. "Please enjoy your swim. I mean it." Elle gave one of her best vicious glares, daring her to say otherwise. But it was laughable. Her sister had never been intimidating. At least not to Alex. Elle was a softy when it came to her.

Chuckling, Eve started back toward the rear of the house. "All right. Maybe we could all take a dip later on this evening?"

"Maybe," Alex said. "We'll talk later."

"I'll take you up on that," Elle called out.

"Sleep well, ladies." Eve waved over her shoulder.

And that was Alex's cue to slip away from Elle and grab her own cup of coffee.

"Okay. Now that Eve's gone." Elle came up behind her. "Don't try to deflect me. You know that won't work. What's really going on?"

"Nothing, all right?" Alex reached up and snagged a mug from the shelf. "I'm just tired of being everyone else's problem. I need to learn to take care of things myself." That much was the truth. She was sick of allowing life to happen to her. It was time she took the reins and controlled her own destiny.

"What the hell is that?" Elle grabbed Alex's arm, and the cup dropped onto the granite with a loud *pop* of ceramic against stone, right before Elle yanked her limb closer for inspection. Her sister stared down at the residual indentations of the bite marks to her wrists. The wound was already about half its original size, but one could easily discern what the pink impressions represented. And if the observer was a vampire, how recently it had occurred, as in the last half hour.

Glancing up, Elle looked over at Michael, and Alex followed her gaze. The thirty-something male stood there in his usual attire of ripped jeans and a graphic T-shirt, this one reading *Face it… You know you're impressed*.

"Will you give us a few minutes alone, please, Michael?" Elle tightened her hold on Alex's arm. A subtle message that said *you're keeping your ass right here*.

"Sure thing," he said and sheepishly nodded, a few

sandy-brown waves dropping onto his forehead. He tossed the towel in his hands onto the counter then strode off toward the front of the house. Michael really was a nice guy. Funny, too. Someone perhaps in her earlier life she might have wanted to get to know better. A time before she'd been turned into something that, if unleashed, could drain him like a juice box. She closed her eyes and mentally shook herself. But her ship called humanity had sailed into the horizon more than a year ago and would never come again.

"You want to tell me what this is all about?" Elle's gaze darted between Alex's wrist and her. "Every one of the warriors in this house is mated, and as far as I know, not injured. So I'm pretty damn sure it wasn't one of them who did that."

"Leave it alone, Elle," Alex grumbled and jerked her arm back.

"What were you doing downstairs?"

Trying to tell her sister to mind her own business was like spitting in the wind: a waste of energy. Closing her eyes, Alex inhaled, needing every ounce of calm she could muster. Elle would never understand why she'd agreed to Markus's deal. Hell, she barely understood it herself.

"You're scaring me, Alex. My imagination is running wild here."

"I had a run-in with Enrique tonight." Alex dropped the first bomb, then resumed pouring herself that cup of coffee.

"Come again?" Elle said. "Marguerite's former commander? When? How?"

Alex faced her sister, leaned her rear against the counter, and took a sip of the hot brew.

"And what does that have to do with why you were

downstairs and how you ended up with a bite on your arm?" Elle crossed her arms.

"Seeing him stirred up a few images—flashes, really," Alex said and sighed. "These blanks in my memory...I thought I could live with them, Elle." She shook her head. "Move forward and try to ignore the holes, but I can't," she whispered. "It's driving me crazy."

Her sister's palms brushed her shoulders. "I'm so sorry," she crooned. "I wish I could help." Her touch fell away. "What happened with Enrique? Did he say or do something, or was it just seeing him that triggered the flashes?"

Alex swallowed hard and weighed how much she should actually reveal to Elle. She didn't need her going off on Markus if there was the slightest chance that he'd still tell her something. If Elle and Arran ganged up on him, he might clam up—permanently. Yet how was she supposed to explain the bite to her wrist?

Pivoting back around, Alex clasped her sister's hand. "Are you positive there's nothing more you can tell me about my time spent in Marguerite's lair?"

"Like I've said, we found you with Markus. He was the one who'd turned you and had apparently been caring for you." Elle cocked her head, her expression questioning. "Is there more going on here?"

"Enrique wanted me to tell Markus hello." There was no reason to go into detail with Elle about the sick bastard's full message. Repeating his words about Markus's claim on her would only upset Elle even more, and there was nothing her sister could do about it. After everything Elle had been through, being turned against her will while freeing Alex from Markus and Marguerite's clutches, she didn't need to hear all of Enrique's nonsense.

"Did you go see Markus?" Elle pulled her hand free and squared her shoulders. "Is that why you were downstairs?" The pulse at her sister's neck throbbed, lifting the flesh in time with each beat.

"Calm down," she said. "I just wanted to ask him some questions."

"And how did that go, as if I need to ask?" Elle scoffed. "Wait." She sobered and snatched Alex's wrist. "Is he the one who did this?" Her eyes flashed a second before her pupils enveloped the white.

Oh shit. This was getting out of hand. "It's not what you're thinking."

"I'll kill him," Elle shouted and spun. "I'll make damn sure he never puts his hands or anything else on you ever again!"

"Stop!" Alex grabbed her, halting her before she could get away. "I agreed to do it."

"You did what?" Elle whirled on her. "Why would you allow him to touch you?"

"We made a deal." Alex ran shaky fingers through her hair, pushing it back out of her eyes. She could do this. "After I delivered Enrique's message, I asked him to tell me more about what happened. But of course, Markus wanted something for answering my questions."

"That bastard," Elle spat. "I can't believe you went through with his blackmail."

She couldn't either. It had been crazy. "I know. But after running into Enrique..." Alex smoothed her palm over her sternum. The knot of frustration sat behind the bone, and sometimes the pressure drove her mad. Persistent. Yet just out of reach. And she was helpless to do anything that would give her relief. "I had to try, Elle. Of all people, I'd think you'd understand. The not knowing...days of my life I can't remember. I can't stand having gaps in my memory like this." She shook her head. "I'm so damn frustrated," she said, her voice tight, cracking. Dammit. She had to get past this. "And I'm sick and tired of feeling like I'm not in control of what's happening to my body. I thought after I'd finally gotten away from that bastard our mother brought home, I'd be safe." Alex laughed, but it was that sick kind of chuckle that bubbled up from your gut that had nothing to do with humor. "But the joke was on me, huh?"

"You have no idea how much I wish I'd been there and saved you from that asshole. Our mother—Anita—should have never allowed that to happen," Elle bit out, her voice hoarse. "She should have never let him stay there." A solitary tear flowed down her sister's cheek. Alex probably should be the one crying, but her tears had dried up long ago. All the sobs in the world wouldn't repair the damage in her heart and inside her head. Ever since they'd been little girls, Elle had always possessed the bigger heart. She may have been the tomboy, but inside, Elle had been the rescuer, endlessly trying to fix Alex's problems for her. But this was something Elle couldn't make better.

"It's not your fault, and Anita's dead." Alex cleared her throat. "All that crap happened a long time ago, and no one can change it. I shouldn't have brought it up."

"That's exactly why I think you should leave this alone, Alex. Don't go digging up what's already over and buried." Elle palmed Alex's cheeks. "We don't know for sure if Markus had anything to do with this or if it's traumatic amnesia. You've been through enough pain."

"You're not the one having to live like this." Alex covered her sister's hands with her own. "My gut says it was him, and I'll be damned if I allow him to get away with this. I can't change the fact that he turned me, and I may not like what's revealed. But one way or another, I'm going to find out what happened, and why, when he let me go, he felt compelled to take another piece of me."

Chapter Four

Enrique drew one more sip from his donor's vein, then lapped at the puncture sites, sealing the wound. He wouldn't want him to slowly bleed out, allowing a decent Calyx to go to waste. Especially since he still enjoyed the male's services.

Sliding his cock free from the human's warm depths, Enrique uncoiled his fist from the man's hair and lowered onto the mattress. He rolled onto his back as his lover groaned and eased down into a prone position next to him.

"You seem in a particularly good mood this evening."

"Yes, I am." Enrique grinned.

"Whatever has put this smile on your face must be pretty damn good." The man pushed up onto his elbows. "Because this is the happiest I've seen you since we lost Marguerite… and Markus disappeared."

A growl vibrated in the back of Enrique's throat at the mention of the traitorous vampire's name. By kidnapping and turning the Enclave's human female last year while

Enrique had been away scoping out a new location for Marguerite's lair, the bastard had somehow led the warriors straight to them. The Enclave had killed his Mistress, and instead of dying with the rest of Marguerite's minions, Markus had disappeared with the self-righteous pricks.

And seeing as Alexandria hadn't denied Markus's presence among the Enclave when Enrique had mentioned his name to her, Enrique's suspicions were confirmed. Marguerite's former commander had returned into the fold of his prior master.

How very nice that Kenric St. James had welcomed his prodigal warrior back into their sanctimonious little group.

Markus should have slit his own throat instead of leaving with that pathetic excuse for a band of vampires.

"Ah, Christian," Enrique began, forcing the past back into the recesses of his mind, in favor of the present. He rolled onto his side, facing his current lover. He threaded his fingers into the ginger's hair and cupped the male's nape. "It's been an enlightening night. While I was out, I ran into some old friends, and in the process, I made a very special new acquaintance."

"Really?" The human's brows lifted over pale green irises, drawing attention to the inked swirls that wrapped his right eye. The male was definitely striking. An added bonus to keeping the Calyx alive and healthy. It really was a shame most of Marguerite's Calyxes, trusted humans who took pleasure in serving as vessels for vampires, had scattered after her death.

Enrique rose from the bed and padded over to the large oak desk on the other side of his basement apartment. The chilled, damp air of the room skated over his nude flesh, lifting the hairs on his body. At the desk, he rounded the corner and yanked open the closest drawer. Flipping through the stack of materials on top, papers scattered as he searched for one in particular.

"There," he breathed. On the bottom of the compartment sat a small manila envelope with the red letter *M* penned in the corner. Enrique pulled it free, flipped it over, and thumbed open the flap. Tipping it up, he shook the contents into his waiting palm. A lone photograph, weathered on the edges from its battle with time, tumbled into his hand. Enrique stared at the image of the lovely dark-haired female and smiled. "I knew there had to be a very good reason Marguerite kept you hidden." The woman captured in the image had an uncanny likeness to his former Mistress, and looked amazingly similar to the female warrior he'd seen taking down one of his DEADs this evening. But of course, she would, since she was the daughter Marguerite had somehow managed to procreate with the master of the Enclave, Kenric St. James.

Christian pressed his chest against Enrique's arm and trailed his fingers down Enrique's spine. The heat of his lover's spent cock brushed Enrique's thigh, the reminder of its presence reawakening his own shaft. "May I ask who that is?" he murmured in Enrique's ear.

Putting his lust aside for the moment, he looked up at the other male. "She's the key to obtaining everything I ever desired."

• • •

"Well damn," Kenric said and dislodged his wrist from

Markus's fangs. "Appears I should have sent Alex down weeks ago, if that's all it took for you to start acting like you wanted to live."

Markus swallowed the last traces of the master vampire's blood, stood, and brushed past him. He rolled his shoulders, already sensing the strength returning to his body. It had only been twenty-fours since Alexandria had fed him, but with the addition of tonight's full meal from Kenric, his vision had already sharpened and his pulse was a roaring waterfall inside his head.

"What makes you think one has a damn thing to do with the other?" Markus scrubbed a palm across his mouth.

"You're so full of shit." Kenric huffed. "Your sudden about-face has everything to do with her."

"For Christ's sake." Markus turned, facing Kenric. "Who are you? Dr. Phil?" He crossed his arms. "Since you seem to know so much, why don't you enlighten me about what you think is going on here?"

Without warning, Kenric lunged, fisting Markus's shirt, lifting him up by the material, and slamming his back against the wall. "I can tell you what's *not* going to happen again." Kenric's upper lip curled, his fangs fully extended. "And that's you putting your hands on Alex."

Markus closed the distance between them even more, putting them nose to nose. "Or what?" The question blurted out of his mouth before he had a chance to reconsider whether or not he should stab at the coiled viper before him.

"Dammit, Markus!" Kenric curled his lips in disgust. "Are you so far gone that every word out of your mouth has to be a lie or an attempt to make me want to kill you?" With one hand, he seized Markus by the throat, holding him in place. "Did you think I wouldn't smell her blood the second I walked in this cell last night?" The Enclave's master shoved him even tighter against the wall. "Did you believe I would be so unobservant and not see the mark on her wrist, even though she tried to hide it?"

Of course Kenric had picked up on nearly every detail of what had gone down between him and Alexandria. "All right," Markus said. There wasn't any reason to attempt and deny it any longer. "You're right."

One dark brow lifted on Kenric's forehead.

"Taunting you has become a reflex—a nasty habit I can't seem to break," Markus said. "Stifling it is like trying not to pick at a scab that you know you'd be better off leaving alone yet, damn, you just can't resist making it bleed."

"You associate me with a scab?" A grimace twisted Kenric's expression as he released the hold on his neck and lowered his arm. "How pleasant."

Shrugging, Markus added, "Well you have to admit, my time here with you and the Enclave is sort of like a healing wound."

"I think you have that backward. Your time with Marguerite is the wound you need to concentrate on healing."

"Point taken." Markus nodded.

"Now," Kenric said and reversed his step, putting some much-needed space between them. "As I was saying about you and Alex. It was clear that more than a heated chat had taken place in here before I'd walked in. But I didn't bring it up in front of Alex because there was more riding the air than the smells of anger and frustration." Kenric swiped a hand over his face. "And it wasn't your scent alone filling the room."

There'd been no need for Kenric to remind him of that fact. Her pheromones were forever imprinted inside his brain. His mouth watered. Even though Kenric's blood had washed down his throat only moments before, Markus could still taste Alexandria on his tongue. Marguerite's blood had been a powerful obsession, but nothing had prepared him for the effect of one sip from Alexandria's vein, and he had no idea how the hell he was supposed to forget. How he was so supposed to pretend every molecule in his body didn't want more. Need more. And inside what was left of his heart, he knew he wasn't referring to only her blood. He wanted all of her—in his bed and out.

"I haven't forgotten how possessive you were over the female," Kenric said.

"I sired her." Markus shrugged. "I take care of what's mine. What can I say; I'm a protective kind of guy. It's my nature." He smirked.

"Well then, I suggest you take that need of yours to protect and focus it elsewhere." Kenric stepped in, his gaze locking with Markus's. "After what you put that female through… Do her this one small favor and leave her alone. You owe her that much."

Hot lightning surged through Markus's veins at Kenric's words and the master's implication that Markus didn't realize the true depth of his sins. The other male had no idea how deep the caverns actually ran. But Markus did, because he'd dug every one of them with his own hands. Yet none of them did he regret more than what he'd done to Alexandria. And he owed her a hell of lot more than his absence from her life could ever make up for.

"She came to me, Kenric," Markus said, shoving his

hands in his jeans pockets and moving away.

"I remember. But if she returns—"

"She wants answers, and she wants me to fill in the gaps." Markus glanced over his shoulder at the master.

"And you getting to sink your fangs into her one more time was Alex's payment for doing just that? A little give-and-take arrangement that you came up with?"

"In a way," Markus said. "But she didn't like what she got in exchange."

"You lied to her," Kenric flatly stated. "And she walked out of here without a damn thing."

"Did you expect anything different?" Markus eased in closer to his former commander. "Like you said, after what I did to her, do you really think I'd be so willing to spill my guts? Fuck, I was the one who did her the favor of going all Magic Eraser on her memories in the first place. So why would I want to undo all that?"

"Perhaps because you know hurting her wouldn't end with Alex. It would combust and spread through this house like a wildfire. And after the way you've responded to my attempts to save you, after the things you've said and done since you've been back inside these walls, causing more pain to what's left of this Enclave is something that would be too tempting for you to resist."

"Not everything is as black and white as you think."

"Is that so…" Kenric crossed his arms and squared his shoulders as if preparing for battle. "What am I missing here?"

"Enrique is sniffing around."

"Tell me something I don't know," Kenric snapped.

"Did Alexandria tell you that he threatened her?"

Kenric's arms fell back to his sides. "No," he said, his tone dipping low. "She and I haven't talked since last night. What the hell did he say to her?"

"Nothing specific. Basically that if I wasn't more careful with her, I'd lose her."

"As if he'd ever be able to touch her within the protection of the Enclave." Kenric flashed the fangs hidden beneath his upper lip. "He's nothing without Marguerite's minions to back him up, and they scattered once she was defeated."

"You'd be surprised what Enrique is capable of once he's set his mind to a goal." Markus understood that statement all too well, since he'd experienced being the object of the male's obsessions. For a second, his mind flickered back in time to when Markus had held Alexandria in his possession and Enrique had revealed his hand.

"You know what I want," Enrique stated. "The game is quite simple, really. And either you decide to start playing, with me, or I go to Marguerite and tell her all about how your priorities have changed. Make the right choice here, and we both win."

For years, Enrique had been under the tutelage of the master manipulator: Marguerite. The male knew how to get what he wanted, and before Marguerite's untimely demise, that had been Markus. And for a short period, in order to protect Alexandria, Markus had given in to Enrique's blackmail.

Bile surged to the back of his throat at the memories of their encounters, but if he had to do it all again to keep Alexandria alive, he would.

"I guess you, better than most, would know, since he'd been under your command during your time with

Marguerite," Kenric said, pulling Markus back into the present.

"Exactly," Markus said. "I know how Enrique thinks." He eased onto the seat of a straight-backed chair and crossed his legs. Shit. How had he not seen this coming? He swallowed hard, forcing the coiled fist of apprehension back down into his gut. "With this new possible threat," he began, "and as you put it earlier, seeing as the Enclave is somewhat depleted, I believe you need me."

"Excuse me?" Kenric took the chair on the other side of the small table. "In what way do we 'need' you?"

"With the Enclave having lost Logan last year, and since I'm no longer here, you're down two males."

"I can do the math," Kenric snapped. "Spit it out already, Markus. What are you getting at?"

A year ago, he would've bet his left nut that what he was about to admit would never pass his lips. But if he didn't do it and something happened to Alexandria… There wasn't any other way.

"I want back in the Enclave."

Chapter Five

FOUR WEEKS LATER

Apparently, even an immortal still felt the burn from a strenuous workout. Alex rolled her shoulders once more, trying to loosen the knots in her neck and upper back from the previous day's training session. She sighed, closed her bedroom door, and strode down the second-floor hallway. Eve had seized her arm, twisted it, and forced her to drop the blade from her fist before taking her down hard. Alex slowed, closed her eyes, and shook her head at the memory. God, two weeks and she still wasn't much better than when she'd first started training.

With a deep breath, she opened her eyes, repositioned her workout jacket, and continued down the hall. Time for another rematch. No matter how long it took her to develop the necessary skills, she couldn't give up—would never give up. She was tired of sitting idle. She wanted out in the field with the rest of the Enclave. And with any luck, that would mean coming face-to-face with Enrique. If Markus refused to talk, something told her Enrique was someone who would. She was willing to bet her life on it.

A few steps away from the staircase, a grunting sound caught her attention. Bypassing the stairs, she crept closer, listening, picking up the resonating beat of a bass guitar. *Music?* Two rooms down, she spotted one of the doors standing ajar. *Strange.* She didn't know anyone occupied that particular room.

Humpf.

She cocked her head toward the guttural noise punctuating the rock tune. A couple of seconds later, she heard the sound again. What the hell was going on in there?

Curiosity rode her hard, and unfortunately Alex had never been known for the strength of her willpower. Before she'd been turned, her hips could have attested to that fact. That was one of the few positive things about losing her humanity. Her new metabolism rocked.

Reaching out, she placed her palm against the wood and eased the door open a few more inches. Billy Idol's "White Wedding" bounced off the walls, bombarding her eardrums, but it only took a second for her to locate the source of the other sound. A male, wearing a pair of charcoal-colored sweats and nothing else, hung by his hands from a metal bar suspended between the two built-in closets. Black and red tattooed swirls trailed from his wrists up and over his shoulders, covering both of his arms. His hair was bound at the nape and hung down his back in a thick black-as-sin mane. A grunt rushed from his lungs as he yanked on the bar once more and pulled himself up until his chin topped the metal. Muscles along his spine flexed and rippled beneath flesh that shone with sweat from his effort.

Arousal swelled between Alex's legs and hardened her nipples into stiff points.

"Holy mother of God…" The words exited her lips on a breathy whisper. She'd never been one who prayed very often, but the sight before her was worthy of a few spontaneous words of worship.

The male dropped from the bar, plucked the remote from the nearby shelf, and tapped one of the buttons, silencing the music. "I was wondering how long it would take before you and I ran into each other," he said. "I'm pleasantly surprised it happened so soon."

The voice… It couldn't be?

As if the world had downshifted and everything was suddenly moving at half speed, he turned.

Air punched from her chest.

Markus.

Except this wasn't the Markus who lived in the small silver cage in the basement. The one who was thin, pale, and almost fragile in appearance. Oh hell no. This was the Markus from her dreams—nightmares—the gorgeous male who'd left her with images and feelings that oscillated among lust, arousal, fear, and rage.

Reflex propelled her back a step. "What the hell are you doing in here?"

"This is my room," he calmly stated, as if the situation were perfectly normal.

"What are you talking about?" Alex scanned the rest of the bedroom. She'd been so distracted by the view, she'd totally missed that the once-empty room now contained all the furnishings of a typical bedroom. Her head spun with the implications of what he'd said.

"How?" She shook her head and waved a finger at his metamorphosis. "You look so…different."

"Yeah." He held his arms wide as if inviting a closer inspection. "It's pretty amazing the power contained in a master's blood, if you actually allow yourself to consume it." He flashed a grin.

Alex backed farther into the hall, yet Markus matched her step for step. "How did you convince Kenric to let you out?"

"Stop running from me, Alex," he said. "I'm not going to hurt you."

Jamming the brakes on her retreat, she lifted her chin. "I'm not running. And it's a little too late, don't you think, for your latter proclamation?"

"You have a point." He crossed his arms and retreated, giving her some space.

"So how did you do it, Markus? How did you get him to believe you actually want to be part of the Enclave again?"

"You did what?" A loud voice that sounded a lot like Guerin rang out from the first floor, distracting her and jabbing a cork in whatever story Markus was about to spout. Alex angled closer toward the stairs.

"I can't believe you opened that damn cage without coming to me first," Arran bellowed, his tone less than civil.

"I guess that means they've heard the news," Markus murmured directly behind her, a ripple of heat skating down her spine. Whether the reaction originated from the proximity of his half-naked flesh, or the fact she was scared to death that was exactly case, who the hell knew at this point?

Alex glanced over her shoulder, her gaze catching the fine dark hairs covering his pecs. She followed them as they rode the hollows and ridges of his ripped abs. The thin trail circled his navel, then traveled lower, disappearing beneath the waistband of the sweats sitting low on his narrow hips. *Damn him.* At the lower section of his abs, he possessed the perfect hard vee of muscles and veins she loved on a man. The kind that arrowed south, straight toward his—

Her mouth went dry, and her breasts tingled, nipples tightening into hardened peaks. She jerked her head up. Markus stood there, staring at her with one slash of a brow lifted.

"Did you get a good look, or is there something more you'd like to see?" He smirked.

"Shut up and get some clothes on," she spat, and proceeded to march down the stairs, doing her best to keep her shoulders squared and her pride intact. God, why did she let him get to her? Or an even better question was: when it came to him, why the hell did her hormones always kick into high gear?

Her heart pounded inside her head with each step, and she didn't miss Markus's chuckle when she made her hasty exit. Which just pissed her off even more. How the other males in the house were going to keep from killing that smart-aleck asshole was beyond her. Because it was all she could do not to storm back up there and personally remove the grin from his face with her bare hands. But murder before breakfast was probably in poor taste.

• • •

"You owed me that much, Kenric," Arran barked from where he stood by the fireplace, facing the commander. Kenric's mate, Emily, the second female after Alex's sister to become part of their dysfunctional family, sat nearby on the love seat. Her apprehensive expression and body language relayed her concern over the tension and anger vibrating around them like a plucked guitar string.

On the other side of the room, Guerin slowly paced the floor, the *thud* of his boots on the hardwood resonating like a metronome in the room.

"Christ!" Arran swiped a hand over his face, then added, "He kidnapped and assaulted my mate. Don't you think I'd want to know you were going to release him?"

"It was my decision to make," Kenric said, his voice low and steady. "Mine alone. Besides, it was only few hours ago that I decided today was the right time for him to join the rest of the house."

Guerin drew to a halt and spun, facing the other two males. "Today was the right time?" His expression twisted. "Are you saying that you've been considering this for a while now, and you didn't discuss it with me?"

"There was nothing more to be said. You knew from the beginning that I hoped Markus would be able to recover from Marguerite's brainwashing and return to the Enclave."

"But at the time, it was more like a fantasy of yours," Guerin snarled, "and not one I shared."

Elle strode into the room from the kitchen and stopped at Alex's side. "What's all the shouting about?" Elle glanced at her sister.

"Me." Markus stepped down from the last stair behind them.

"Shit!" Elle whipped around, clamped onto Alex's wrist, jerking her closer as if attempting to shield Alex from the intruder with her body. Alex stumbled forward, but managed to grab on to Elle's arm.

"Elle…" Alex protested. "What are you doing?"

"What am *I* doing?" Elle's perplexed gaze flickered between her and Markus. "What the hell is *he* doing here?"

"Well, that's the question of the evening, isn't it?" Arran inserted himself between Alex and Elle, his mate, and Markus, his former partner.

Markus released a short crack of laughter as if amused with Arran's protective move. "You worried about me getting too close to your mate, partner?"

"You lost the right to call me that the moment you sank your fangs, and other various parts of your anatomy, into Marguerite," Arran spat.

"That was a long time ago, Arran." Markus shook his head and proceeded farther into the room toward the master of the Enclave. "If Kenric can let go of the past, don't you think you should give it the old Boy Scout try?" At the commander's side, he faced the others in the room. "After all, Kenric was the one betrayed the most, yet he's willing to give me a second chance." Markus tapped first Guerin, then Arran with his gaze. "Your numbers are down, warriors. You need me. And hey." Markus smiled. "I'm willing to let bygones be bygones."

Arran roared and launched at the grinning male.

"You arrogant son of a bitch." Guerin also surged toward Markus.

"That's enough," Kenric bellowed and appeared in front of their new team member, blocking their attack. Yet Alex never saw him move. The warriors froze in their steps, their wills seized. A powerful feat only a master such as Kenric could accomplish. Alex's breath hitched and her pulse quickened at the sight.

"Now…" Kenric said, ratcheting his tone back down into the range of civil conversation. "Do we think we can keep from killing one another long enough for me to speak?" As if the master vampire had reeled his power back down a measure or two, the males managed slight nods. "Good." Kenric inhaled deeply and released them.

"Damn, I hate when you do that." Arran rubbed his nape. "I always end up with a bad case of fucking whiplash when you let go."

"Then stop giving me reasons to do it," Kenric drily stated.

"*Pfft.*" Arran lowered his arm and drew his mate to his side once more.

"I knew my decision to release Markus and invite him to return to the Enclave would be met with a great deal of reservation," Kenric began, taking a stand beside the fireplace. He leaned his shoulder against the mantel and crossed a leg over his booted ankle. Standing at more than six foot four with short, thick black hair and eyes the color of the sea, Eve's father emitted power—confidence. The dark warrior was an impressive sight, and Alex could easily see why Emily was so enamored with her mate.

Yet as captivating as Kenric was, Alex found her attention wandering. Drawn to the darker male to his right, the one the others in the room tossed daggers at with their eyes, as if he had a target painted on his chest.

And it was disturbing.

Not the part where the warriors and their mates wanted to kill him. Nope. That she understood. She'd wanted to do the same not five minutes ago. But the part where every time his gaze brushed hers, a fire kindled low in her pelvis.

What's wrong with me?

Maybe when a male turned a female it wasn't uncommon for a lingering attraction? Except no one had ever mentioned she should expect that type of physical reaction to Markus. Elle didn't seem to have the same problem, and Markus had also been her sire. But she'd also said he hadn't been the one to feed her during the change. A Calyx by the name of Christian had been sent to take care of her need for blood. Perhaps that had made the difference?

There was only one problem with her theory, though: confirmation. She couldn't just walk up to anyone in the house and say, "I've got the hots for Markus. Do you think my body's reaction to him has to do with the fact he's my sire and he exclusively fed me for so many weeks?"

Alex mentally shook herself. Nope. No way was she dropping that bit of news on anyone.

"I can't imagine why," Guerin uttered, jerking her back into the moment.

Shit! Had she spoken out loud? A cool sheen of sweat beaded from her pores, and her heart raced.

"I understand you're pissed off, Guerin," Kenric said.

Oh, thank God. She inhaled deeply, trying to calm her pulse.

"I didn't discuss my decision with any of you beforehand because I knew this would be your response," the commander added. Restless grumbling resumed around the room.

"Are you okay, Alex?" Elle whispered, her sister's hand

brushing her arm. "You look pale." She stepped in closer. "And you're sweating."

"I'm fine." Alex frowned, shrugging off her touch.

"It's your proximity to Markus, seeing him again, isn't it?" Elle shook her head, scowling.

Yes. But not in the way you're thinking.

"God…why did he have to ever let that bastard out?" Elle mumbled. "Go back upstairs for a little while and lie down."

Alex clenched her fist, holding on for patience. "You don't have to mother me," she bit out as quietly as possible. "I said I'm fine."

"What's wrong with Alexandria?" Markus's deep voice sliced through the other conversations in the room, sending a spark of electricity down her spine. Alex jerked.

Elle whipped around. "That's none of your business," she replied, her tone razor sharp. "And I would highly suggest the more distance you keep between my sister and yourself, the better for your health."

"Elle," Alex hissed and attempted to tug her back. This was only going to make the situation worse. The room was already so thick and heavy with tension, all it needed was one strike of a match for it to blow.

"Alexandria…" Despite Elle's warning, Markus strode forward.

And the fuse sparked.

"You're either deaf or a dumbass." Arran charged the offending male, reared his arm back, and swung, connecting with Markus's face in a loud *crack* of bone against bone.

"Holy crap!" Alex gasped and jumped out of the way.

Guerin surged toward the fight, but Alex wasn't sure if he

meant to break them apart or get his own piece of Markus. Either way, the moment he came within striking distance, the prodigal vampire rotated onto one leg, then struck with the heel of one boot straight into Guerin's midsection.

Alex grimaced as air burst from the male's lungs on a *humpf*. He stumbled back, clutching his gut. Damn, that had to hurt.

"You son of a bitch," Arran shouted, then swung once more. This time, the blow landed near Markus's diaphragm. Markus doubled over from the impact. A second later, wheezing, Markus straightened and eyed the snarling vampires.

"Is that all you got?" With the back of his hand, Markus wiped a smear of blood from the corner of his mouth. Growls rumbled off the warriors. "Come on then." He lifted his chin, beckoning them. "You know you've been waiting for this day. Don't hold back." Markus opened his arms, his fingers splayed.

What was he doing? Then it dawned on her. Where was Kenric? Why hadn't he put a stop to this? Alex did a quick search of the room and found the commander standing with his arms crossed, intently watching the events unfold. Emily stood near her mate, one hand covering her mouth. Her expression matched exactly what Alex was primed and ready to do: she was a half second from jumping between the males and putting a stop to the madness.

"Don't play that shit," Arran bit out.

Guerin fisted the front of Markus's shirt. "Since when the hell have you ever been a martyr? Fight, you asshole. Where are your damn balls?"

"But isn't this what you both wanted, a pound of my

flesh?" Markus looked between the two males. "I thought I'd give you your opportunity. Let you get it out your system. Because after today"—his upper lip curled off his fangs—"you won't get another chance."

"Fuck you," Guerin spat, and shoved the other vampire. Markus stumbled but quickly regained his footing.

Arran turned around, flexing his fingers open and closed, his brows drawn, lips in a taut line. Elle crossed the room to her mate's side.

"Okay," Kenric finally spoke up, drawing everyone's attention. "Now that we've appeased our beasts, maybe we can at least try to tolerate one another's presence. Because like it or not"—Kenric scanned the room, connecting his gaze for a moment with each person—"this *is* the Enclave. The men and women in this room are all we've got, and dammit, we have one another's back."

Chapter Six

"What do you mean Seth Keller is dead?" Enrique hissed, and pitched the glass tumbler in his hand at the wall of his apartment. It shattered against the brick, spraying jagged shards onto the wood floor.

With a firm grip on the cell phone at his ear, Enrique jerked the straight-backed chair out from his desk with his free hand and plopped onto the seat. "This can't be true," he continued. "How do you know this?"

"From what I hear," his contact on the other end of the receiver said, "Seth, his lover, plus several of his colony were slaughtered several months ago…maybe even a year now."

What the fuck? Seth had been obsessed with tracking the alleged born-vampire, one who was rumored to walk in daylight. Seth was his best prospect for the kind of wealth and connections he needed in order to get his hands on this female. Many thought the German master had been crazy—that he was on some kind of bigfoot hunt, searching for something that didn't exist.

Luckily for Enrique, having been in Marguerite's service for many years before her untimely demise, he'd once or twice, when she hadn't thought he'd been within earshot, overheard her boasting about a very special child she herself had carried. But because Enrique had valued his continued existence, he'd never asked Marguerite any questions on the subject. Besides, she'd been a master of deception, and the idea of a vampire female conceiving was implausible.

Thusly, he'd never dug around for any further details. The risk would have been too high if any word traveled back that he'd been snooping into his Mistress's business. If Markus had learned of any indiscretion on Enrique's part, he wouldn't have blinked at the opportunity to toss Enrique's ass at Marguerite's feet for sacrifice.

Not that Enrique wouldn't have done the same.

With Markus, though, he would have taken a different route. He'd have used the info, as he had with the male's feelings for Alexandria, to further blackmail the gorgeous vampire for yet another fuck. He sighed. Like all good things, he and Markus had eventually come to an end.

"A master traveling with another vampire from the States," his contact replied, snagging his attention and yanking him back to the present.

"Repeat that," Enrique demanded. "Who did you say killed Seth?"

"I said I had heard that a new master, along with another vampire, had entered the area unannounced. Word is..." The informant paused for effect. "He, his partner, along with a couple of others, raided Seth's home, eliminating him, in order to rescue someone the crazy bastard had been holding."

"Is that so…" Enrique stood, his mind racing. *Kenric St. James and one of his Enclave.* It had to be.

"That's the rumor. Whether it's true or not, I have no way to verify. But I haven't seen Seth in a very long time. Neither has anyone else I know."

"Thank you for the information, Stefan. You've been very helpful." Enrique tapped end call on his cell and dropped it to the table.

"My bet is"—Enrique stroked his chin, eyeing his lover who rested on his side, watching him from the bed—"Markus ran his mouth to Kenric about the possibility of a long-lost daughter, and they jumped on a plane to Europe." Enrique unbuckled his belt, pulled it free, then shed his pants before climbing onto the bed with the redheaded man. He stroked the Calyx's cheek and grinned. "I wonder if Seth finally got his clutches on his precious born vamp, and the Enclave came to her rescue?"

"Sounds logical," the human replied.

"I wonder if she knows her daddy's Enclave is responsible for her mother's demise?" The excitement of the topic, in addition to the naked man in his bed, had his cock pulsating and rock hard. He nudged his lover's thigh with his shaft.

"She'd have to know, since she's living with them," the other man said and smiled, returning the thrust.

"True. Very true, Christian." Enrique lowered his hand and traced the dark pink circle around the human's nipple.

Christian's eyelids lowered. "Still, I don't understand why she would've stayed after what they did."

"I do," Enrique said, thinking back to how protective Guerin had been of the female. "Kenric's second-in-command, Guerin." He lifted his brows at the other male.

"Ah." Christian smirked. "She's found someone in the Enclave whose bed she doesn't want to leave." He trailed his fingertips lightly down Enrique's arm. "I can...understand the appeal." He glanced up, meeting Enrique's gaze, his green eyes bright with mischief.

"Exactly," Enrique said. "The good thing is, she's not going anywhere. Bad thing, she's in the heart of the Enclave, which makes the act of extracting her nearly impossible."

Christian grinned. "You said 'nearly.'"

Enrique lifted the corners of his mouth, exposing his fangs. "That's where you come in."

Chapter Seven

"It's been a week now." Eve circled behind Alex. "How is it to have your sire freely roaming the house?"

Alex spun, sensing Eve's strike, and blocked the female's incoming arm aimed at her throat. "You give him too much credit," Alex retorted, swiping her brow with her forearm. Training with Eve three times a week in the Enclave's gym was tough, but so far it hadn't been nearly enough. No one needed to tell her that her sparring skills weren't even close to being considered eligible as an active member of the Enclave. The bruises, sore ribs, and joints relayed that message loud and clear.

"What do you mean?" Eve matched Alex move for move, making sure to keep herself at Alex's back.

Tightening her fists, Alex mentally checked her fighting stance. *Concentrate.* She couldn't allow Eve to gain the upper hand. Her attempt to distract her with conversation about Markus wasn't going to work. Yet despite her best efforts, images flashed across her mind's eye of when she'd first seen him after his release. The way his muscles had glistened and bunched while he'd pulled up on the bar in his room. The way the swirls of red and black along his arms appeared to be alive, moving with each flex and release of his biceps. Her pulse notched a little higher.

Stop it! she chided herself.

Alex tossed her head, attempting to shake the memory from her mind as well as a few stray tendrils of hair from her eyes. "'Sire' is too kind of a word. You mean what's it been like to have the male responsible for attacking me and then holding me prisoner walking around free?"

"Yeah. That." Eve suddenly appeared in front of her.

Faster than Alex could visually follow, Eve leaped, gaining some air time, twisted, and landed a blow with her heel to Alex's gut.

Oxygen punched from Alex's lungs, the force of the impact knocking her back a couple of feet. Spots swirled in front of her eyes. *Damn.* With a tight hold on her midsection, Alex focused on the bright blue mat covering the floor. *Breathe.* She blinked, trying to chase away the stars. *In and out.*

"Are you okay?" Eve's Nikes appeared in her line of sight. But Alex couldn't quite get her vocal cords to respond yet. "Alex?" Eve dropped to a crouch and glanced up at her. Alex closed her eyes and nodded. Yeah. She would live. Her pride? Not so much.

"You need to learn to expect the unexpected, Alexandria," a deep male voice from the doorway said.

Oh dear God. Not now.

She didn't need to raise her head to identify who stood there. The way the sound lifted the hairs on her arms and made her heart sputter told her who had been watching.

Eve stood. "She doesn't need your input, Markus."

Alex straightened, the ability to draw a deep breath resuming.

"After the blow Alexandria just received"—Markus approached, raking his gaze from head to toe over Alex—"I'd let her be the judge of that."

Her stomach flipped as if she'd topped the first hill on a roller coaster and was about to go on the ride of her life. Alex crossed her arms over her chest.

"You arrogant son of a…" Eve shook her head, clamped her mouth shut, and moved in closer to the male. "We're doing just fine without your interference," she added.

"Yes. We are," Alex chimed in.

"Then you won't mind if I observe your technique?" Markus backed off the mat. "It has been a while since I've been out in the field. I could be rusty." He shrugged.

Eve glanced her way, the fire in her eyes mirroring what Alex knew her own had to resemble. "I think I've had enough for one day," Alex muttered.

"Are you sure?" Eve eased toward her. "Don't let him get to you and ruin your progress. You're doing fine. If you want to keep going, I'm here for you."

"I appreciate it," Alex said. "You're a good friend. But let's continue this tomorrow, if that's okay?" Alex rotated her shoulder, loosening the muscle.

"Sure. We can call it." Eve strode over to one of the chairs in the corner of the room and Alex followed. The heat from what had to be Markus's gaze warmed her spine. Eve grabbed her towel, and Alex did the same. "Same time tomorrow night?"

"Sounds good." Alex painted on a smile as Eve started to leave, then halted when she realized Alex hadn't moved.

"You're not coming with me?"

"*Uhm…*" Alex couldn't help but glance across the gym at the tall male with his dark hair loose around his shoulders. Instead of sweats, this time he wore a pair of dark jeans and a white short-sleeved shirt stretched taut over his arms, his bold tattoos in brilliant contrast against the cotton. His presence somehow filled the expanse of the open space and set her on her edge. "Markus and I need to talk."

They definitely had to set some boundaries.

"You're sure?" Eve followed Alex's gaze, concern wrinkling her forehead. "This vampire has unresolved issues. He may be saying he's let bygones be bygones, but believe me, honey, after all I've heard, let's just say I'm not convinced yet."

"I'm not sold either," Alex said. "As they say, actions speak louder than words."

"You got that right." Eve wiped her neck with the towel and headed out. "I don't think he'd be stupid enough to try anything with you in this house. I just don't trust that he's not up to something."

"I know. But I'll be fine," Alex said.

"Okay." Eve nodded. "Catch up with me later," she said over her shoulder and disappeared through the door.

From the other side of the gym, Markus followed Eve's exit with his gaze, then turned his attention to her. "You're not running out on me, too?"

Alex dropped her towel back on the chair and strode toward the male. "Do I have a reason to run?"

"Not from me." Markus met her halfway, his arms relaxed at his sides.

"Good to know," she said. "But when it comes to me and this house, you need to keep your distance."

"A guy can't even get in a workout?"

"Dressed like this?" Alex pointed at the boots and jeans. "Pleeaasse. You didn't stop in here for exercise."

He glanced down at his clothes, then up at her from under a thick set of lashes, and the stormy gaze she'd remembered as a dark void shone with mirth.

"Guilty." He smiled, and this time the effect went straight to her knees. Alex quickly compensated and repositioned her stance.

Get a grip, girl.

"I was passing by and saw you two sparring," he said. "I couldn't resist coming in to watch."

"You need to work on your impulse control," she quipped.

He smirked. "I was serious earlier, though. You need to work on detecting the subtle clues of your opponent's next move. Expect the unexpected."

"Tell me something I don't know. My ribs would appreciate me becoming a better student. Sooner rather than later." She massaged her side.

"We could help each other, you know."

She froze for a moment, her palm against her side. "Pardon me if I don't jump at your offer." Alex hit him with a droll stare. "You don't have the best reputation for coming through on your end of a deal."

"This is different."

Alex rolled her eyes. "I don't have time for this. My only reason for talking to you—"

"Let me help you with this," he said, cutting her off.

"You're relentless!"

"It's important you learn how to properly defend yourself." He closed the distance between them.

"On that, we agree." She glared up at the male in front of her. "If I'd been better at protecting myself, maybe neither one of us would be in this situation."

For a split second, an odd expression washed over his face, but it was gone so quickly she couldn't put her finger on the emotion. Had it been regret? Fear? Probably neither one. More than likely it had been her imagination, because in its place, the cool facade Alex was so familiar with stared back at her.

"That's something we'll never know," he said, his tone low and gravelly. "But we can do something about today." He strode off the mat, and in a matter of seconds, Markus had his boots off and shoved against the wall. "Now." He wheeled around, yanking his shirt over his head and tossing it to the floor.

Dear God... She swallowed hard, willing her body to not react to his. He rolled his shoulders, and it was as if the tats covering his arms and pecs had a life of their own. Hypnotic, if she were to stare for too long. She forced her gaze up.

Determination gleamed in his expression. "Let's get started," he said, resuming his place in front of her.

"You can't *truly* be serious," she said, shaking her head. Markus had lost his damn mind if he thought she was going to fight him.

"Why would you think I'm kidding?"

"Because..." She couldn't spar with him! Her mind whirled, searching for a proper excuse for her brain's rejection of the idea. She just...*couldn't.* Way too much contact.

"Because..." he repeated, and held out his hand as if

waiting for her to plop the words from inside her mind into his palm.

"You're a man!" The words tumbled from her lips. But not just any man. He was *Markus*. The male her head said she should hate. Yet her body responded to him as if he were Vin Diesel mixed with the swagger of Alexander Skarsgard and sprinkled with the deliciousness of Enrique Iglesias. And damn if she subconsciously wanted a bite of all that yummy goodness.

But that was the problem. She didn't dare sample any of what he had to offer, unless she wanted to dance with the devil himself.

"I'm a man." Markus nodded, his lips drawn taut. "Last time I checked I was, indeed, still male."

"Then you know why this isn't a good idea." Having made her point, Alex marched off toward her gym bag.

"That's exactly why this is the perfect idea."

"You need a reality check, bucko," Alex shouted over her shoulder. "You and I aren't doing this."

"Bucko?" His feet thumped against the cushioned vinyl behind her. "Since when have you ever held your tongue when it comes to me?"

She shrugged. "Maybe I'm trying something new. This is me attempting to be civil." Alex hefted her gym bag onto her shoulder and faced him, but the expression meeting her was not what she'd expected. Markus stood, his cheeks flushed with his effort to keep his mouth clamped tight. "Don't you dare," she grumbled.

Laughter burst from him, ricocheting off the walls of the open space.

"What is so damn funny?" Her hands went to her hips

and her bag fell.

"You." He sucked in a breath. "My hot-tempered vixen…civil?" He tossed his head back with laughter once more. She would have found this new, relaxed side of him sexy, if it weren't at her expense.

The temper he so nonchalantly mentioned boiled like a kettle of oil in her gut, the fire overflowing and heating her chest, her face. Before she could think better of her action, Alex charged forward and slammed her palms into his chest. "Stop it!"

Except she may as well have pounded at a brick wall for as much as he moved.

His head rolled forward, and he glared down at her. "Stop what?" he taunted her. "Laughing at you?" He smiled and chuckled. "Why should I, when you amuse me so?"

God, how this male infuriated her! "Well, then…" She smiled sweetly, holding tightly on the leash to the rage doing its best to consume her. Alex needed to make this count. "By all means, allow me to continue amusing you."

Rearing back with her right leg, Alex swung her knee forward and upward with all her might. Straight into Markus's groin. The large vampire gasped and doubled over, both hands grasping for his no doubt disappearing testicles.

Satisfaction bloomed like a warm brush of morning sun across her flesh. *Oh, he so deserved that.* She couldn't stop her grin if she wanted to. And she definitely didn't want to.

Heading for the door and a swift exit, Alex brushed past him. But before she'd taken two steps, Markus grabbed her arm.

Shit! Alex spun, her fist ready and aiming for his jaw. She swung.

Markus blocked.

Damn him!

He pivoted. Kicked.

Alex blocked. *Yes!*

She punched. Markus easily deflected her and tossed one of his own toward her jaw, but Alex was ready and knocked it away.

"That's right," he said. "You saw it coming, didn't you?" He whipped around, his heel coming for the side of her head. Alex ducked, avoiding the kick, but returned his attack with her fist targeting his face. Except this time, he was ready. Markus weaved and dodged the blow. "Good," he said. "Stay ahead of me."

He blurred to her left, wrapping his arm around her throat. Alex's breath hitched from the sudden contact. Instinct drove her hands to his forearm. He tightened his hold, the heat of his body clinging to her back and short-circuiting her brain.

"Think, Vixen," he murmured at her ear, sliding his other arm up and around the back of her head, locking her in his grip. "How are you going to make me release you?"

Her pulse thundered in her head, but she wasn't sure if it was panic or from his proximity. *Damn.* She couldn't allow him to get the best of her. Alex searched and found the hand and elbow of the arm behind her head. Driving all of her reserves into her upper body, she pushed and loosened his hold enough to wiggle her head through the gap. She spun, keeping a tight hold on his arm, twisting it. He grunted, but she didn't let go. Not yet. Instead, Alex delivered a forward kick into his rib cage. His head was lowered, and she released him, prepared to take him to the floor with an elbow to the back of his neck. But as she readied to deliver the blow, he wasn't in the same spot.

An arm came out of nowhere, clipping hers up and back before impacting her chest and slamming her back onto the mat. Air whooshed from her lungs, and she squeezed her eyes shut. Hard palms seized her wrists a moment before Markus's weight covered her.

She lifted her eyelids, and the storm-gray irises that plagued her dreams stared back into hers.

"Anticipate my moves, Vixen," he whispered.

Her heart raced.

Her chest heaved with each breath. And it had everything to do with panic *and* Markus's proximity.

She should feel completely trapped, yet Alex couldn't find her voice to demand he let her go. Her gaze fell to his sinfully full mouth. God, how would it feel to have him kiss her, devour her with those lips the same way he'd drunk in her essence—as if she were his first taste of cool water after surfacing from the fires of hell?

His gaze lowered, and she licked her lips. "Yes," she breathed.

But she had no idea if it was an answer to his first demand on anticipation, or the question his eyes had relayed. Either way, her answer was the same.

Then his mouth was on hers, hot, smooth, and dangerous, stealing her breath with its contact. He glided over her lips, gentle at first, nudging, seducing. She moaned, and unable to deny him, parted her lips, inviting him in. His tongue brushed hers, and her nipples pebbled; her hips rocked up, pressing into his, needing more, wanting more. She gasped, shocked at the intensity of her body's response.

Markus groaned, released her hands, and his palms cupped her head. Holding her steady, he deepened their kiss like a man starved, and she offered everything he needed. Her head spun as if she were on an out-of-control carnival ride. *Too much.* Her heart raced and her gums tingled, releasing her fangs. She wasn't ready for this. She had to get away. Groaning with desperation, she drove her fingers into his hair and bit down, sinking her fangs into his bottom lip. He hissed and jerked.

"Get off me," she spat.

He glared down at her in silence as the tip of his tongue appeared and slowly licked away the droplet of blood from his lip. Her lower abdomen clenched at the sensual sight.

"I said move," she chewed out. "Or do you need a repeat of my knee to your groin?"

Markus lifted his hip, making way for her to scurry from beneath him.

Without looking back, she made short work of retrieving her bag, trying to ignore her jelly-filled knees. She bit back a groan and started for the exit. The door to the gym had never seemed as far away as it did at that moment.

Passing him where he still sat on the mat with his arms draped over his bent knees, heat flared up from her chest and into her cheeks. Even though things had never gone that far, she understood what others meant by the walk of shame.

"For the record…" he called out.

Alex captured the doorframe with her hand and paused.

"You kissed me back," he said.

She lowered her lashes and white-knuckled the wood. *Oh, please kill me now*, she silently prayed.

Because this time, Markus wasn't lying.

Chapter Eight

Alex pressed the button inside the console in the Mercedes E-Class, lowering the top on the convertible. The warm summer night air rushed inside, lifting her hair and teasing her neck. She allowed her head to fall back onto the padded leather rest, closed her eyes, and let the sounds of the night along with the rumble of the engine drown out her thoughts.

"Thanks for getting me out of the house," she said to her sister.

"You looked like you could use a change of scenery," Elle replied. "Besides, I'm getting to hang with my baby sister. Why wouldn't I jump at the chance?"

Alex scoffed. "You're crazy." She opened her eyes. "With that gorgeous male specimen you have for a mate at home, I'm the last person you should want to spend your evening with."

"Well…" Elle smiled, flipped the turn signal, and slowed the car. "I do admit, he is pretty easy on the eyes and his many, many skills do not make me want to leave his side very often," she drawled.

"TMI," Alex cried out, and covered her ears.

Laughing, Elle turned onto the streets of downtown Elizabeth Bay. "Actually, he's on patrol tonight," she said, sobering. "So this is great."

At the slower speed, Alex studied the locals with their packages in hand, their partners hooked on their arms, smiling at each other and strolling the sidewalks. "I like to just sit and observe the humans sometimes—watch the way they come and go with their family and friends…it's like vicariously reliving my life through them."

"Yeah. I know what you mean," Elle said quietly.

"You know what's weird, though?" Alex glanced over at her sister. "It's only been a year, but what it felt like to be them already seems like a really, really long time ago."

Elle nodded. "I think that's what's called acceptance."

"Maybe," Alex said. "It doesn't feel like that most days. There's a part of me that's pretty damn angry." She sighed. "You're not still pissed off, Elle, about what Markus took from you? I don't get how you can just let it go so easily."

The car suddenly veered to the right into an open parking space, taking Alex by surprise and jamming her against the door. Elle hit the brakes and shoved the car into park.

"What the hell?" Alex smoothed her palm over her bruised shoulder.

"You think I let what Markus did to me just roll off my back?" Elle shook her head. "Alex, you have no idea how that ate away at me, boiled inside my gut like a cauldron of hate. I *despise* the fact that it was Markus—his bite, his blood—that turned me and not the male I love," she seethed. "When I came around and was conscious enough to fully understand what had happened, I wanted to rip the flesh from my body. Knowing that another male's blood, not Arran's, ran through my veins." Her sister swallowed, choking back what had to be disgust. "Coming to terms with that reality, knowing it was something that could never be undone, was one of the most difficult things I've ever had to accept."

"But you did," Alex quietly added.

She nodded. "Having my sister going through the same thing, and helping you to understand a world that was completely new to you, helped me to push past my anger and to focus on the things I could control."

"Plus, you had Arran."

Elle smiled, and the deep love she held for her mate shone in her amber-colored eyes. "Yes. After everything was over, and you had been safely returned to me, becoming Arran's mate made my life complete. Even though the decision to become a vampire wasn't mine to begin with, knowing we'll spend an eternity together makes it easier not to dwell on the negative."

A wave of loneliness swamped Alex, souring her stomach with her own self-pity. And she hated it. Hated feeling sorry for herself. That wasn't who she was. She didn't begrudge Elle one moment of her happiness. Her sister deserved having a mate who loved her totally and unconditionally. There were times like tonight, though, when she wished there was someone in her life who made her soul light up when she talked about him. Someone whom she couldn't imagine waking up without.

"Having him there for you had to be wonderful," Alex muttered and directed her attention to the storefront outside the car. The lights inside lowered to a dim glow, mirroring how she felt most days, as if she were functioning with only a partial charge. Only half alive.

"It must be closing time," she said, trying to shake herself out of her woe-is-me state of mind. She was a fighter, not a loser.

"You'll find someone, Alex."

"I know," she said, and popped the release on the door. "Let's get out of this car and walk down by the water."

She had to get out of here before things got any mushier.

"All right. We can do that." Elle raised the top of the Mercedes, then exited the vehicle and joined her on the sidewalk.

A few minutes later, they strolled the docks, listening to the water lap at the sides of the boats. That was one of the things she loved about her sister. Elle didn't require conversation. She enjoyed just "being" there for her as much as Alex did without the required heart-to-heart.

"I heard you've been training with Eve," Elle said.

Or so Alex thought.

"That's right."

"Any reason for the sudden interest in mixed martial arts?"

"Just thought it was time, that's all," Alex said.

"Time for what?"

A straining, gurgling-like sound crested on the night air, bringing Alex to a halt. "Did you hear that?"

The noise was eerily familiar to what she'd heard when she'd been out with Eve and Guerin during a DEAD attack.

"No. What?" Elle stopped and surveyed the area. "Are you trying to change the subject on me?"

Another soft groan came from a few feet away, where a stack of storage crates sat just outside the glow of the scattered lighting. "That." Alex nodded in the direction of the disturbance.

"Oh God," Elle whispered. "That doesn't sound good."

Alex jogged ahead, with Elle right on her heels. Together, they rounded the stack of abandoned crates. Hidden in the shadows, a large male held another by his throat against the ground, his back to them. The trapped guy bicycled his legs. The effect impotent in his attempt to get away, as the smell of fresh blood permeated the enclosed space. This wasn't your ordinary attempted murder.

This killer was of a different species altogether—a vampire.

Elle charged, grabbing the vamp by his hair and shirt and yanking him back. "Get off him!" she cried out. "You're killing him."

The male hissed and wrenched himself out of her hold. His eyes were wide, pupils dilated, crimson stains smearing his mouth and chin, battling with the tangle of red hair clinging to his face. Even in the dark, thanks to their preternatural vision, the scene was a grisly sight.

"Get the fuck away from me!" He swung, claws extended, going for Elle's head. But Alex leaped, catching his arm before it could make contact with her sister. He roared and snatched his wrist, trying to break her grip on him, and it was all she could do to hang on.

"Christian?" Elle's voice was soft, hesitant.

His struggle ceased, and the vampire twisted his head in her sister's direction.

Alex studied him. *Christian?* One of Marguerite's

former Calyxes? The one Markus had ordered to feed Elle after he'd kidnapped and turned her?

"It is you, isn't it?" Elle eased closer, assessing him. "Oh my God. You're a vampire? I barely recognized you." She shook her head.

"Gabrielle?" He stumbled back and spun around. He grabbed the bottom of his shirt to wipe at the evidence on his face, as if that would make everything okay.

A slight gurgle came from the vampire's victim, drawing Alex's attention. "He's still alive," she said. *Thank God.* "We need to call 911 and get the hell out of here."

"You could have killed him, Christian," Elle snapped and moved in behind him. "What were you thinking? Do you want to become a mindless Death Euphoria addict—a DEAD?" She tugged at his arm.

"I was just so damned hungry," he rumbled.

"Didn't your sire teach you anything?"

He released a sick-sounding laugh.

Elle glanced at Alex, then Christian. "How long ago were you turned?"

Shrugging, he looked over at Elle. "A week, maybe." He shook his head. "It's all been kind of a blur since Enrique dumped me here. I've had to figure this shit out on my own." He drove his bloodstained fingers through his hair.

"Enrique?" Alex's heart stuttered, and she edged closer to Elle and the new vamp. "Enrique did this to you?"

"Yeah. That's what I said, wasn't it?" he barked.

Adrenaline laced Alex's veins, making her hands tremble. "Where is he?"

"How the hell am I supposed to know?" His fangs glinted beneath his upper lip. "The bastard put my ass on the street. You think he's on my Christmas card list?"

"Whatever, you two," Elle interjected. "We need to call an ambulance if this guy's going to have any chance of making it."

"Shit. You're right." Alex glanced back at the injured human. "Help is coming," she whispered and quickly made her exit from the scene.

Elle called emergency services as they hurried back to the car. Once there, Alex opened her door and turned back to the others. With tattooed swirls circling his right eye and his wrists, and bloodstains on a ratty T-shirt, the dude appeared one part gangster and one part lost puppy.

"You've got to get rid of that shirt," Alex said. He looked down at his front side. "You look like you've just stepped off the set of a *Saw* movie."

Christian pulled the offending material over his disheveled head of red hair, revealing a wide expanse of lean muscle and a narrow waist. He looked a hot mess, but beneath the unkempt appearance, the male could have easily passed for an Olympic swimmer.

"What are we going to do with him?" Alex pinned Elle with a pointed stare.

"Hello?" Christian said. "I'm standing right here. I'm not an idiot. And I'm definitely not anyone's damn charity case." He started to march off.

Good grief. Alex sighed. "Hey genius," she called out, and Christian slowed to a stop. "Where are you planning to go?"

He tossed her a look that said he'd rather claw his eyes out than give her the satisfaction of an answer. "Why do you give a shit?"

A part of her didn't, really. He was acting like an ass. But he'd recently been in contact with Enrique, had lived with Marguerite and Markus when she'd been their prisoner, and he might possess valuable information about what had happened to her.

"Because you're too new to be out here on your own without guidance," Elle said. "Look what happened tonight." She braced her hands on her hips. "You were mere minutes from turning into a DEAD."

"What are you suggesting?" He faced them.

Elle's worried expression said she was thinking the same as Alex. She wanted to take him back with them. Except Kenric would shit a brick if they brought someone into Enclave headquarters without vetting the male through him and Guerin first.

"Are we doing this?" Alex tightened her grip on the door.

"Okay. Stop talking like I'm not fucking here," he said. "I got enough of that from Enrique. If you're not going to include me in what's going on then I'm out of here." He tossed his hands up and started to leave.

"We have a place you could stay for a while," Elle said. "That is…if you're interested?"

Christian drew to halt, glancing back at them once more. "I'm listening."

"I'll have to make a phone call first," her sister continued. "But you were there for me when I was turned, so let me be there for you. I can't make any promises, though. There are others who would have to approve of you staying with us."

"With you?" Christian strode closer. "Are you suggesting I bunk—"

"With the Enclave," Alex said.

Chapter Nine

Markus hit the guide button again on the remote control, searching for something, anything to take his mind off the clock. Alexandria had left with her sister more than three hours ago. He hated every damn minute she was out of his sight and his immediate protection. And this "sitting on the sidelines" shit sucked.

Strumming the fingers of his free hand on the leather arm of the den's couch, he punched the button selecting the Syfy channel: a storm was brewing when suddenly a great white shark flew out of a tornado and consumed some guy in free fall from a helicopter.

"Oh, fuck me," Markus groaned. "Seriously?" He tossed the remote across the room and shoved up from his seat.

Heavy boots trampling on the wood floors in the other room snagged his attention. Awareness sizzled inside his veins, and instinct had him smoothing a palm over his chest.

Alexandria had returned.

Following the sound, Markus strode into the large living space. Kenric and Guerin huddled near the fireplace in deep discussion about something. Movement in the corner of his eye caught his attention, yet he didn't have to look to know Alexandria had entered the room. But she wasn't alone. Behind her, a familiar face cautiously made his way inside.

Christian.

Except the male didn't quite look like the same Calyx he'd left behind at Marguerite's estate. Instead of the well-kept blood donor Markus recalled, Christian resembled one of the dirty and half-clothed residents of the New York slums from more than a century ago, when Markus had been a boy.

Christian's squared shoulders and erect spine conveyed confidence and a lack of fear. But Markus noticed the mix of trauma and desperation lingering in the male's eyes. He looked much like the humans who had begged for a coin or a piece of bread.

Understanding the origin of anguish and worry in the expressions of the homeless from his past had been easy. Question was, what put that look in Christian's eyes—or rather, who?

The redhead followed Alexandria, with Elle bringing up the rear. Markus leaned against the wall and crossed his arms, waiting for the story regarding Christian's arrival to unfold. As if Arran had been expecting everyone, his former partner trotted down the stairs and greeted his mate. So the whole gang was gathering around the bonfire.

This would be good.

The new guy eyed the others one by one, but when his gaze fell on Markus, he came to sudden halt. "Commander?"

His brow furrowed, and he took a hesitant step toward Markus.

Oh, give me a break. Like he didn't know I was here.

"Christian," Markus said, lowering his arms and pushing away from the wall. "What the hell are you doing here?"

The tall, fair-skinned man edged closer and that's when his individual scent registered over the others. Blood and... vampire. Markus drew up short. "You've been turned," he said.

"Yeah," Christian replied.

"What happened?" Markus gave him a once-over. "You get tired of being the donor? Thought it was time you were the one with the fangs?"

"Markus," Kenric warned. "Take it easy."

Markus shrugged. "It's a valid question."

"I wanted it," Christian said. "If that's what you're asking."

"Okay." Markus nodded. "I get that. Then what's your story? Why do you look like you're about one gulp away from turning DEAD?"

"Enrique Mateo," Arran interjected, drawing Markus's attention. "That's what happened to him. Gabrielle called earlier. She and Alex stumbled on Christian feeding and stopped him before he went too far. He said Enrique had done the deed and then dumped him on the street a few nights ago."

Tendrils of foreboding snaked their way up Markus's neck. "Enrique, huh?" Putting them toe-to-toe, Markus sneered at the newbie. "What would make him do such a thing to you?"

Christian met him glare for glare. "I don't know. He's a

damn ass, I guess. Enjoys watching others suffer. Much like you and Marguerite, don't you think?"

Something that felt like a smile tugged at Markus's mouth. The kid had guts. But he wasn't fooling him. Markus seized the other male by the back of the neck, yanking him hard until they were sniffing each other's pores. "Don't fucking lie to me, Red." Markus's fangs stabbed his lower lip. "Why the hell are you really here? What kind of game is Enrique playing?"

"For God's sake!" Elle appeared at their side. "What are you doing?"

"I don't know what the hell you're talking about," Christian spat, and groped at the hold on his neck.

"You know exactly what I'm talking about." Markus wasn't about to let up. Enrique was after something. And he bet his ass Christian was his puppet.

"What makes you think Enrique has anything to do with this other than setting Christian up for a walk through hell as a DEAD?" Elle grasped Markus's free arm.

"What's the deal, Markus?" It was Arran this time. "Where are you going with this?"

"I don't know what you think I know," Christian chewed out. "Enrique can kiss my ass. There's no game."

Without waiting for permission—like that was fucking happening—Markus mentally drove fast and hard into the male's neurons. Flashes of nameless faces whizzed by on the vampire's recent bloodletting parade, until Markus spotted the image he sought. Enrique.

Conversations were too scrambled to be of any use. Since the male's turn had occurred so recently, anything that had happened near the timeline of the event would still be an electrical rat's nest. Yet Markus hoped he'd get lucky and Christian's memories would reveal some clue or evidence as to the other bastard's agenda. But it was a damn long shot.

The young vampire groaned and struggled against the rapid, forceful mental invasion.

"Markus…" Kenric's voice sliced through his brain, but he ignored him. He had to know if Christian's presence had anything to do with him or Alexandria. One thing Markus knew for damn sure, Enrique would never get his hands on her.

Various images of the male maneuvering around what looked like an apartment. Markus flicked that shit aside.

Christian on his back with Enrique over him—inside him—then the dark-skinned vampire behind Christian, thrusting.

Fuck.

Markus's gut roiled. Those were scenes he could have done without. His own memories with Marguerite's former commander were still too fresh inside his head. Markus barreled through.

Enrique's face appeared beside the male, grinning—arrogant—ivory-white fangs fully extended.

More.

Come on. Give me something more. Show me what the hell you're up to.

The Spaniard dove for Christian's throat and the memory morphed to white static, as if the television station had suddenly gone off the air. Christian slumped.

"Son of a bitch." Markus stumbled back, leaving the others to catch the new guy. The abrupt disconnect had Markus spinning. He grasped the nearby chair, steadying himself, and shook off the swarm of bees buzzing inside his head.

"Dammit, Markus!" Kenric slammed a hard palm to his chest, shoving him back a little farther. "Was that really necessary? The guy has already been treated like a piece a trash and dumped on the street. We bring him here with the illusion of safety, then within minutes, you're playing Scrabble with his brain." Kenric sighed. "He's only days out of his turn. What the hell did you think you'd be able to piece together?"

Choking back his rage, Markus swallowed hard before finding his voice. "I'm not buying his shit about Enrique tossing him out," he bit out.

"Then come to me first before you take things into your own hands," Kenric ordered. "We're a team. Try to remember that." The commander looked back, checking on their new arrival. Christian had recovered well enough and was burning a hole through Markus's head with the flaming daggers of his glare. Kenric refocused on Markus. "Let's talk."

The Enclave's master brushed past him and opened the double French doors to the library. Markus shot Christian one last *kiss my ass* look, rotated on his heel, and followed the other vampire inside the dimly lit space.

Four overstuffed coffee-colored leather chairs sat across from each other in front of the cold fireplace. Numerous books lined the windowless expanse of the walls from floor to ceiling. One of those ladders used to find novels on the highest shelf stood locked to its rail and shoved to the other side of the room.

"By the way, I like what you've done with the new place." Markus performed a spin-and-survey maneuver before perching on the arm of one of the fine cowhide-covered chairs. "Have you added to your collection? It looks even bigger." Markus spread his arms wide for emphasis.

"Since when did you start talking so damn much?" Kenric shook his head. "Before Marguerite, you hardly said two words to anyone other than Arran."

"Well…" Markus began. "Being beneath—and on top of—Marguerite changes a man, wouldn't you say, sir?" Markus smiled. "That is, if you survive long enough."

Kenric grunted. "True. And rarely for the better."

"My point exactly about Christian," Markus said, and stood. "He's been Enrique's fuck buddy for God knows how long. They probably hooked up right after Marguerite's demise and her Calyxes were left behind—if not before."

"And you think Christian could be a threat to the Enclave because of his association with Enrique?" Kenric leaned onto the opposite chair and crossed his arms. "What would they be after? Enrique was Marguerite's pawn, not the mastermind. After Eve, Guerin, and Alex's run-in with him, I did my own investigation into Mr. Mateo." Kenric stood. "My informants tell me he doesn't have any significant following and appears to be keeping things quiet, staying mostly to himself."

For some reason, that bit of info didn't make Markus's gut feel any better. Unease still ran like an icy stream in his veins. "Yet isn't it the quiet ones you always have to worry about?" Markus raised a brow at the master. "It doesn't sit well at all with me that Enrique got that close to Alexandria. He and I weren't the best of friends when we served Marguerite."

"And you think since Christian and Enrique have a

connection, Christian may try to hurt Alex for Enrique to get back at you?" Kenric frowned. "I think you're reaching, Markus. That cell has left you a bit paranoid."

Frustration's ugly head reared inside Markus. "I know what the hell I'm talking about, Kenric. I'm not fucking delusional." He braced his hands on the library shelf.

"Alex lives in the heart of the Enclave," Kenric said. "Even if what you're saying is the case, Christian would have to be an idiot to try anything with her inside our walls. I have a hard time believing Enrique would go to such elaborate lengths to hurt Alex. She's safe here, Markus. Believe me."

This was a sorry-ass waste of his time. But he wasn't surprised Kenric didn't believe him. Too much shit had gone down between them, and he doubted any member of the Enclave would ever take him on his word.

"Sure," Markus muttered and gave him a nod. "If you say so." Alexandria's protection would have to fall on his shoulders alone.

• • •

Several days had passed since he'd last heard from Christian. Enrique drummed his index finger on the aluminum shell of his laptop, staring at the clock on the toolbar. In less than sixty minutes, the sun's rays would be licking at the horizon, singeing the edges of the darkness, burning it away. And he still didn't know a damn thing!

Whether or not his plan would run smoothly rode on the redhead's coming through. On whether or not he could pull off an Oscar-winning performance for Markus and that tight-ass excuse for a master vampire.

The cell phone on his desk vibrated, yanking Enrique's attention from his laptop. Snatching the smartphone up, he checked the display and couldn't stop the grin forming on his mouth. *Christian.*

With a slide of his finger across the glass, he answered. "You're inside?"

"Worked just like you said it would," Christian said in a hushed voice. "Sorry it took so long for me to contact you. I'm finally back out on the streets tonight to feed with Elle and Arran. Once I got them to give me a few minutes alone, I tracked down the female you'd planted with my phone."

"Good, good. I knew they'd never be able to resist the urge to rescue a lost and abused puppy." Enrique snickered.

"Didn't hurt that the Enclave member who was out the other night happened to be the female I'd fed for Markus during her turn. She had this whole 'I owe you one' complex."

"Absolutely perfect." Enrique kicked back in his chair and propped his legs up on his desk, his boot heels releasing a solid *thud* on the wood. "I couldn't have planned that any better." He snagged a pen from its holder and tapped out a melody on the laptop's case. "Looks like whatever god is up there is on my side, for once."

"Yeah," Christian said. "Markus and I had our little meet-and-greet the first night I moved in. The bastard tried his damnedest to put my brain through a fucking sifter looking for proof that you're behind my sudden appearance."

"And…" Enrique tossed the pen onto the desk and his boots slapped the floor.

"And just like you said. He couldn't find a damn thing," Christian said. "My head's still too messed up."

Smiling, Enrique stood. "Excellent."

He stood and yanked on the thick curtains behind him, opening up his moonlight view from the top floor of his new apartment building that overlooked the docks. Moving as soon as he'd kicked Christian to the curb had been the most prudent decision. That way even if his new vamp developed an ugly case of a conscience, he could honestly say he had no idea where to find him.

This was going to work. With Christian on the inside, he'd have access to the intel on the Enclave's movements. Precisely, Kenric's daughter's movements. He needed to know everything he could about the female. And once he had the proper buyer in place, which was only a matter of time now, getting his hands on her would be that much easier.

"Over the next few days, you need to get them to trust you," Enrique said.

"No problem," Christian whispered.

"You get me everything you can find on that female."

"Eve," Christian said.

"Say again?"

"The female in the photo. They call her Eve."

"Eve, then." Enrique shook his head. *How appropriate, Marguerite. No one ever accused you of not being imaginative.* "Help me to get the information we need to get our hands on her, and I'll make sure you're a *very* happy man."

The call went dead, leaving Enrique chuckling to himself. Why not promise the redhead anything he damn wanted? Didn't matter. Because once the Enclave figured out who'd ratted them out, the male was as good as dead.

Shame, though, in a way. Enrique sighed.

He'd been a good fuck.

Chapter Ten

Alex leaned her head back and under the shower's warm spray, working the shampoo from her hair. She was ready for tonight. For weeks she'd been training. Eve had finally given her the thumbs-up with Kenric, and he'd agreed she could go out on a trial basis with Guerin and Eve. Not that Elle hadn't done everything in her power to dissuade Alex from the entire idea of becoming more than a resident of the Enclave.

Hell, no. Alex wasn't about to back down. She needed this. Needed the purpose. The empowerment. Needed to feel like she truly belonged somewhere again.

Squeezing the water from her hair, she moved out of the stream. Her next obstacle would be to remain out of Markus's path for as long as possible. So far, she'd managed to steer clear of him ever since their encounter in the gym. Despite her best efforts to keep the memory buried, it came barreling forward, knocking the strength from her knees.

Alex leaned against the wall for support. Closing her eyes, she was helpless against the surfacing images. Markus over her, his hair brushing her arm, gooseflesh rising in its wake. His lips on hers, stealing her breath, her will. Her nipples pebbled, and her sex swelled. Even as a memory, Markus consumed her.

With her fingers splayed flat against her stomach, Alex glided her hand south over her wet abs. God, how she needed. She groaned. Just one touch and maybe the constant knot of tension—yearning—inside her would finally uncoil. Slipping her fingertips through her soft curls, she parted the moist folds between her legs, searching for the aching bundle of nerves at the apex. Her fingertip nudged the sensitive nub, and her breath hitched at the contact.

"Oh, God," she sighed, squeezing her eyelids tight. A shadowed face loomed in her mind's eye. Alex gulped. *Please. No. Go, away. For once. Why can't you stay buried inside my head?*

"You're your mommy's dirty little girl, aren't you sweetie?" The man chuckled. "Fuck, you're a pretty thang." The heavy weight of the man pressed down on her, nearly smothering her as he shoved her legs apart. His wide and calloused hand groped at her private parts. Alex chocked back a sob. "A dirty, dirty girl," he drawled.

"No," she cried out, and yanked her hand away from her groin. Curling her fingers, she straightened, but before she could consider the consequences, frustration had her slamming her fist into the wall. The tile released a loud *pop* beneath her knuckles and fractured. "Dammit!" Alex drew back, wringing her hand and flexing her aching fingers. "Stupid." She shook her head and turned off the water.

After popping the door on the shower, she tugged a bath sheet from the bar, wrapped it around her, and stepped from the stall. Padding over to the counter, she grabbed the extra towel she'd left there and started drying her hair. She was almost twenty-seven years old. A grown woman. What had been done to her by her mother's boyfriend had been almost twenty years ago. She flung the towel from her hands onto the counter, gritting her teeth. So why the hell did it still mess with her head?

Shoving the memories back into their temporary vault, Alex brushed her teeth. Even more frustrating was the fact that the only man who'd ever elicited the feelings of pleasure—sexual pleasure—from her and made her feel as if she could be a real woman was the man everyone hated.

She plopped the toothbrush back into its holder and twisted the faucet handles to their off position. Alex swiped a wide path across the mirror, revealing her reflection through the steam. Violet eyes, clouded with confusion and anger, stared back at her when something odd occurred to her. When she'd thought about Markus a moment ago and those who hated him, she'd referred to everyone else, excluding herself. When had that changed? Didn't she still hate him? Shouldn't *she* be at the top of that list?

She'd fought to hang on to her anger, the bitterness, but she couldn't move forward if she still lived in the past.

Eve had taught her that.

Perhaps the message had finally sunk in. God knew she was ready to move on—do something—with the new life she'd been handed.

Pushing away from the sink, Alex tucked the thick cotton a little more snugly across her breasts and headed back to her bedroom. She'd left the bathroom door slightly ajar and, reaching out, she pulled it wider and crossed the threshold. And stopped dead in her tracks.

Markus leaned against the opposite wall of her room. Dressed in black from head to toe, his jaw revealed a dark shadow of a beard, minus the goatee. With his thick tattooed arms crossed over his chest, he looked like a coiled lethal weapon waiting to pounce on his prey. Her stomach flipped. Any woman with an ounce of common sense would hit the door and not look back. So why did the sight of him have the opposite effect on her? Instead of running, she had the crazy urge to toss her towel to the floor and drop to her knees at his feet.

Hadn't she thought the word "crazy"?

"You weren't invited in here," she said, her tone icy.

"You've been avoiding me," he said and moved away from the wall, bringing himself closer.

Alex had always believed her room was large, more room than she really needed. But at that moment, the four walls weren't nearly wide enough. Markus's presence absorbed all the oxygen in the confined space. Her heart galloped at his approach. Finding her next breath was more difficult with every beat.

"Yes, I have," she said. "So get out." She dodged left, but Markus countered, halting her escape.

"No," he said, smiling.

Glaring up at him, heat from her rising temperature radiated up her neck and into her face. "No?"

"Not yet." He shook his head.

Fire sparked in her veins and with an open palm, Alex swung for his face. But before her flesh met his in a satisfying *whack*, Markus's long fingers cuffed her wrist. He jerked her forward, and her chest slammed into his, punching the air from her lungs. Yet she had a feeling the sudden vacating of oxygen from her cells had nothing to do with the impact and everything to do with the man himself. Her jaw dropped, and she did her best to form coherent words. A rebuke for his actions, but for the life of her, she couldn't find her voice.

With his free hand, Markus pinched her chin with his thumb and forefinger, forcing her to look at him. His nostrils flared, and fire swirled around the storm clouds of his irises. God help her, that shouldn't be so damn sexy, but the sight made her knees wobble.

"How else am I supposed to get a chance to talk to you alone?" One dark slash of a brow lifted. "Besides, I heard a bang coming from your room when I was passing by. I knocked, but you didn't answer. I checked the door handle, discovered it was unlocked, and I let myself in. You were in the shower, and it sounded as if you were okay, so I thought there was no time like the present for us to clear the air."

"You're just so damn innocent and heroic, aren't you?" she spat. "That still didn't give you the right to sneak into my room." Then it dawned on her how long he'd been waiting for her. "Oh my God..." she muttered. "You've been out here this whole time. Watching me."

That did it. Her claws were out. Alex yanked hard on the hold he had on her wrist, wrenching it. With her other arm, she punched in the region of his kidney. Yet her struggle only culminated with him wrapping himself around her, drawing her tight against him. Using his larger legs against hers, he moved her in reverse, not stopping until her back was pressed against the wall. She might as well have been a

Fiat going head-on against a tank. Arching, she shoved her hips into his upper thighs. The unmistakable hard outline of his erection pressed into her lower abdomen. *Oh God.* Her heart stuttered, and as if someone had vented the lid on her rage, the fight drained out of her.

Hesitantly, she glanced up from under her lashes. Markus stared down at her, unfazed. His expression an unreadable mask. He had to know she'd felt his arousal. Yet instead of taunting her with its presence, he loosened his grip on her and cupped her cheek.

"I know you're pissed at me," he rumbled. "I'm a bastard. I get that." He lowered his head, his mouth too damn close to hers for her brain to handle. Alex tugged her lower lip in with her teeth for strength. "What I want to know, though, is why there are fresh bruises on your knuckles?" He slid his hand into hers and brought it up between them, her fingers on display as evidence. "You weren't scheduled to spar this morning."

How had he noticed that small detail? More importantly, how did he know her schedule? Mentally she rolled her eyes. What was she thinking? This was Markus. Devious was his middle name. "That's none of your business."

He gently squeezed her hand. "Does this have something to do with the sound I heard outside your door?"

Glowering, she evaded and searched for some kind of quick excuse. Damn, at times like these, she wished like hell she were a better liar. Even when they'd been kids, she'd never been able to fool Elle. Their mom? Well, that was another story. Getting away with stuff had been easy since her mother had spent most of her days stoned out of her mind. But the man before her was nothing like Anita Stevens.

"Maybe?" She shrugged. It was the best she could come up with under the pressure.

"Talk to me," he demanded.

"Kiss my ass," she snapped. She wasn't about to tell him the reason for her bruises. That she'd hit the wall out of frustration because she hadn't been able to masturbate—to orgasm—*ever.*

"Don't tempt me." He flexed his hips, pressing his swollen length into her, reminding her of their position.

"You need to get out of my face."

"Why?" He smirked. "I kind of like having you like this. Up against a wall. My body against yours. You all nervous and hot. Your pulse strumming away inside my head."

He'd gotten one thing right. She was about to jump out of her skin. "Stop it," she demanded.

"When did you last feed?"

"I-I…" She blinked from the sudden change of subject. "I don't know." She thought back for a moment. When had she last fed? "A few days ago. Maybe a week?"

"That's what I was afraid of."

"You?" She arched a brow. "Afraid? My, my, will wonders never cease?"

"Don't get used to the idea."

"Don't worry."

"You can't go out tonight at less than full strength," he said.

"I'll do whatever the hell I want. I'm not your prisoner any longer." She shoved against him, but the effort had little effect on him.

"You need to feed," he stated, his words as firm and immovable as his body. "Now."

"And who are you suggesting I do that from? You?" she scoffed.

Lowering his lashes, he inhaled through his nose once more, and based on his expression, she could have sworn he'd just sniffed his favorite pie. "Do you find the idea so distasteful? You used to take my vein on a regular basis."

"Like I had a choice," she grumbled, not holding back on the hostility.

"Tonight's not that different," he said, the control in his tone slipping, revealing an edge of desperation underneath. "You're heading out in less than an hour. And unless you want to screw up, get yourself injured and kicked off Kenric's team before you've even started, I suggest you take what's right in front of you."

Damn him. He had a point. She'd been so consumed with the training aspect of preparing for tonight, she was about to make a foolish rookie mistake—placing herself and her partners at a disadvantage by not being at her full strength. If something happened to Eve or Guerin because of her carelessness and lack of planning, she would never forgive herself.

"Besides," he said, "and I don't admit this often…to anyone."

His thumb caressed her chin, the tip skating over the base of her lower lip. Electric tingles that didn't play fair arrowed straight for the bundle of nerves between her legs.

Ignore them. He's doing this on purpose to rattle me.

"You could say I kind of owe you one from a few weeks ago."

"Yes," she replied, thankful for the reminder that she was supposed to be pissed at him. "On that point I can definitely agree with you. Especially since you didn't fulfill your end of the bargain."

"Your perspective." He cocked his head. "Not mine."

God help me. He is so infuriating.

"I was only referring to the blood donation." Markus reached up and pulled his hair away from his neck. "Take what you need." He tilted his head.

"You're not serious." He wanted her to feed from his throat?

"Do I look like I'm kidding?" He lifted his chin, beckoning her.

Like a magnet to its perfect polar opposite, her gaze collided with the thick rope of an artery running the length of his neck. His pulse lifted the flesh there, and inside her head, the beating of his heart resounded like a jungle drum, taunting her. Calling her.

"Come on, Vixen. Fast and hard," he coaxed. "Take it."

Her gums tingled with the lengthening of her fangs. Maybe she would take him up on the offer. After all, wasn't his throat the least he could offer? Her fingers curled into fists, her nails digging into the soft tissue inside. "Payback's a bitch, you know," she said, her mouth watering.

"From you, darling," he said, and there was no way she could miss the sound of the smile in his voice, "I expect nothing less."

She struck.

Sure, deep, and without mercy, her fangs sank into his artery. His breath hitched. And with her first hard draw on his flesh, he groaned.

Alex gulped, and her taste buds sparked. Reflex had her swallowing again. And again. Her skin heated, burned. Except the scorching sensation in no way resembled pain.

God, no. She was alive.

Every pore.

Every nerve ending radiating out from her spine had awakened.

She'd sipped from countless, nameless humans since she'd become a vampire, yet none of the feedings had ever ravaged her control. It was as if her cells recognized his, and a switch had been flipped.

Mine.

Her sex pulsed with hungry need. Arousal rushed from her, swelling her folds. She moaned, arching her hips into his.

"Damn," Markus bit out, pulling her tighter into his embrace.

Yes. This wasn't like her, but dear God, at that moment, she didn't care.

She spread her legs, needing something. Anything. Markus's leather-clad thigh slid between hers. Perfect. Straddling his firm leg, Alex rocked onto the thick muscle. The pressure. God, the pressure was so damn good. She gasped against his skin, her head a dizzying rush of desire.

"Vixen...Fuck." Markus dug his fingertips into her back. "Use me," he murmured. He thrust higher, harder, working himself against her pussy. And nothing had ever felt so divine in her life. "Whatever you need."

Scoring his scalp with her nails, Alex rode the hard presence between her thighs. She lapped at his skin, and the taste of his flesh, his essence, transported her to a hot summer night with the tide swirling around her ankles. Exotic, sweet, and sultry. Her pulse hammered inside her head, drowning out all reason, all conscious thought. She was lost to her body's demands.

A whimper left her throat, and as if Markus understood exactly what she needed, he pulsed his leg back and forth. The new angle and movement pressed into the apex of her sex with divine precision. Pleasure swirled like a growing vortex within the swollen bundle of nerves between her legs. *More.* Alex twisted her fingers in his hair and pumped her hips.

"Let go, baby," he whispered. "It's yours."

She groaned. God, how she wanted it.

"Take it, dammit," he rasped.

Suddenly, as if the pressure had grown too high for her to bear, the bubble exploded on her pleasure. Her head fell back, bumping the wood behind her. The muscles in her arms and legs tensed, and her spine arched. Rapture tore through her on a blinding tidal wave of sheer ecstasy. Her body quaked. The world around her shimmered, vanished, leaving only the man whose arms circled her and held her to earth as bliss pulsed through her core.

"That's it, baby," as if from a distance, Markus whispered, stroking her back.

Too soon her tremors calmed, and the euphoria of her orgasm waned. Markus loosened his hold on her and eased his leg back. But keeping his body next to hers, he didn't let go. Thank God, because at that moment, she wasn't sure she possessed the ability to stand on her own two feet. Threading his fingers through her hair, he cradled her head. Her arms dropped to her sides, the strength in her limbs depleted. Alex dragged her eyelids open, and his hooded stare slammed into hers. Lust, fiery hot, swirled in his gray eyes. His mouth hovered mere inches from hers, his breathing ragged.

And the reality of what had happened hit her like a

roundhouse kick to the gut.

Markus had let her use him. Worse yet, she'd taken what he'd offered. All of it. And he'd given her the best—the first—orgasm she'd ever had.

Damn him.

She reeled, torn between the near irresistible urge to kiss him or to punch the snot out of him. Swallowing hard, she forced the growing knot of desperation down into the pit of her stomach.

A deep rumble vibrated off him as his body went rigid, pressing the hard length of his cock against her. Alex's spine stiffened. *Oh God.* Lifting her chin, she fisted her hands in anticipation of his next action. No way would she get away with what she'd done without the male demanding something in exchange. Because history had taught her well: nothing good came without a price.

"Are you okay?" His words came out hoarse, strangled. Yet that wasn't the most unusual thing about his question. Asking her about her health at that moment had been the last thing she'd expected.

"Excuse me?" she croaked.

A roughened palm stroked her cheek, and it was all she could do not to lean into the caress. But she'd already allowed her guard to fall further than she'd ever anticipated.

"If I let go, are you okay to stand?"

"Oh…" She glanced down at where his body was still connected with hers, helping to hold her upright. *Oh, shit.* Neither of them had moved since…since. Yeah. Alex planted her palms against his pecs, cleared her throat, and nodded.

"Good," he muttered under his breath. Untangling his fingers from her hair, Markus took a couple of steps back.

Her bath sheet slipped, but she managed to snag it and tighten the material around her before she lost any more of her dignity. Pushing a lock of hair out of her eyes, she inhaled deeply, gathering her courage to face him. What would he expect from her now? He was an aroused male with needs. Of that there was no question. She'd felt the very large evidence of it pressed into her.

How long had it been since he'd been with a woman? Had he…satisfied those particular cravings since he'd been freed? A flash of uneasiness she refused to define roiled inside her gut at the thought of him with another, thrusting, straining for his peak until he roared with the ferocity of his release. Her heart clenched at the visual image. A familiar *click* sounded in the room, and she jerked her head up. Blinking, she scanned the space around her. A clawing blow of emptiness struck behind her breastbone, taking her by surprise.

Once again, not what she'd expected from him, or from herself.

Markus was gone.

Chapter Eleven

Markus slammed the door to his room and kept moving. He couldn't stop and think or his head would explode. His heart raced, and his chest heaved with every breath. Slapping a palm over the residual wound left behind by Alex on his neck, he rubbed across the bruised flesh.

"Stupid," he chided himself, pacing between his walls. He was a fucking idiot. Behind the confined space of his zipper, his cock throbbed with each step. With a death lock on his molars, he drew to a halt and snatched the straight-backed chair from in front of his desk. Roaring, he swung hard, tossing it across the room. The chair crashed into the wall with a loud *bang*, shattering the wood. Broken pieces scattered across the floor, never to be put back together again. A lot like his life.

Walking away from Alexandria had been one of the most difficult things he'd ever done. He choked on a laugh. "Hobbling" away was a better word, since making a quick exit when his cock had felt like a brick between his legs had been no easy task. But he'd had no choice. For him, or for Alexandria.

If he'd remained in her room one second longer with the scent of her orgasm thick in the air, clinging to the insides of his nostrils, his control would have snapped. And she deserved better than what he had to offer: a mate with a soul so tarnished and frayed that he'd lost his grip on his ethical compass. *A mate?* He choked back a laugh. Since when had he begun to entertain the idea of her in a more permanent role in his life? Mere days ago he had lain wasting away in a cell. The only reason he'd worked so damn hard to convince Kenric he'd turned over a new leaf was to keep her safe, not bond with her for an eternity. An unfamiliar sensation, yet one not at all unpleasant, surged through his veins at the thought of waking with her in his arms each night for the next century and beyond. *What the hell?*

Reaching low, he shoved the heel of his hand against the swollen length of his erection, willing the arousal to let him go. He grunted. "Shit!"

Squeezing his eyelids shut, he tried his best to force the memory of her into the dark recesses of his mind. Alexandria with her head thrown back against the wall, shuddering in ecstasy. But he succeeded in only burning the image into his neurons. He slapped his palms on the window frame in front of him and his forehead tapped the warm glass. His cock pulsed, demanding attention. Beads of sweat popped from his pores, and a cool, thin trail ran down his temple.

On a groan, he relented and pushed away. Treading across the threshold to his bathroom, he reached for his zipper, tugged on the metal, and opened his fly. His erection sprang free, the head wet with pre-cum. The sound of his pulse was a mantra to the need for release strumming inside his veins.

How long could he go on like this? Every evening after rising, he inhaled the sweet traces of vanilla and honey lingering in the hallway. The scent confirmed Alexandria had recently passed down the same path. She was so damn close, yet forever out of his reach. But he'd have to learn to deal, for as long as he had to. His discomfort was a small price to pay as long as she remained safe.

Over the last several weeks, though, his palm and his dick had become quite the BFFs.

Having to jack off on a regular basis to ease the ache was a situation the old Markus would never have tolerated. He grimaced at his reflection in the mirror. When he required a female, finding one to satisfy his needs had never been an issue. There had always been an ample number willing to bend over and give him a warm, soft place to relieve his itch. Yet whether he liked it or not, he couldn't bring himself to seek out another. There was only one, who with a single look had captured his heart and made him fantasize about all the ways he wanted her. Against the wall. Beneath him. Straddling his hips, with her hair fanned out behind her as she screamed his name.

He curled his fingers around the hypersensitive flesh between his legs, and his breath hitched from the contact. Grasping for the counter with his free hand, he steadied himself. "Motherfucker," he gritted out.

During those months when he'd been secured inside his cell beneath the mansion, he'd kept her memory locked down. If he didn't see her, smell her, he could forget her.

Almost.

At least that was what he'd tried to convince himself.

Sliding his palm over the slick head of his shaft, Markus groaned from the sensation. His eyelids shuttered. *Dammit.* He'd never be able to forget. Not now. Not after the way she'd straddled his thigh, her hot pussy nearly searing the leather between them. She'd ridden him until her release had detonated like a round of TNT, coming close to destroying his control in its wake.

He stroked down his cock, and his rod bucked against his hand. Grinding his molars, he spiraled his palm back up the length. His balls tightened, the cum inside a flood ready to rupture the dam holding it back. Goddammit, this wasn't going to take long.

Once. Twice more, he pumped his straining shaft when the lid suddenly erupted on his orgasm.

"Fuucck!" Markus's fist jerked beneath the sensitized head as jet after jet of cum hit the granite in a violent spray of pleasure.

Growling, he worked the last drop of his orgasm from his shaft and uncurled his fingers.

Moments later, his head still buzzed as he cleaned up the evidence of his release, washed his hands, and prepared to head downstairs. He'd never be ready to stand there like a helpless spectator as Alexandria left for her first patrol, but at least he'd be calmer. Good thing, since when he'd heard that Kenric had agreed to allow her to accompany Eve and Guerin, he'd wanted the master's head.

But he had to play it cool, sit back, and be all fucking agreeable if the Enclave's commander was ever going to sever his leash.

However, not being an active member of the team didn't mean he wasn't going to stay within earshot of Elle while Alexandria was out there. If there was trouble, one of the three would call in for backup. He'd gotten the vixen to feed before she'd left. Renewed their connection. If she needed him, he'd find her. With or without the Enclave's help or permission.

Downstairs, he strode toward the kitchen. Alexandria's voice reached his ears before he crossed the threshold. He braced a shoulder against the archway and listened.

"So you and Guerin usually handle Monday, Wednesday, and Friday while Kenric and Arran take Tuesday, Thursday, and Saturday night," she said.

"That's right," Guerin chimed in. "We rotate as to who works Sunday. After a while, or if something comes up, we'll switch. Just for some variety."

Business as usual. At least she sounded okay. Not that he'd expect any different. Alexandria was too strong-willed. Eve and Guerin would never suspect a thing, unless she wanted them to know.

Markus pushed away from the wall and proceeded into the room. Conversation around the table ceased. His boots thumped off the wood as he made his way over to the coffeepot. He didn't have to look up from his cup to know Alexandria's gaze tracked him.

"Please don't let me stop whatever it is you're discussing." Markus placed the carafe back in its place and looked up. Guerin, Eve, and Alexandria were seated around the table. Whom he hadn't picked up on was Christian kicking it at the far end. Nursing a mug of the dark brew in his hand, the redhead was leaning back in his chair, ignoring the others, as if he were right at home.

At that moment, the rest of the big happy family filed into the room. Arran headed straight for the coffee. A lot had changed since Markus had jumped ship for Marguerite's madness, but apparently, the blond warrior's fondness for the roasted bean hadn't.

Kenric and Emily closed in on the dining table. The commander's arm circled Emily's waist, keeping her close, silently declaring the female his. They came to a stop near Guerin and Eve as Markus eased onto one of the barstools at the island.

Close.

But not too…in their face.

What the hell. He could play the part of the considerate guy when need be.

It was easier this way, for everyone, if he didn't grab one of the chairs and slide up to the wood, pretending as if they wanted him there. He wasn't a damn fool. Arran barely tolerated his presence. And Guerin. Well… Markus glanced over at the Enclave's second-in-command. As usual, whenever he and Guerin were in the same room, the male kept Markus in his sights. As if at any minute Markus would draw his blade and slit someone's throat. Fuck him. Did he look that damn close to the edge?

Lowering his mug to the bar, his mind wandered back to when he had lain in his cell waiting for his next breath to finally stall in his lungs. Maybe Guerin wasn't that far off the mark? But the members of the Enclave weren't the ones in his sights.

Markus brought the brew to his lips once more, his focus landing on their newest roomie. Kicked back in his chair and dressed in what looked like a new leather jacket and jeans, Christian sipped from his cup. The new vamp's attention wagged between the window and conversation at the other end of the table about their agenda for the night's patrol. Markus bit back a laugh. The male was trying too hard to pretend he wasn't absorbing every detail. He was about as subtle as a foghorn.

Markus didn't give a flying fuck that Kenric and Elle were all warm and cozy with the newbie parking his shit with the Enclave. He didn't trust the bastard. The redhead's previous location had been up Enrique's ass—or vice versa. That alone was reason enough to not like the prick. Trusting him around Alexandria and the rest of the Enclave? Well, that was a completely different game. Christian would need to show him more than dirty clothes, fangs, and a sob story before he was a player on that team.

In the meantime, until Christian exposed his hand, Markus would have to settle for watching and waiting. And unfortunately for their guest, neither was his strong suit.

Breathing in the warm steam off his coffee, Markus allowed his attention to drift toward the brunette on the far side of the table. Alexandria had dressed in the typical DEAD hunting gear of all leather. And damn if the female didn't look as if she'd been born to wear the rawhide. She wore a form-fitting black jacket with a silver zipper that rose diagonally across her chest and held her full breasts snugly in place. The collar flipped upward around the delicate flare of her throat, bringing attention to her porcelain skin and high cheekbones. He couldn't see from his angle, but he was sure the leather encasing her legs included a set of daggers strapped to each thigh.

His perusal roamed upward to where she'd secured her long dark tresses behind her head. Perhaps it was his imagination, but her cheeks appeared a shade pinker, her violet eyes even more radiant. Behind his mug, a grin spread on his mouth. She'd never admit he was partly responsible for her healthy glow. And despite its recent release, damn if his cock didn't twitch at the memory.

"Tonight's your big night, Alex," Kenric said from his position behind Eve's chair. "Are you ready?"

Alex looked up, her gaze brushing Markus first before settling on Kenric. "More than you can imagine."

Her words rang through him like the striking of a bell on round one of a prizefight. But Markus didn't like the damn odds.

"Christian," the Enclave's master called out, and the male's head popped up. "Have you thought about what you'd like to do now that you've had some time to adjust to your new life?"

"Uhm…" The new guy rubbed a palm over his lingering shadow of a beard, then shrugged. "I'm not sure. Why? You need me out of here?"

"No," Kenric said. "That's not what I'm implying. I ask because I thought you might want to consider finding out a little more about the Enclave while you're here. You might find it's something you're interested in pursuing."

A loud cough burst from Markus's throat. Hell, he nearly choked at the vampire's insinuation that Christian should consider joining them. All heads drifted his way.

Guerin leaned back in his chair. "You have something you'd like to interject, Markus? Maybe a few inspiring words for our new vampire here?"

"Nah, man." Markus shook his head. "I think there's plenty of that spilling out of your mouth for the both of us." The bottom of his cup met the granite beside him with a *clank*, and he made a beeline for the Enclave's master. It was time he evened the playing field.

Moving in behind Kenric and Emily, Markus leaned within earshot of the master vampire. "We need to talk."

Emily glanced over her shoulder at him, then slid from her mate's hold. "I'm going to grab myself a cup of coffee before Arran finishes off the pot."

"I heard that," his former partner interjected from the other side of the island, carafe in hand.

"I wasn't whispering."

"This can't wait until after we're done here?" Kenric crossed his arms.

"No," Markus said. "It can't."

"I think we're ready to head out, anyway." Guerin stood from the table, looked toward his mate, then at the few empty pieces of tableware.

"Yeah." Eve nodded. "I'm good to go." She rose and Alexandria did the same.

"I'm set," she said.

"All right, then," Kenric said, surveying his team. "Stay safe."

"We intend to," Guerin said with a possessive hand resting low on Eve's back as they rounded the table.

Christian pushed back in his chair at the same moment and stood, striding into the path of the approaching couple. "You know, something's been bugging me for the last several days, and I finally put my finger on what it is."

The sudden interjection of dialogue from the brooding

new vamp drew everyone's attention. Guerin and Eve came to a stop and faced Christian.

Shoving his fingers into his hair, Christian pushed the thick red strands back out of his eyes. "You remind me of someone," he said, wagging a finger at Eve.

"Really?" Eve's smile was hesitant as she looked between her mate and the younger vampire.

"Yeah." He nodded. "Except for the eyes, you look a lot like my former Mistress, Marguerite."

A loud *crash* resonated off the walls of the kitchen, drawing everyone's attention. Elle stood, her eyes wide with what was left of a coffee cup at her feet. "I'm—I'm sorry about that," she muttered. "I can be so damn clumsy sometimes." She lowered onto her haunches and began gathering the broken shards into her palms.

"Are you okay?" Arran made his way from around the island and toward his mate.

"I'm fine." She shook her head. "It just slipped."

"No worries," Michael said, appearing out of nowhere. Markus had been so absorbed in his own thoughts, he hadn't noticed the human's arrival in the room. "I'll grab a broom and dustpan." The Enclave's thirtysomething cook and driver disappeared back into the large pantry, then emerged seconds later with the said tools in hand.

"Don't you agree, Markus?" Christian asked.

"Excuse me?" Markus squared his shoulders.

"About Marguerite," the redhead reiterated. "Doesn't Eve bear a striking resemblance?"

"Maybe." Markus shrugged. "If you say so. I don't see it."

"How can you say that?" Christian gave Eve another

once-over. "They could have been sisters."

"Listen," Guerin began and moved to intercept the newcomer, tossing his arm over the other male's shoulder. "Since you're new around here," he continued, his voice a low rumble of warning, "I'm going to give you a onetime pass." Then with his face in the other male's, he added, "Marguerite is a subject we prefer not to discuss."

Christian glanced over his shoulder and gave Eve a sheepish look. "I didn't mean any offense," he said.

"None taken." She shook her head and grasped her mate's hand. "We better get moving."

"You're right." Guerin joined her, resting a hand on her hip. Passing Elle, Alexandria palmed her sister's shoulder, her gaze brushing his in the process, before striding over to meet up with her team. The trio headed toward the exit, leaving apprehension a clawing, living force in Markus's chest. He had to do something, and that meant going to Kenric.

"We need to talk." He brushed past the Enclave's master. "Now." Markus marched into the library adjacent to the kitchen. The *thud* of Kenric's boots echoed behind him. There wasn't any sense in again bringing up his suspicions to Kenric about Christian and Enrique. They'd already been down that road and had hit a dead end. Kenric was convinced of Alexandria's safety inside his walls. And Markus didn't have a shred of evidence to prove him wrong other than his gut instinct. Frustrating as hell.

But one thing Markus did know was that he couldn't stand around any longer doing nothing more than sucking up the oxygen inside the mansion's walls. He needed to take matters into his own hands. He needed action.

A few paces into the room, Kenric's deep voice filled

the space. "You forget yourself, Markus," he said, and the door banged shut, drawing him back around. "You're not the commander in this house."

Before he could respond, the master vampire slammed into his chest. If it weren't for the tight grip the male had on his shirt, Markus's feet would have left the ground, and his back would have been having a nice meet-and-greet with the bookshelves. "I'll only allow you to push me so far," Kenric added, fangs flashing from beneath his upper lip. "before I give you one of two choices: your cell, or your head?"

"What happened to the diplomatic master we all know and love?" Markus sneered, showing off his own set of sharp teeth.

"Oh, he's still here." Kenric lifted a brow. "Believe me. Or you would have been dead a long time ago." With a slight shove, he released Markus from his hold. Markus stumbled back a couple of steps before regaining his balance.

"Touchy tonight." Markus chuckled and repositioned his shirt with a roll of his shoulders.

"I tolerate a great deal around here, Markus. I'm patient like that." Kenric settled into one of the dark brown over-stuffed leather chairs and crossed his legs. "You, more than anyone, should be well versed." His mouth twitched. "I also realize the warriors on my team are all alpha males. You're bound to argue, fight, and test boundaries. It's in your nature." The Enclave master laced his fingers over his chest, his elbows resting on the soft sides of the chair. "But when you trample over the lines by giving *me* orders in *my* home, you need a reminder of who is in command of this operation, and those aren't always gentle."

"Point taken." Markus flexed his fist. The urge to tear

into something or someone rode him hard, and if he didn't find release soon he would go fucking mad. Breathing hard through his nostrils, he dialed back his tone. Prior to Marguerite, he'd spent more than two decades with Kenric and his team, but all those years had been piss in a toilet the moment that sadistic bitch had gotten inside his head. Because after that, his status as an Enclave warrior had spiraled down the drain. If he was ever going to be officially allowed back on the inside and placed on patrol, he had better learn to leash his temper. God knew he needed out of the damn mansion for more than a feed. He shook his head, the tips of his fangs aching from the tight hold of his jaw.

"I'm glad we understand each other." Kenric dipped his head in acknowledgment. "So what was so important that you needed my immediate attention?"

Moving in behind the large chair facing the other vampire, Markus curled his fingers over the sculpted top. "I'm ready to get back to work," he said, impressed with the amount of calm civility he was able to muster in his voice.

Kenric lowered his hands to the arms of his seat. "I take it this urgent need has something to do with Alex?"

"I admit," Markus began, pushing away from the dark leather, "I don't like her being out there alone. We've already discussed my concerns about her safety with Enrique coming around and Christian's coincidental appearance."

Tossing his head back, Kenric released a short laugh, then rolled his chin forward. "For your sake and continued health," he said, any remaining humor now dissipated from his words, "I won't share your opinion of Guerin with him about his ability to serve as an adequate partner to Eve and Alex."

Like Markus cared.

"What I'm saying is, I've paid my dues." Markus rounded the chair and perched on the edge of the seat, his forearms propped on his thighs. "My head's on straight, Kenric," he said, meeting the other male's icy blue glare with a hard one of his own. "You need me out there on the streets. Not in here sitting on my ass!" His nails scraped over the metal tacks adorning the leather.

"Getting antsy, are we?" Kenric gave him a wry grin.

"What was your first damn clue?" Being stuck in this mansion shackled his wrists from fully protecting Alexandria.

Kenric leaned forward, erasing some of the space between them, his mouth a grim line. "I think we have to ask ourselves another question first. Is there a warrior in the Enclave who is ready for you?"

Despite his best efforts, the flame on his temper blazed hot. Markus's spine went rigid. "What the hell are you getting at?"

"No one in the Enclave works alone." Kenric shook his head. "Not any more. And I have no intention of making any exceptions. You may be ready, but what *you* need to work on is healing the distance between you and your partner."

Son of a bitch.

Markus shoved from his seat and trudged toward the cold fireplace. Bracing his palms wide on the mantel, he stared down at the hearth.

"So what you're saying is Arran holds the key to me ever reclaiming my status." The serrated edge of resentment sawed at the bone covering Markus's heart.

"You need a partner, and since, as you know, Elle manages all our IT and communication needs, and she doesn't have any desire to work in the field, he still has a vacancy," Kenric said. "So I suggest you try to make nice."

Smart-ass. Markus swallowed back the retort, and the echo of a sour taste welled on his tongue, screwing his mouth into a grimace.

He and Arran, *making nice*.

Like that was ever going happen.

Chapter Twelve

Two in the morning, and still Alex hadn't run into anything more interesting than two half-lit humans groping each other in an alley.

"Damn," Alex muttered under her breath, watching as the young girl grabbed her lover's hand while tugging her skirt back into place with the other. Laughing, the couple scurried away and out of the darkened corridor. "I thought we really had something this time."

"Itching for battle with a few bad guys?" Eve tossed her arm over Alex's shoulder and grinned down at her.

Her pulse quickened at the thought of getting her claws into a DEAD vampire, followed by a nearly undeniable urge to scream, run, or climb the damn wall in front of her. Her skin prickled. Sucking in a deep breath, she reached up and massaged her upper arms with her palms, doing what little she could to rub away the sensation.

"Just a lot of nervous energy, I guess," she said. "I've

been waiting, preparing for this night for so long, you know. And then…" She groaned low in her throat, and dropped her arms to her sides. "Nothing but a couple of horny college kids."

"Don't worry," Guerin said, passing Alex on her left. "You'll get your chance to go to work. Unfortunately, there's never enough blood to satisfy Elizabeth Bay's DEAD population. They'll be here. And sadly," he crossed his arms over his chest, his biceps straining the short sleeves of his black T-shirt, "there's never an issue of a warrior growing complacent, even after we've culled their population. Soon enough, another young vampire or two will lose control, kill, and take the plunge into addiction." Guerin pulled a dagger from the sheath at his thigh, flipped it blade over hilt, and snatched it from the air with his palm. "Guess that's what they call job security." He smiled, flashing the tips of his fangs, and winked at his mate.

Eve stepped away and covered Guerin's dark scruff of a beard along his jaw with her hand. "You're a morbid kind of guy, you know that?" She patted his cheek.

"And it turns you on, doesn't it?" His smile broadened. "Come on…admit it."

"Are you giving me an order, Guerino?" Eve's voice lowered to a challenging, husky purr.

Alex cleared her throat, suddenly feeling, once more, like the awkward third wheel on a voyeuristic journey. After what had gone down between her and Markus, then walking in on the action in the alley, the last thing she needed was another reminder of… What had happened. With him.

As if she'd been able to get *him* out of her head for even one second.

"*Uhm…* Guys," Alex called out. Eve glanced over her shoulder, her long dark ponytail swaying. Alex gave her a quick wave and quirked a smile. "Still here."

"Sorry." Eve's brows rose and she grinned at Guerin. She smoothed her palms down the male's chest. "Later." She sauntered away, calling a halt to their heated exchange. Except based on the fire glowing in Guerin's eyes, Alex wasn't sure if her friend's assurance to pick up where they'd left off had been a warning or a promise.

Guerin seized Eve's arm, reeling her back in. The breath left Eve's lungs in an audible gasp a second before his lips claimed hers for a brief, yet hungry, kiss.

Oh, yeah.

Definitely a promise.

Alex's fists clenched over the complete adoration the two held for each other. She couldn't imagine ever forging a connection with a man on such a level. Not like what Eve and Guerin had. The love between them burned so deep and hot that even the others in their path felt singed by their passion.

Not to mention the trust. Without question, they had each other's backs.

She'd discovered that sexual chemistry wasn't a problem between her and Markus. What she'd felt and experienced earlier with him had been amazing. Hours later, she still hadn't come down from the endorphin rush. Yet for there to be something more—something that went beyond chemistry and orgasms—there had to be trust.

But the word "trust" and Markus didn't meld as perfectly as peanut butter and chocolate. Not. A. Chance. It was more in line with a dish of hot sauce and ice cream. Strange as hell and singed the tongue.

A muffled cry sounded, yanking her back into the present and lifting every hair on her body. Reflex had her drawing her dagger from its sheath at her thigh. Out of the corner of her eye, Alex noted Eve and Guerin both going for their weapons.

Closing in on her partners, Alex whispered, "So I wasn't the only one who heard that?"

Eve shook her head. "Unfortunately for someone, that wasn't your imagination." The trio hurried toward the sound of distress, their boots silently gliding over the residual puddles of rain. The ability to levitate was another gift from her vampire arsenal that she'd learned to use during her training—cool as hell.

Steam rose off the cooling pavement around them, and with the fog rolling in off the bay, it formed a white veil at the end of the alley. As they closed in on the narrow street running horizontal to the corridor, the unmistakable grunting and growling sounds of DEADs in the throes of a feeding frenzy greeted them. But even with their preternatural sight and hearing, the pea soup in front of them made it difficult to discern exactly what lay ahead.

Alex tightened her grip on the hilt of her blade. Her pulse leaped, fueled by the adrenaline leaking into her bloodstream. This was it.

The real deal.

Her initiation into the Enclave...by blood. She swallowed hard in search of the moisture abandoning her mouth.

Moments before they breached the end of the corridor, Guerin came to a stop and pointed upward toward the building's roof. Eve nodded. Her mate was going for higher ground, leaving the two of them to make a frontal approach. Hopefully, the view through the haze from five floors up was better than what they had from ground level.

Alex watched as the Enclave's second-in-command leaped two stories and grasped a small section of a brick window ledge. Finding small handholds where he could, he treated them to his best Spider-Man impersonation and scaled the wall for the remainder of his journey up.

Not long after his ascent, Eve glanced back at Alex and held up three fingers. Through Eve's mental connection with her mate, Guerin had communicated his findings from his aerial advantage. Three DEAD vampires.

One for each of them.

With a flick of her wrist, Eve motioned for Alex to follow. Dressed in curve-hugging black leather from top to bottom, Eve cut through the fog like a panther on the hunt for her prey. In mere seconds, they were on top of the macabre scene. Alex ground to a halt, her legs frozen by what—who—were beneath the Euphoria addicts.

Oh, no...

Beside a battered green Dumpster, three DEADs were in the process of draining the drunken couple from the alley. The two had apparently decided to finish what they'd started in the shadows—when they'd been interrupted.

Alex blinked and covered her chest with her arm, as if the act could shield her heart from the gruesome truth. If only she, Eve, and Guerin hadn't entered the alley? If only they hadn't chosen that particular path, maybe the couple would still be alive? Nausea reared its insidious head inside her gut.

Maybe I'm not as cut out for this as I thought?

Alex squeezed her damp palm around the curved hilt of her dagger. The yellow glow from a nearby streetlight sliced through the fog, illuminating the growing crimson pool beneath the victims and the DEADS at their side. Unbidden, her mind flashed back a year ago to the basement of Wicked Ways. That night, she'd been a naive human on her back, her life essence spilling onto the floor and into the vampire at her throat. Cold sweat beaded along her hairline and trickled down her neck.

Don't do this, Alex!

Lowering her arm to her side, she inhaled deeply through her nostrils. *Stay in the moment.* She had to concentrate on the here and now. Like a bass drumbeat, her pulse thumped inside her head. She forced her gaze away from the man's and woman's lifeless bodies and drilled her focus onto their predators. She needed this. Needed to balance the scales and correct what she had the power to change.

"Well, well…" Eve drawled and sauntered a little closer, drawing the DEADs' attention. The beasts had been so engrossed in their feeding they hadn't even heard the Enclave's approach. The bloodthirsty animals' heads swiveled in their direction, their mouths and chins stained with the thick garnet fluid. "Look what we have here," she added, fisting a dagger in each of her palms.

The trio hissed, slowly rising from their crouched positions. "Well, if it isn't a couple of Enclave bitches," a dark-headed male snarled right before swiping away some of the bloody drool from his chin with his sleeve. "I guess we must be too tame, boys, to justify a team of males." He cocked his head, cracking the bones in his neck.

"I think I'm just a tad bit offended," one of the DEADs

said, this one with a head full of dirty-blond hair. He frowned and stepped over the limp body of the human female, joining his partner in crime.

"You know, Bubba…" the first vamp began, reached behind his back, and pulled his own blade. "I do believe my feelings are hurt, too."

"Yeah," the last one yelled out, as if he'd been left out of the party. He rolled his thick shoulders and rounded the feet of the man he'd drained. "But I can think of a few ways you ladies can make it up to us." Running a wide palm over his bald scalp, his thin lips twisted into a vile grin.

Alex was willing to bet before he'd been turned and become an addict, the male had already been a sexually depraved bastard. Even after the introduction of the vampire antigen, a brain that was fucked up in the light of day retained all its original pathways in the dark of night. Nothing got scrubbed or purified all snowy white and innocent.

No such luck for the world. The tarnished gray matter was now housed inside a superhuman shell. And capable of even more debased acts than before.

"If you mean by me sinking my blade into your blackened heart?" Eve raised her dagger, the serrated point aimed in his direction. "Then by all means, allow me to apologize." Mirroring her stance, Alex lifted her weapon.

The DEADs didn't have to say a word; the expressions on their faces easily read *can you believe this chick*? They glanced at one another as if to challenge who would make the first move.

A *thump* sounded behind the bloody trio. They spun, claws extended.

"Let me help you make up your minds," Guerin said

from his crouched position, a dagger in either raised fist, blades pointing downward. He looked like an assassin who'd just leaped out of *The Matrix*, and Alex couldn't help but grin at the perfection of his surprise entrance. "I'll go first." He sprang toward the males, his movements a blur of slice-and-dice precision.

Clamping down hard on her jaw, Alex leaped into the action, aiming her booted heel for the depraved bastard with all the "ideas." Her foot slammed into his chest with a satisfying *thud* and knocked the addict back. He hit the pavement, his ass skidding across the wet surface until he came to a sudden and spine-cracking stop by the light pole.

Baldy groaned and rolled onto his side. "You bitch," he spat, shaking his head. "I'm going to make you fucking pay."

Alex marched toward the vamp, her dagger firm in her palm and ready for action.

That's it, you savage asshole. I'm coming for you. Based on the grunts and curses emanating from behind her, Eve and Guerin were making short work of clearing two more DEADs off the streets of Elizabeth Bay.

At the bloodsucker's side, Alex grabbed a fistful of his shirt's collar and hauled him up, ready to shove her blade home. The male lunged to his feet, knocking her off balance. Seizing her upper arms, Baldy surged forward, connecting his forehead to hers with a sharp *whack*. Stars exploded before her eyes, and the world tilted off-kilter. *Dammit.*

He twisted, swung his leg up and around, aiming for her face.

Shit!

She ducked, his foot breezing past the top of her head. Rebounding, Alex straightened and jumped on his back. *Got him!* She managed to snake one arm around his throat while targeting his throat with her blade. The DEAD roared and bucked, doing his best to throw her. But Alex wasn't about to let this one get away. The edge of her weapon found the soft flesh at his neck and dug in.

"Shit!" the DEAD reared back, trying to knock her free. "You fucking bitch," he spat. "Kill you!"

Fangs burst from her gums, and a growl, originating from somewhere low in her gut, rolled from her throat. She dragged the silver-plated knife across his throat, putting an end to his impotent threats. A crimson fountain sprayed from the sizzling wound. The bald DEAD staggered, clawing at her arm as his life-giving essence emptied down the front of his shirt. Taking advantage of his weakened state, she released her hold, spun, and finished the job with a stab of her silver-coated dagger to his heart. Eyes wide, pupils swallowing every inch of the white space, the DEAD crumpled to the ground. His body swelled, blistering from the toxic reaction to the metal. Then, as quickly as the decomp process had begun, *pop*, the body imploded, his remains turning to ash.

Sliding her blade back into its sheath, Alex caught up with Eve and Guerin. The second-in-command pulled his weapon from the deceased DEAD and straightened. Eve had already taken care of her target, and what was left of him had begun to scatter in the breeze.

"You did well." Guerin nodded as she approached the couple.

Eve's gaze lifted to what had to be a giant goose egg on Alex's forehead, and she grimaced. "Ouch," she said and brushed aside a few stray locks of Alex's hair for a better look.

"That's what happens when your head slams into one of theirs," Alex said. She ran a few of her fingers over the bruised lump, the flesh sensitive to touch.

"Damn." Eve frowned. "We're going to need to work on your ducking skills." Her frown lifted into a teasing grin.

"Ha, ha." Alex rolled her eyes. "I should probably check in with Elle." Alex lowered the zipper on her leather jacket, reached in, and pulled out her cell. "I'm sure she's about to jump out of her skin wondering how things are going out here."

"That's a good idea," Eve said. "Put her out of her misery." The tall brunette strode over to her mate, and the two proceeded to rehash the last few minutes of the battle while inspecting their weapons.

Alex tapped the stored number in her phone for the Enclave. Elle answered on the first ring.

"Alex?"

Grinning, she replied, "Yes, it's me."

"What's happening out there?" Elle's tone was light, attempting to hide her anxiety, but Alex knew her sister. She could only imagine how many empty bottles of diet soda and blueberry Pop-Tart wrappers littered Elle's desk. Her go-to foods when she was worried.

"I'm fine, Elle," Alex said, trying to put her mind at ease. "We're all okay."

"So, all's quiet on the docks?" Something tapped the phone, and a swallowing sound registered through the connection. Elle had taken another swig of her drink.

"At first, yeah, it was," Alex began. "But we just downed three DEADs." She glanced over at her partners. Guerin had his cell out. "I think Guerin is arranging for a cleanup of a human couple the addicts took down."

"Oh, damn." Elle groaned. "Are you sure you're okay?"

Alex's thoughts wandered back to the moment they'd found the two people bleeding out beneath the DEADs. The scene had hit her harder than expected, but after she'd shaken it off and gone to work... She breathed deeply, reveling in the blossoming sense of empowerment, the satisfaction that had come from taking action. She'd made a difference. "For the first time in a long while, Elle," she whispered, and a strange—considering her battle with the DEAD—yet pleasant warmth filled her, "I'm really okay."

"You don't know how happy I am to hear you say that."

"You don't know how good it is—" Movement out of the periphery of Alex's eye caught her attention. She spun. Her breath hitched. "Oh shit..." Emerging from the fog, at least five more DEADs stood before her.

"Alex!" Elle shouted. "What's going on?"

"Hello, beautiful," the one in front said, his elongated fangs dripping with drool.

"More DEADs," Alex muttered, dropped her cell, and dived for the dagger at her thigh. "Eve!"

Her palm found the hard, smooth grip of her dagger. She wrapped her fingers around the hilt and yanked it free. A sharp burning sensation exploded in her abdomen. Air punched from her legs. Her knees buckled.

"Alex!" Eve's voice rang out, but it was too late.

Alex hit the pavement, her hand seizing her midsection. Hot fluid seeped between her fingers. *Damn, damn, damn.* She'd really screwed up.

Chapter Thirteen

Two more reps.

Straddling the weight bench, Markus curled his arm, lifting the seventy-pound dumbbell for another round. Sweat beaded on his flesh. The droplets dripped off his forehead, stinging his eyes, as he watched the black and red tats stretch around his biceps. His right arm had already been punished for the last half hour, so he couldn't allow his left to feel ignored.

Jaw clenched, he lowered the weight, drawing in a long breath through his nostrils.

"Who the hell are you pissed at?"

Markus glanced up to find Arran standing in front of him, his blond hair pulled back and bound at his nape. Christ, he didn't need Arran riding his ass tonight. He yanked on the dumbbell once more, air hissing through his teeth. With his free hand, Markus flipped him the one-fingered universal sign for do not disturb.

Tossing a towel over his shoulder, Arran scowled and crossed his arms over his dark blue wifebeater. "You've been in here for the last two hours," Arran said.

Damn. He knew the vampire was blond, but he didn't think Arran was so dense he couldn't read when a male wanted to be left alone. He lowered the dumbbell, but this time, Markus allowed it to roll from his palm. The weight hit the wood floor with a heavy *thud*.

"Kenric's promoted you to gym monitor now?" Markus swung his leg over the bench, stood, and snatched his own towel from the seat behind him. "And I've exceeded my limit?"

"Nope, on either," Arran said, unfazed by Markus's sarcasm.

Shit. Must be losing my touch.

"Just an observation," Arran added.

"Sweet Elle must not be keeping you *occupied* enough..." Markus made a quick pass over his brow and face with the terry. "Seeing as you're spending your time monitoring me."

"Fuck you," Arran growled, shaking his head. "You may act like you've changed in front of Kenric"—his lip curled back, eyes narrowing—"but in my gut, I know you're still the sick son of a bitch who would betray every last one of us if the price was right—or the pussy hot enough." Arran released a guttural sound of disgust and headed toward one of the two treadmills that faced a wide flat-screen TV.

"You don't know shit," Markus chewed out. The phrase fired off right before Kenric's words came charging back like a swift kick inside his head: *You may be ready, but what you need to work on now is healing the distance between you and your partner.*

Arran rotated on his heels, a slow spin followed by a glare that declared he wanted a piece of him. "Oh, I do know you, Markus," he snarled. "That's the problem. A problem I'm willing to fix right now." Arran tossed the towel from his shoulder to the floor and stepped forward.

"Seriously, man?" Markus crossed his arms. "We're going down this road again?"

"From what I've seen, you've never left it." Arran didn't stop until they were nose to nose. "Bottom line…" Arran inhaled a sharp breath. "I don't trust you, Markus. You're unstable. Dangerous. In my opinion, your presence is a threat to the Enclave."

"Please, don't spare my feelings." Markus quirked a corner of his mouth. Yeah, the words stung, but Arran wasn't saying anything he didn't deserve.

Arran rolled his eyes. "Can't you be serious for even one damn minute?"

Diverting his attention to the big screen on the opposite wall, Markus rubbed his palm across his face and over his head. This was his chance. The door had been cracked. A knot, coiled and barbed, pulsed inside his chest. He glanced back to his former partner, swallowed hard, then found his voice. "Tell me what I need to do to prove that I'm the same male you used to know. That you can trust me."

Fuck.

That was hard. But Markus kept his tone steady, never wavering from the other vamp's glare. "Tell me what that is, Arran, and I'll do it," he continued. "Seriously."

Shaking his head, Arran took a step away from him and spun, giving the other male his back. As if it had been festering somewhere deep in his gut, an agonized groan surfaced and spilled from the Enclave warrior. "How dare you?" Arran whipped around, fire swirling, flashing around his irises. "After everything you did to Alex, my mate, *and* the Enclave, I don't even know how to respond to that. How can you even expect me to—"

Pain, hot and tearing, sliced through Markus's abdomen, blinding him to whatever else Arran was about to say. His breath stalled in his lungs, and he doubled over.

"Markus!" Arran shouted. "What the hell's wrong with you?"

The room tilted, and he stumbled back. Arran grabbed his biceps, stabilizing him.

"Talk to me!" the warrior demanded.

Giving his head a shake, Markus did his best to knock away the stars from his line of sight. "Shit," he grunted, his voice rusty.

With his palm still pressed to his abdomen, he massaged what felt like a burning hole in his gut. His chest ached as if someone had a chokehold on his heart. What the hell was happening to him?

"I don't know, man," Markus managed to get force out between breaths. "I was fine." He glanced up at Arran while trying to unfold his body from the fetal position it was determined to assume. Fuck that. "Then this sharp pain, like a knife cutting through me..." Markus looked down at his bare midsection and pulled his hand away, half expecting to find his palm dripping with blood. That's when it hit him. Icy tendrils of panic slithered on a fast-moving current through his veins, nearly shutting down his ability to function.

Alexandria.

"God, no!" Fear launched his body back into action.

He lunged for the door, slamming his shoulder into Arran's, knocking him out of the way. "Alexandria!"

"Markus!" Arran called out. The heavy fall of footsteps behind him relayed that the other vampire followed him down the hall. "What about Alexandria?" The warrior's voice echoed off the narrow corridor's walls.

"Something's not right," Markus called over his shoulder.

"How do you know that?"

Markus dug his fingers into the flesh over the epicenter of the pain, choking back the suffocating knot of fear in his throat. "I feel it."

As if someone had tripped up his former partner's sprint down the hall, Arran's footsteps faltered. Glancing back, Markus captured the other male's gaze. Anxiety greeted him in the vampire's stare. He understood all too well what Markus meant. "Oh, fuck," Arran groaned and charged forward.

By the time he reached the mansion's basement, the heart of the Enclave, Markus's pulse had morphed into a jackhammer inside his head. And judging by the elevated pitch of Elle's voice as they neared her desk, unfortunately, it appeared his instincts hadn't been wrong.

Something *had* happened to Alexandria.

Dread spilled like a putrid oil slick inside his gut. Its stained fingers melded with the pain there until he was sure nothing would be able to hold back the bile crawling up his esophagus. Enrique had made good on his threat.

Rushing past him toward his mate and the Enclave's commander, Arran reached Elle first. "What happened?" he asked, glancing at the anxious female, then Kenric.

It took everything inside Markus not to be the one in

the master's face demanding answers. Instead, he hung back, his claws digging a trench inside his palms.

"It's Alex and the rest of the team," Elle said, her voice tight with anxiety. "She called, and at first, she sounded good. They'd run into a few DEADs, but Alex said she was okay then she suddenly whispered, 'more DEADs,' and called out to Eve right before I lost her." She glanced over at Arran, then Markus for the first time.

"Lost her?" Markus edged closer. "Lost her how?"

"What are you doing down here?" she snarled.

An inferno raced inside his veins, and he was sure his irises were burning a fiery red. But at that moment, he didn't give a shit if Elle was upset or not. No one was going to keep him away.

"Don't worry about him." Arran cupped her cheek, drawing her attention back to the details. "Is there anything else? Have you heard from Guerin or Eve since then?"

"Not yet," she said. "I tried calling back the second the line went dead, but no one's responding yet. I think Alex may have dropped her cell, because after she called out for Eve I heard a loud *pop*."

Arran looked to Kenric. "What area were they patrolling tonight?"

Kenric started to respond, but Markus didn't have time for this shit. Alex needed him now. Not minutes from now.

"I've heard all I need to here." Markus headed toward the stairs. If he left things up to them, she'd be dead. And he wasn't about to allow that to happen. He'd been too lax about her safety, allowing others to protect the only damn thing in the world that mattered to him. His reason to exist.

"Markus!" Kenric called out. "Where are you going?"

"To find my female," he said, not giving a fuck what anyone thought about his claim to Alexandria. Following the ache in his soul and body, Markus phased from the mansion into the night.

Moments later, he coalesced onto a shadowy back street, and the grunting sounds of a battle filled his ears. Automatically, Markus dived for his back pocket and the blade he was sure to find tucked inside. Instead, his palm discovered nothing but his sweats. "Idiot," he grunted under his breath.

He'd been so out of his mind, he'd left without changing or grabbing a weapon.

Scanning the immediate area, he counted about a half dozen DEADs a few feet ahead of him along with Eve and Guerin in the center of the bastards. The addicts had them walled in, their daggers flashing in a constant merry-go-round of a fight. But the duo were holding their own. Good thing, because at the moment, they weren't his primary concern. Besides, Kenric and Arran would arrive soon and save their asses.

Markus edged closer, his heart pounding, searching for the only person on the planet who gave him a reason to rise each night. Alexandria had to be alive. His brain couldn't comprehend any other alternative.

A pair of mangled human remains lay in a twisted lump near a garbage bin, but their scent along with the vibrating hum in his blood stream told him neither was Alexandria. A wave of relief swamped him as Markus swept the shadows. Where the hell was she?

"Markus!" Guerin called out a split second before something solid came down hard across the back of Markus's head.

Fuck!

He didn't have time for this. Jarred, but not stunned, Markus spun, bringing one booted leg up in a sweeping move. His heel slammed into the DEAD's flank with kidney-crushing accuracy. A grunt burst from the vampire as the male careened into the nearby wall. His head bounced off the brick, releasing a loud *crack* as the two-by-four he'd used as a bat toppled from his hand onto the street.

Prepared for the next attack, Markus whipped back around, his fists in front of his face. That's when he noticed the other crumpled body lying in the shadows. The lump of muscle he called a heart stuttered at the sight.

His knees struck the pavement at her side, rattling his jaw. Yet he had no recollection of when he'd moved. A ring of crimson pooled beneath Alexandria's back. A groan, born from the tormented depths of hell, rolled from his throat and filled his ears.

With hesitant fingers, he reached out, aching to touch her again. He cupped her cheek with trembling fingers. Shallow, warm puffs of air left her parted lips and teased his palm.

Enrique is responsible for this. Harsh breaths exited his nostrils, and his fingers curled.

"I swear to you," he rumbled to her still form. "I will make him pay. Before this is over, Enrique will experience pain he never knew possible."

He had to get her out of there. Markus swallowed hard against the restriction in his throat. Fuck it all. He had to take her somewhere Enrique would never look. A place not even the Enclave knew about.

A growl reached his ears at the same moment another hard blow rammed into his back. Claws dug into his shoulders as fangs, sharp and tearing, sank into his throat.

"Son of a bitch!" Markus roared, and surged to his feet. Swinging his arms out to his sides, he flung the bastard off him and turned on his heels. "You want a piece of me?" he shouted, his voice devolving into that of a savage primitive beast. His fangs jabbed his lower lip, aching for retaliation. "Come and take it."

Two of the motherfuckers stood facing him, their clothes torn and filthy. Saliva and blood dripped from their chins. Nothing mattered except their next kill, another dose of Death Euphoria screaming into their bloodstream and straight to their brain cells.

The one to his left lunged first. More than likely, the bastard who'd jumped him—back for more. And Markus was more than happy to give it to him.

Markus leaped, and the two collided in midair. Claws and fangs clashed, blood spraying as if two hundred–plus pounds of wingless raptors fought for dominance. Only one would come out on top, and it wasn't going to be the hissing cocksucker with a nasty-ass drool problem.

The ground rose up to meet them with bone-jarring intensity. Air punched from both their lungs on a hoarse grunt. Markus rolled away and onto his feet as the other vamp flipped into a crouch, his knuckles resting on the pavement. His partner in crime joined him at his side. Their features morphed, becoming half man, half wolf. Both males were too young to fully shift into an alternate form. Yet both were ready to pounce.

Time to put an end to this grisly circus.

Moving with preternatural speed, Markus targeted the one on his right, meeting the creature head-on. The addict reared up onto his legs, claws and fangs extended. Before the bastard had a chance to sink either into his flesh, Markus grabbed the back of its head with one hand, his chin with the other…and jerked. The beast slumped to the street.

A roar unleashed from the remaining DEAD. Reaching deep inside for one more burst of power, Markus spun, his own claws extended, driving them deep into the other male's neck. The wounded vampire staggered, a crimson fountain erupting from his open artery. Like a great oak that had finally succumbed to the logger's ax, the DEAD toppled.

"Damn!" Guerin hissed.

Markus jerked around, his breath coming in harsh pants. The broad fellow Italian vampire and his mate had taken care of their mob of addicts and were surveying the remains around Markus's boots.

"I don't know what the fuck you're doing out here." Guerin's upper lip curled as if he'd detected something rotten. "But…thanks." The word left his mouth in a rush, as if he had to get it out as quickly as possible before the poisonous spines surrounding the syllable pricked his tongue.

Whatever.

The Enclave's second-in-command flipped his dagger, blade over hilt, then proceeded to snuff the carcasses.

"I don't need your gratitude," Markus huffed, and rushed back to Alexandria's side. Helping to save their asses hadn't been the primary point of his arrival. The woman bleeding out before his eyes was his main concern. Hell, she was the only reason he hadn't walked into the sun's rays before now. He stared down at her still form, his insides a quivering mess. She had no idea how beautiful she was to him. Not just her looks. Even though they were stunning. Her spirit for life and her sharp mind enthralled him.

Markus slid his arm underneath her neck. His fangs pierced his bottom lip, stinging the soft flesh with his effort to be gentle. Her head wobbled. "Shit," he bit out the curse.

"What are you doing?" Eve dropped to her knees on the other side of Alexandria. Reaching over Alexandria's shoulders, stilling him from moving her farther, she glared up at him. "We'll take care of her." As if she had every right to claim possession.

"Like you did tonight?" he spat, his own stare never wavering, matching her fire for fire. "I don't think so."

"She wanted to be out here, Markus," Eve said. "And she did an amazing job. No one expected an ambush like this."

"Why didn't you hit them with that famous sonic blast of yours I've heard about? Rumors are you took out five men when you and Guerin were under attack in Germany." Markus slid another arm under Alexandria's legs, lifted, then cradled her next to his body. She didn't flinch from the change in position—didn't utter a sound. His heart jerked, the thump a physical punch to his breastbone. "You could have prevented this." Eve's eyes widened, but he couldn't tell if it was pain or guilt clouding the blue in her irises.

"Enough, Markus!" Guerin snapped.

Eve eased back, and they both stood.

"Don't ever speak to my mate with that tone again." Guerin strode closer, pressing his chest to Markus's shoulder. "Or I'll make sure you look like what's left of those DEADs," he said, the words coming out as if dragged over sand.

Markus hissed, clutching Alexandria a little tighter. "Don't fucking threaten me."

"I couldn't risk it," Eve said. "If I'd used my mental pulse on them it would have taken out the DEADs, but it could have injured Guerin and Alexandria, as well. Not to mention that it would have left me drained and unable to protect myself or anyone else if more of the bastards had shown up."

"Guerin!" another male voice called out, one Markus didn't need to look up to identify. Kenric had arrived. More than one pair of boots thumped against the pavement sounding their approach. Arran had probably joined the Enclave commander as well.

Fucking hell.

He had to get Alexandria out of there and heal her wounds. Her injury appeared deep, and she'd lost a great deal of blood. But hopefully, the blade hadn't done major internal damage that couldn't be repaired by replenishing her blood supply.

"We're out of here," Markus muttered and began to step away.

Guerin's head snapped back around. "Hold up," he ordered. "We've got this. I'm taking Alex back to the Enclave and to her sister." Guerin reached for her.

Heat flared up from Markus's chest, a fiery burst of rage so primal that it took even Markus by surprise. "Mine!" The single word erupted from Markus's throat.

Guerin snatched his hand back. "Markus...what the hell are you doing?"

The Enclave's second-in-command's words echoed inside his head as Markus phased and the world faded to shimmering particles.

Chapter Fourteen

Sweet God in heaven!

Alex couldn't get enough of the honeyed elixir flowing across her tongue.

She moaned. Gulped. Unable to stop the process if she tried, her throat convulsed on the fluid and another moan bubbled up. What a delicious way to wake up.

The rich, intoxicating essence filling her mouth warmed her from the inside out. More than that, it electrified her. Made her squirm; her core ached from the excruciating emptiness. Breaking the seal of her lips on the warm flesh, she gasped, desperately in need of air.

Only one other source had ever affected her this way. But after their last encounter, *he* was off-limits. He couldn't be here. *This was…* Alex beckoned the image of her current donor to her mind, yet nothing appeared. Wait. She searched the sluggish stream of memory again. *Nothing.* How and when she'd started her current feeding was a total blank.

Why couldn't she remember?

Panic swamped her senses, making her head spin and her stomach roil. Her heart lurched into a staccato beat.

Inhaling deeply through her nostrils to quickly still the contents of her stomach and pulse, Alex dragged her eyelids open. One small crack. Whoever had their wrist in her mouth apparently hadn't wanted her dead—yet—but to be on the safe side, she didn't want to alert her mystery donor that she was fully conscious.

Blurry tan walls, dimly illuminated by a soft glow, filled her vision. No pictures decorated the plain surface. She glanced lower. A dark blue sheet covered her lower half. *Dear God...where am I?*

As if her brain cells were lagging a second or two behind her nose, the scent lodged in her nostrils finally registered: chocolate laced with cinnamon.

Recognition flung her eyelids wide.

Markus.

The thick liquid in her mouth stalled in her throat, choking her. Alex coughed. Gasped, and coughed again.

"Easy," he crooned and removed his wrist from her mouth.

Maybe if she closed her eyes again, squeezed them really tight, it would all somehow be a dream?

"Alexandria...?" Her donor rose from the edge of the bed, rocking the mattress.

Nervously licking away the traces of his essence on her lips, she watched for his movements in her peripheral vision. *Damn.* Why did he have to taste like heaven iced in a coating of sweet sin?

A moment later, he came into view. He'd covered his

broad torso with a solid black T-shirt that left his colorful tattooed arms bare. Unable to resist, she lifted her lashes to take in the rest of him, meeting his gaze. Lines she'd never noticed before fanned out from the corner of his gray eyes, and shadows formed dark circles beneath them. If she didn't know better, Alex would have sworn he looked like a man who'd been up for hours worrying about his female. But the idea of Markus sitting vigil at her bedside was ridiculous enough to make her laugh. And if she weren't so damn tired, she might have done so at the thought.

"Hey there, Vixen," he said, his mouth twitching. "You with me?"

"I'm here, aren't I?" she rasped and grabbed for more of the linen, tugging it up over her chest. Through the cotton, she detected her clothing was still in place. Yet the extra material between her and the overwhelming presence of the alpha male in the room somehow made her feel better. "Speaking of here," she added, "where the hell am I?"

"You're at my place," he said as if it were perfectly normal that she was there and in his bed.

"Your place?" Alex flickered her gaze from one side of the drab room to the other. "Your 'place' is in the Enclave mansion, and this is not your room." She reached down, pressed the heel of her hands into the firm mattress, and pushed herself up. This was craziness, and she was getting out of here. Sharp pain cut through her side and caught her by surprise, stealing her breath. "Shit!" She gasped, froze, and braced her palm over the ache.

"Take it easy," Markus demanded. Before she could blink he had his arm around her. "You're not completely healed yet. Lie back down." He gently pressed against her shoulders, as if she'd readily submit to his orders. Nice try.

Alex shrugged, dislodging his hands. *Healed?* Anger sent her fangs punching from her gums. "What did you do to me?" she snarled.

Straightening, Markus peered down at her. "News flash, Vixen. I pulled your ass off the street after a DEAD tried to gut you." He crossed his arms over his chest as if he were some kind of hero.

Yet a cold chill ran down her spine from his story. Twisting her fist inside her sheet, she mentally pounded at her brain for proof of what he was telling her.

Think, Alex!

Eve's face flashed before her. She'd been with Eve. Yes. And Guerin. They were on patrol, and it had been her first time out. Suddenly, as if the tab holding back her memories had been pulled, images of that night spilled out like a raging flood. Everything made sense again right up until the point where she'd been stabbed. Markus hadn't been out with them that night. So when, and why was she with him and not back at the Enclave? Did that mean…? Oh, God… A crawling, sickening dread swelled up from her stomach.

"Where are Eve and Guerin?" Alex threw back the sheet covering and despite the tearing pain in her side, swung her bare feet over the edge of the bed. "Are they…?" Grabbing hold of the headboard for support, she pushed up from the mattress.

"Hold up!" Markus grasped her upper arms, holding her in place. "Don't push yourself."

"Answer me!" she shouted, knocking his hands away. "Just answer me." She lowered her voice, doing her best to stay sane and not take his head off before he gave her an answer. "Are Eve and Guerin still alive?" Alex swallowed hard, forcing the wave of nausea back down. They couldn't be dead. Life just couldn't be that cruel. The thought of never seeing her friend, hearing her laughter, watching the way her eyes lit up with love and mischief every time her and Guerin's eyes locked…

"Last time I saw them, they were very much alive," he said.

The lungful of air she had no idea she'd been holding rushed from her. "Oh, thank God," she uttered. Before she could think twice, Alex reared back and slammed her fist into Markus's shoulder. "Why didn't you just say that?"

The impact sent a jarring pain arrowing through Alex's joints, rocking her. Another twinge in her side had her grasping her abdomen. "Son of a…"

Plopping her rear back onto the mattress, she sucked in a stabilizing breath.

"I told you that you weren't completely healed yet," Markus grumbled, his tone scolding.

"Please spare me." Alex rolled her eyes and scooted farther back onto the bed. Gritting her teeth against the strain on her wound, she began lifting her legs. But before she could get far, Markus's wide palm circled her calves, taking their weight. Even though she still wore her leather pants, his touch sent an electric hum through her nervous system. "What are you doing?"

Too freaked out by her body's reactions, self-preservation had her yanking free from his assistance. The additional effort tugged on her freshly healing abdomen muscles, but she'd rather take the pain. Pain was simple. Uncomplicated. One dealt with it until it was gone. And if you were lucky, the affliction left you unscarred.

Alex wasn't sure she could say the same about prolonged contact with Markus. Would she escape unmarked?

Stepping back a couple of inches, Markus glared down at her, his gray eyes darkening into a brewing storm. God, she could almost picture the hairs on the back of his neck rising with his temper. "I was only trying to help you get back into bed," he chewed out.

"I've been putting myself into bed for years." She gritted her teeth, refusing to allow him the pleasure of hearing her grunt as she adjusted the pillow behind her back. "I don't need your help."

With a slow shake of his head, the thick fan of his dark lashes drawn to half mast, he said, "You are so damn stubborn."

Alex blinked and lifted her chin. "Oh pleasssee," she huffed. "You could teach a master's class on the subject."

His nostrils flared. "Just stay put," he bit out, and strode toward the room's door. His fingers flexed open and closed at his sides. He was leaving. The big-ass vampire was actually walking out on her.

"Oooh, no you don't!" she called out. Her temples throbbed. The male was beyond infuriating. "We're not done here. I don't even know where the hell I am."

"I told you." Markus paused with his hand on the doorknob and glanced over his shoulder. "This is my home. You're safe."

"I'm safe." She nodded and half laughed. "That's supposed to make everything all hunky-dory? And you can stroll away without explaining anything to me?"

"We can talk when I get back," he said as if she were the

one aggravating him. Her own imaginary hackles rose.

"Where do you have to go that's so damn important?" She crossed her arms over her chest.

"I need to feed," he said, his fangs glinting off the soft yellow glow of the room's lamps. She'd been so flustered and angry, she hadn't noticed them until now. "You're going to need more blood if you're going to heal properly. So until you can take care of it on your own..." He faced the door once more. "I need to hunt."

The reality of what he was saying dawned on her. Once again, Markus was refilling her with his blood. Life had gone full circle. Yet this time, he'd saved her instead of having been the one to take her life. Emotions whirled inside her head and her heart, like a spinning kaleidoscope of rage, denial, gratefulness, and affection. And she had no idea which one to settle on or feel.

"Don't try to leave," he added, pulling her from her mental chaos. "You don't know this area, and as a young vampire, you're too far away to phase back to the Enclave."

Too far away from the Enclave? The phrase looped inside her fuzzy head until she was sure she'd understood him correctly. *I will not freak out. I will not freak out.*

"What have you done, Markus?" The words left her lips in breathless disbelief.

He didn't turn around. Even though her voice had been soft, Alex knew he'd heard her. His auditory capabilities were not in question. The vampire had at least a century on her.

"Look at me!" she yelled.

But her demand had absolutely no effect. Instead, what she got in response from him was one simple statement.

"What I had to do."

Markus twisted the doorknob, opened the door, stepped through, and closed it behind him with a sharp *click*.

Anger steamed inside her like a teakettle left on an open fire for too long. And Alex was ready to blow her top. She would never be his prisoner again. It didn't matter that, according to his story, he'd saved her from the DEAD attack. One act of heroism did not make her his property.

Gritting her teeth, Alex made her way back out of bed and onto her feet. Hell if she was following his stay-put orders. She was no one's trained Labrador Retriever.

After a calmer scan of the small space, she noted the absence of any windows, plus another door off to her right she assumed led to a bathroom. Images of a similar windowless enclosure flickered inside her mind: the basement room where Markus and Marguerite had kept her captive. She closed her eyes and balled her fists. History would not repeat itself.

Holding a steadying palm to her abdomen, she padded around the bed in search of her boots. She spotted them by a chair shoved in the opposite corner of the room along with her leather jacket. Dried blood coated the front as well as a jagged tear near the bottom from where the blade must have entered her abdomen. The hairs on her arm stood on end at the gory sight. She'd witnessed the other warriors returning from their patrol with similar stains on their clothing. But somehow knowing her flesh had been the one torn by the blade that had done the damage to the leather chilled her bones.

Alex tugged the hem of her black cami up, exposing the puckered skin of her wound. Markus had been right about the status of her injury. The site was closed, and she was better, but anyone could tell it wouldn't take much to reopen the wound. Plus, the gnawing pain in her gut wasn't from the DEAD's blade alone. She was hungry. Despite the fact that Markus had recently fed her. A telltale sign she wasn't 100 percent. *Dammit!*

After slipping on her boots, she made her way to the door. Time to see how much of a captive she actually was in this place. With a firm grip on the knob, Alex tested the lock.

Click.

Her breath hitched, and the door opened. On a long exhale, she pulled the door wider, revealing a staircase lit by a single bulb. He hadn't locked the door. Still gripping the dull brass-colored knob, Alex stared up at her access to freedom. Her heart thumped like a wild horse trapped in his stall. So why wasn't she bolting up the stairs?

Dammit. She groaned and her head lolled on her shoulders. It shouldn't matter.

"You're such an idiot, Alex," she cried out into the empty stairwell. "Why do you keep looking for some small glimmer of evidence that the vampire still has a soul?"

Just because he hadn't locked her inside didn't make him a good man. He'd basically kidnapped her to "save" her. At least that was his story. How many sane men did that kind of thing?

None.

That was how many.

To any other person with half a brain, the fact that she was standing on the other side of the door would change nothing. More than likely, leaving her access to the outside world had more to do with his confidence that she was still too weak to get away.

Yet for Alex…the warm twinge of relief said she wanted to believe there was more to it.

That didn't mean she wasn't ready to get the hell out of there. She'd deal with his bruised feelings and disappointment that she hadn't obeyed him later. Basically, he would have to get over himself.

Slowly, Alex made her way up the steep flight of stairs. Not a pleasant experience, considering her abdomen felt as if it wanted to split with each step. At the top, another door greeted her. This one locked from the inside and released by a single twist of the knob.

Thank you, Mr. Santini, for your show of good faith. Or for whatever had made him forget to lock up.

Opening the final door, Alex crossed the threshold into the last place she'd ever expected: the kitchen of a log cabin. She stepped farther into the room, breathing in the earthy scent of cedar and oak. Based on the worn appearance of the floors and the dilapidated state of the minimal furnishings, the home appeared quite old.

The idea of Markus, the male who seemed to appreciate the finer things in life, ever owning or living in a cabin didn't gel. Yet he'd claimed this was his. She sighed. The history lesson as to why he owned the place would have to wait for another time. She had to get out before he came back.

Alex hurried across the small living space toward the door. After making quick work of the dead-bolt latch, she flung it open and exited onto a narrow covered porch. And into the darkness of a foreign wilderness.

"Markus," she whispered. "Where have you taken me?"

Chapter Fifteen

Brilliant orange and yellow ribbons painted the tops of the trees in warning of dawn's approach as Markus coalesced in the den of his cabin. The familiar scent of the wood beams and floors infiltrated his nostrils as the view of cobwebs clinging to faded blue drapes assaulted his retinas. Sights and smells from a time he'd long tried to forget. But for the last twenty-four hours his timeworn refuge had once again served him well.

Ghosting through the interior door to the basement, Markus reappeared on the stairs on the other side. After a repeat visit to the streets of the closest town off the mountain, Markus had once again refilled his system with a blood supply. With any luck, after this evening's feeding, Alexandria should have what she needed to complete her healing.

Then what?

He paused on the wood planks and stared down at the soft glow of light below him. How the hell was he supposed to convince her that staying put with him—the male who'd, yet again, taken her from her friends and family—was in her best interest?

Stealing her away to a safe place to heal, then returning her, was something she'd probably give him hell about, but eventually would get over. Abducting her, healing her, then holding her here against her will... Yeah, that was a shit sandwich he'd have to feed her, and he doubted he'd ever get the flavor to pass as Subway.

Sighing, he glided the remainder of the treads to the bottom. There, he spotted the raven-haired vixen asleep where he'd left her on the bed. Her long locks fanned out behind her on the pillow like an obsidian wave of silk. His palm literally itched to run his fingers across its surface. *Fuck.* He'd give his right nut to feel those tresses glide down his chest. Skate over the head of his shaft. His cock twitched at the thought. A low rumble vibrated in his chest. Fantasies better left suppressed, since that's all they'd ever amount to: wishful thinking—no matter how he felt about her.

Markus lowered the satchel in his hand to the floor and Alexandria stirred, a soft exhale leaving the perfect curve of her pink lips. He closed his eyes at the sound, willing the rush of blood swelling his rod to back the hell off.

Her lashes fluttered, and it didn't take much to realize the moment her vision had cleared and settled on him. Alexandria rolled to her back, tugged her sheet a little tighter with one hand while managing to push up with her other.

"You're back," she said, and cleared her throat.

"You stayed." Markus sauntered farther into the room.

"Like I had a choice."

"I didn't lock the doors." He settled on the padded seat

of the chair near her bed.

"Of course you didn't." She glared at him. "Why would you, when there was nowhere for me to go? Unless I wanted to go up in flames under a pine tree while hopelessly lost in that damn forest." She tucked the hair falling in her eyes back behind an ear. "Bastard."

"Maybe." He shrugged. "But you're alive. And I think you'd prefer to stay that way."

"Where am I, Markus?"

"The only place I'm sure my enemies will never find you."

Her gaze narrowed on him, a violet wand of electricity lifting the hairs on his arms. "By enemies, you mean Enrique."

Markus stood, his lack of response all the answer she needed. With his back to her, he shrugged off his leather jacket.

"You still haven't actually answered my question. Where is this place?"

"The mountains," he said. It didn't really matter if she knew or not. She was too far away to phase directly home.

"Dammit, Markus. I swear you must be king of the non-answer." She chewed the words out. "I figured that much out myself." A long and forceful breath exited her lungs. "At least tell me why you feel all this is necessary to protect me from Enrique? I couldn't be any safer than with Kenric and the rest of the Enclave."

"Is that so?" He snarled, spun, and closed the distance between them in two large strides, not stopping until his shins slammed into the bed rail. Her eyes widened at his swift, driving approach. But she didn't flinch. Of course not. Alexandria wouldn't dare risk revealing a weak spot in the wall he knew she'd built in his honor. "Then how the hell do you explain the hole you got in your gut?" He pointed at her abdomen and raised his brows. "Because that's how I found you with *your* Enclave, wounded and flat on your back in an alley."

"They're *your* Enclave, too," she said, her voice low and hoarse-sounding.

"Used to be, Vixen." He curled his fingers and retreated. "Past tense."

"So what's your brilliant plan?" she huffed. "How long do you plan on us staying here?"

"That depends."

"On what?"

"How long it takes for me to put an end to Enrique and whatever game he's trying to play."

"You know it's only a matter of time before my sister hunts you down. She found me before when I went missing in Fairfield." One delicate eyebrow arched in an arrogant taunt. "And if you think she won't find me again…" She shook her head, smiling. "You're dead wrong."

"Not this time, Vixen." He grinned. "I can assure you," he added, making sure his tone conveyed the rigid confidence in his words. The edges around her smile faltered. Message received.

They wouldn't find her because he'd never told anyone about his cabin embedded in the rock at the top of Grim-Reaper Mountain—the name adopted by the locals because of its treacherous slate face, and the number of people rumored to have never been seen again after attempting to explore its steep forest on the opposite side. The legend possibly created and supported in later years by a certain vampire who'd resided at its peak. One who had wanted to be left alone.

Not even his father had known about his sanctuary. Markus's stomach pitched at the mere thought of the Santini family patriarch. The cabin on Grim-Reaper Mountain had been the one thing that was truly his when he'd been human. A quiet place in the world where he could escape when the noises inside his head became too much to bear.

Markus strode to her bedside. "Move over," he ordered.

"What?" Her brow crinkled. "You're not getting in here with me."

"I need room to sit," he said. "Not to fuck you." She blinked, looked up, and Markus couldn't help but challenge her stare with one of his own. "Unless there's a different kind of feeding you had in mind." He shrugged. "I aim to please."

Alexandria slowly shook her head, her violet eyes darkening. "Is asshole the only language you speak?"

"Nope. I'm bilingual. But when I'm around you, it's the only language you seem to respond to."

"God, you're just so…" She groaned, driving her fingers through her hair. "I'm still baffled as to why Kenric let you out of that cage," she spat.

"It's my hidden charm, sweetheart." Markus stroked the overnight growth of stubble on his chin. "If you're real nice, I'll show it to you."

"Oh, please," she drawled. "Spare me." She crossed her arms. "Why can't you just go around to the side of the bed?"

"Because, if you don't mind, I'd like to alternate which wrist you're sinking your fangs into."

"Fine." She relented and scooted over a few inches on the king-size bed.

Settling on the spot next to her, Markus dug deep, tightening the reins to his control in preparation for her touch. Feeding and caring for her before had always been a challenge. During that time, he'd made sure she was his responsibility alone to keep nourished. No other male had dared to touch her without fear for his continued existence. From day one, something about her had triggered his primal side. An immediate connection he couldn't explain because he'd never experienced it with another female before. He'd wanted her, body and soul, but there had been Marguerite, so he'd been motivated to keep a certain…distance.

But this was a different situation.

Ever since Kenric had released him, Markus had found that the more he was around her, the harder it became not to give in to his primal urges. Harder not to take her beneath him and make her his in every way fathomable. Bury himself deep inside her over and over again until the desire for his next breath, the next moonrise, was irrelevant.

But that was impossible.

Because if he ever spilled his seed inside her—marked her—he'd be lost. She'd own not only his heart, but his mind.

He'd never let her go.

Alexandria deserved so much more than the stained monster that was Markus Santini. And he wasn't talking about the fact that he was a creature of the night, but who he'd been before and after the change.

Markus stretched his arm and offered her his vein. Delicate, soft fingers encircled his wrist. Her hands were so much smaller, her touch more gentle. Yet at that moment, he was grateful to be sitting, because unbeknownst to her, she alone held the power to wobble his knees.

Lowering his eyelids, he braced himself for the sharp, excruciating pleasure of her bite.

"Do you like being a vampire?"

Opening his eyes, Markus cocked his head at the beauty beside him. She held his arm in front of her mouth, yet her focus wasn't on her next meal, but him. Her stare held that familiar look Alexandria got when she'd mentally dug her heels in and had no intention of moving on until she'd gotten her answer.

Shit.

Talking about himself was his least favorite activity. Yet he didn't believe anyone had ever asked him that question.

"Sure." He shrugged. "Who wouldn't like being more powerful and essentially immortal?"

"Why am I not convinced?"

"Why regret what I can't change? I am who I am."

"How old are you, anyway?"

"What the hell is this?" He pulled his arm free and stood. "An interview for your school paper?" He didn't do this. Looking back never did a damn bit of good.

"Touchy much?"

"I'm not a heart-to-heart kind of guy." He rolled his shoulders, loosening the knots. "It's not my thing."

"All I asked was your age. Not when and to whom you lost your virginity."

Shit. She was right. Not that he'd tell her.

Glancing over his shoulder, he glared down at her, meeting her dogged stare. One that said *come on, you ass, loosen up.* A message telegraphed to him from the only person on the planet who could pull it off and live.

"One hundred and forty-five."

Her eyes widened and a satisfied smile bloomed on her face. Yeah. She'd won this round.

"You're an old man." Her smiled morphed into a sly grin.

"I like to think of it as experienced," he said.

"Oh, I see." She nodded. "That's how it is."

"How what is?"

"You're sensitive about your age."

"I'm not 'sensitive.'" If she were a male, that word would have been the last thing he ever uttered.

"If you say so." She shrugged.

A low growl of frustration erupted from his chest.

Alexandria pointed at him. "I make my case."

"Bullshit." Markus waved her off and plopped back down on the bed. "You're supposed to be feeding, not talking." He shoved his wrist back in front of her. "Please, put this in your mouth."

"Are you trying to tell me to shut up?"

"Oh, don't tempt me, Vixen."

She laughed. Actually laughed. With him. And it was the most glorious sound he'd ever heard. It filled his ears and wrapped his body in an electric veil of warm sunshine. Christ. What he wouldn't give to hear that every day for the rest of eternity and to be the one to cause it.

"As you well know, when it comes to my memory of what happened while you and Marguerite held me, I'm a little sketchy," she began, her violet gaze going somewhere distant before coming back to him. "But I'm willing to bet this is the most civil conversation you and I have ever had."

"You're probably right."

"It's nice. Don't you think?" Her expression transformed,

becoming soft and warm. Damn near inviting.

And dangerous as hell.

"For a change of pace," she added.

Unable to take another second more, he looked away. "Yeah. It's good."

Too damn good.

"Tell me more about you," she said, and the request hit him like a sucker punch to the ribs. Totally unexpected and temporarily knocking him speechless.

She'd lowered his guard and come in for the kill. Yet on his next breath, and before he could stuff it all back down where it belonged, he found himself spilling more than he ever had about himself.

"I was born in America—New York—but my mother and father were Italian immigrants." What the hell was he doing? He didn't think about, much less discuss, those days. To anyone.

Out of the corner of his eye, Markus noted the expectant and pleased look on the face of the female—the only person in the world that he'd lay down his life for. So, for her…he'd talk.

"Born and bred in South Carolina," she said. "But I've always wanted to go to New York."

"You wouldn't have liked the city I knew back then," he said.

"Not a nice place when you were growing up?"

"That's being kind." He stood, unease growing under his skin like a prickling rash. He had to move. She was too damn close, his proximity too near to the only thing he knew that was *nice* and good in the world, especially when touching the ugliness of his past.

"Tell me," she softly urged.

"You asked me a moment ago if I liked being a vampire." Markus eased back around, facing her. "To be honest, I really don't know how to answer that question." He reached over and tugged the chair over until he could lower onto the seat. Settling his forearms on his knees, he allowed his mind to roll back. "I was twenty-five when I stumbled onto my first vampire. His name was Phillip Durand, and I thought that he intended to kill me." He lifted his head, meeting Alexandria's attentive gaze. "And I was so fucking glad."

Her eyes widened, her delicate lips parting on a soft inhale. "You wanted to die?"

"More like, I deserved to be put down. I just wanted it to end. When Phillip snatched me that late night in the alleyway, as I was walking back after I had finished taking care of my father's business, I was…relieved." Markus lowered his head, studying the stains on the toe of his boot.

"But that's not what happened."

"No. I woke up the next night in some run-down underground room of a brothel. Sick. Disoriented. But not dead." He grunted. "I resigned myself that my new state of being had to be some kind of penance for my crimes. Perhaps evidence that there must be a God, and he'd sentenced me to spend the rest of my days as an immortal monster who would never see the sun or his family again." He looked up at her from under his brows. "A punishment better than death."

"But why?" Alexandria shook head. "What had you done that made you think you deserved such a harsh judgment from God?"

"My job back then was to 'take care' of the people who

owed my father money and didn't pay."

"Your father was part of the Mafia?"

He nodded.

"He was the head of the family. What's called the God-father. Except he was my actual father. I handled things for him, and I was very good at my job." Images zoomed past his mind's eye. Pale faces, their eyes open, unseeing. Bullet holes gaping in their foreheads. Ice settled in his gut, a cold churning brew of nausea.

"You were his assassin," she said, her tone morose. "And you hated it?"

"I was my father's firstborn son." Markus rose. "Loving or hating whatever job he had me do didn't matter. My directive was simple: do the job right. Make him proud, or better yet, don't embarrass him. I followed orders."

"I think I understand now," she softly interjected. "Death was your only way out."

"For a while…" Markus strode around the end of her bed. "Before I was turned, that is, this place served as a refuge. The only thing that was all my own and didn't belong to the family." He glanced around the room, memories of when he'd sneak away and head down south to check on its progress as it was being constructed playing back inside his head.

"I see," she said. "That's why you had this built."

"I paid off a few men with my own money to come up here and quietly do what was necessary to build the cabin. I wanted an underground bunker like this for storage in case I ever needed a backup plan." He stopped and wrapped his fingers around the footboard. "I didn't know then, but building this hideout turned out to be a godsend. I ended up needing it more after I became a vampire than I ever had when I was human."

"You lived here after you were turned? What about your sire?"

"He was killed not long after he created me, so I moved here right afterward. It served me well for a few years."

"Had to be pretty lonely," she said, and he could have sworn for a moment a glimmer of compassion resonated in her expression. But he knew better than that. How could she ever feel anything but resentment when it came to him?

"There were times..." His mind traveled back to the endless days he'd spent staring at the basement ceiling, the lack of contact with the outside world, other than a quick feeding, suffocating. He may as well have been stuffed inside a plastic bag with the air slowly being drained away. "But back then, I believed it wasn't anything less than I deserved."

"And now?" She cocked her head, sending an obsidian waterfall of hair falling over her shoulder. His shaft jerked at the sight. Hell. It was all he could do not to make the leap over the foot of the bed rail, cover her body with his, and breathe her in until he was flying high on her scent.

This had to stop. His mind had gotten muddled reliving the past with emotional foolishness. "And now this conversation ends."

"So why the Enclave?" she asked, completely ignoring him.

"I said I'm done," he barked.

"Did you feel like the Enclave was an opportunity for you to redeem yourself of your past sins?"

He stalled, seizing the bedpost with his fist. She was right, again. Maybe he hadn't consciously realized it at the time, yet that had been exactly why he'd joined.

"You thought maybe this time around you could be the one to save a few human lives," she said. "Pretty damn honorable for someone who's supposed to be such an evil monster, don't you think?"

"'Honorable' is not the word I'd choose." He scoffed. "I'm still a killer, Vixen. The Enclave was just a different uniform."

"After what you've shared with me about where you've been, I'm not so sure about that."

How could she use the word "honorable" when it came to him? Especially after what he'd done to her and so many others? Markus turned toward her. "Have you lost your mind?" He marched closer. "Did that stab wound drain your blood volume and take the rest of your memory about our history along with it?"

"Well, excuse the hell out of me," she snapped. "And here I was about to feel a little bit of compassion for you and maybe a smidgen of forgiveness for all the shit you put me through."

"Don't waste either on me." He hovered inches from her face. "You'll only be disappointed."

"You think so, huh?" She leaned forward, forcing him to straighten. Alexandria swung her legs over the side of the bed. "Perhaps if you'd take the time to knock some of that damn baggage off your shoulders, we could actually get to see the real you! And then, who knows what kind of person we might find under all that weight?" Alexandria's hands came up as she stood, her palms hovering at his chest as if she were leery of getting burned if she made contact.

His breath stalled inside his chest. He was too damn

petrified to breathe, or to move, in case the slightest twitch scared her away.

"Maybe there would be someone there who is worth my time." Gently, the pads of her fingers brushed the surface of his T-shirt, and the sensation sent a spark of awareness straight to the head of his cock. Air rushed from his lungs, and he grabbed her wrists, holding them in place.

"You're wrong, Alexandria," he said, his voice raw.

"I don't think so. But if you keep this *I don't fucking need anybody* kind of attitude up, we'll never know." Shaking her head, she yanked her wrists free, then cried out and clutched her side. She stumbled back against the bed.

"Shit!" Markus grasped her shoulders, steadying her. "I should have fed you before now, instead of allowing myself to get distracted!"

"Stop it!" She grabbed his biceps. "For one moment, would you stop blaming yourself for everything?" she whispered, yet her words resounded inside his head with the clarity of crystal wind chimes—the notes pure and awakening.

Instinct drove him to cup the cool flesh of her cheeks. He had to. There was no other choice. She made him want to touch. To feel. Her lashes lowered, and she leaned into his palms. And his heart warmed, melted. God, how he wished he possessed the power to freeze time and never let this moment go. Never let *her* go. "Okay," he uttered. She opened her eyes, and dreamy violet irises stole his will. "This time— for you—anything you want." He drew closer, exposing his neck. "Feed, Alexandria. Let me take care of you."

He swallowed hard, steeling himself for her bite. Not for the pain. But for the excruciating pleasure it would bring. The gentle stroke of her fingertips brushed his face as she moved aside a stray lock of his hair that had come free from the band at his nape. A tremor rolled down his spine. God only knew how his sanity would survive having her this close again. Yet he was powerless to deny her.

She struck, sending a sharp twinge of lightning through his bloodstream. His jaw dropped in a silent scream as ecstasy burned a path of lust to his cock. Markus drove his hand into her hair, holding her in place against his throat. His head lolled. The room tilted, then spun. He wrapped his other arm around her waist, steadying them both. The dull yellow glow of the lamps morphed into a blazing ring of fire in the periphery of his vision.

"Fuck," he groaned.

Heaven and hell had collided.

Chapter Sixteen

She wanted him.

Maybe it was the weakness from the injury or the hunger for his blood, or she was just damn crazy. Whatever it was, Alexandria had never wanted, needed, another man like she did Markus. Of course, she'd experienced the pull of desire that came with feeding from the opposite sex, and she'd learned to control it. Yet with him, what he awakened inside her went beyond a mere sexual craving. Stirrings that, dammit, she refused to examine or to explore deeper. This had to be lust. Pure and simple. Well, maybe not so pure, but perhaps once sated, they could both get past whatever *this* was between them. Because even if she wanted to analyze how she felt about Markus—about them—the effort would be futile. This was Markus, the Enclave's traitor; how could she ever think there could be more?

She smoothed her tongue over the wound, closing the vein. Gooseflesh rose under her ministration, and knowing she'd caused the reaction from the alpha male had a rush of excitement coursing through her. She clutched the thick muscles of his arms and looked up. His gaze met hers with a firestorm of black and gray.

"How am I supposed to walk away from you when you touch me like that?" he said, the words coming out sounding flayed. "Look at me like that?"

"Like what?" she managed to ask in a steady voice, though inside, she was flying apart.

"Hungry," he said. "But not for blood," he added in a deep, rumbling voice that had her mind picturing things no good girl should crave.

Her knees weakened, yet it had nothing to do with her wound. Keeping her grip on his arms, she eased onto the bed, pulling him down over her until his lips were mere inches from hers. But he didn't move. Instead, he released his hold on her hair and seized the beam on top of the headboard with his hand as if he needed it to draw strength. The veins in his arms bulged in stark relief against the muscle.

"What do you want from me, Vixen?" He gripped her chin with the fingers of his free hand and smoothed his thumb underneath her bottom lip. She shivered. "If it's more of my blood you desire? It's yours." With a tug of his hand, he lifted her head, forcing her to look at him. Her mouth lost all of its moisture. She tried to swallow, but nothing would budge. "But you have to tell me." Markus breached the sensitive flesh of her lip, skating over it with a brief flick of his finger, but he may as well have licked her clit. She quivered, and arousal rushed from her depths. "Where do we go from here?"

"Kiss me," she whispered. Markus's hand slid to the

back of her neck. "I want you to kiss you me."

His mouth slammed down on hers. She'd released the beast in her room, but for some insane reason, Alex wasn't the least bit afraid. She wanted everything he had to give. He licked at her bottom lip, she opened, and he dived inside. Alex moaned from the delicious invasion. He tasted hot, rich, and forbidden. Her pulse was a raging storm inside her ears. God, he was right. She was so damn hungry.

Driving her fingers into the long strands of his hair, she worked the band at his nape free. The weight of the glorious dark locks streamed across her palms. Thick. Silky. Even better than she'd imagined.

Gently, Markus lifted her and moved her farther onto the bed. And then he was there, on the mattress with her. She fell back on the pillow, and his broad frame loomed over her. A part of her couldn't believe they'd come this far. But after tonight, after what he'd been willing to share with her, she wanted so badly to trust him. He wasn't the total monster she'd once believed.

Markus planted his hands on either side of her head, his hair falling over his shoulders fanning around them like a shield from the outside world. "I want you so damn bad," he said, his voice tight, strangled.

"I'm here," she breathed.

He lowered himself until his chest brushed hers. His mouth glanced off hers, his lips performing an erotic dance that made her forget to breathe. "You have no idea how you tempt me, Vixen."

She moaned, her legs scissoring against the ache inside her pussy.

"I want to taste your everything," he rasped. "Consume

you."

Her core tightened at the thought. "Yes." She groaned, arching into him.

His mouth came down on her throat, and the tips of his fangs lightly scored a path down the side. She jerked, nearly coming undone from the sensation.

Gathering the hem of her shirt with his fingers, Markus tugged it upward, not stopping until the cool air had her nipples pebbling. "Damn." The curse exited through his clenched teeth.

He edged lower, placing his mouth above them. "Perfect." He sighed. Then his tongue flicked the tip of her breast. Her back arched, trying to bring him closer. Needing more.

"Markus," she gasped. But he didn't make her beg much longer. His mouth captured the tight bud, licking and sucking the orb. She cried out from the torturous pleasure. Yet he didn't stop there. He moved to the other breast, repeating the process until she squirmed.

"God...Markus," she groaned. "Please." He had to do something. She was on fire.

"*Shhh...*" He proceeded lower, trailing nips and licks along her abdomen until he reached the waistband of her pants. "Are you sure, Vixen?" He glanced up, his fingertips on the button.

Oh yes. At that moment, she'd never been more sure of anything in her life. She nodded. And before she could blink, Markus had the leather open and peeling away from her ankles. Chills skated over her flesh, but it wasn't from the temperature of the room. It was the way the large male hovering over her naked body looked at her. She'd never forget this moment. Markus devoured her with his gaze. The

intensity primal and possessive. She'd never felt more wanted. Cherished.

Large calloused palms splayed over her thighs, nudging them wider. Alex complied, spreading her legs, making
room for him to wedge between them. She moaned. God,
she'd never been more aroused, her folds more swollen and
aching for a man's touch.

His lips parted; his chest heaved as if he couldn't get
enough air into his lungs. "So fucking beautiful."

Markus reached up one of her legs, lifting it a few inches
off the bed, and kissed the sensitive inside near her groin.
Alex whimpered, threading her fingers into his hair. It was
either that or scream. Then he did the same to the other.
So damn close. Christ, why didn't he touch her where she
needed him most?

And then he did.

The tip of his tongue brushed over the apex of her pussy,
and she cried out. Needing something to ground her, Alex
grabbed the bedding, twisting it in her fingers. "If you stop, I
swear I'll kill you," she rumbled.

He chuckled, and the sound waves vibrated off her clit
like tiny pulses, making her shudder. "Vixen, I'm nowhere
near done with you. Not until I've wrung every scream out
of your limp body."

"Oh God," she muttered, and squeezed her eyes closed.

His fingertips traced the edges of her folds, then, using
the pads of his thumbs, he opened her wider. Panting, she
thrashed her head back and forth.

"Look at me," he rumbled from between her legs.

What? She stilled, but kept her eyelids tightly shut. No
way could she watch as he touched her.

"Look at me," he demanded, this time a little louder.

Alex parted her lashes. Markus smiled up at her, his eyes simmering with a sultry fire. "That's it. Watch me taste you."

Slowly, so agonizingly slow, he placed his tongue over the opening to her pussy, then dragged it upward until he'd laved every inch of her. And the shock wave rolled over her body. She gasped. Markus licked his lips.

"Fuck," he rasped. "Hot and delicious."

"You are so bad," she whispered.

"You have no idea, baby," he rumbled. Then his mouth was on her again. Licking, sucking her flesh, working his way up toward her throbbing bundle of nerves.

"God, yes," she mumbled. "Markus."

He circled the swollen nub with his tongue, taunting and teasing her. Her core ached. So damn empty. She needed his mouth on her. Needed him inside her.

"I-I…Markus." She closed her eyes, unable to take it anymore. "Please…" The only word she could manage to utter, but it didn't matter. He seemed to anticipate her needs. Knew exactly how to take her to the edge, dangle her there, then when she didn't think she could take another moment, he took her higher.

His mouth closed over her clit as two fingers sank deep inside her. The universe zoomed into sharp clarity. Suddenly nothing else existed, nothing mattered except the male between her legs and the exquisite things he was doing to her body. A tremor rocked her, and her core clamped down on the thick intrusion. So incredibly good.

"Oh God…" she groaned. It was too good.

Alex's back arched, and she could have sworn she'd taken flight. A scream resonated in her ears, a sound unlike anything she'd heard before. Yet it was her.

On its own accord, her pelvis rocked into him over and over again. She grasped for his head, pressing him tighter against the center of her pleasure. Behind her eyelids, stars danced. Her limbs were lighter than air, and she never wanted to come down.

"Markus..." His name was a moan inside her throat. She sighed, and gravity slowly regained its hold on her body. His fingers slid free from her, and the delicious pressure inside disappeared. She bit back a groan of displeasure from its loss.

She glanced down and met Markus's satisfied smile. "You look quite proud of yourself, vampire," she said, her voice hoarse.

"I am a male who takes pride in his work." Bringing his hand forward, Markus slid two of his fingers into his mouth. His gaze never left hers as he proceeded to lick them in a slow and methodical manner. A process that said *these are the digits that were inside you. The ones that made you come again and again. And you are delicious.*

Dear God, the way his mouth, his lips, moved over his fingers... Her orgasm was too fresh, too recent. As if she were a junkie struggling through rehab, flashbacks of the way he'd drawn the pleasure from her clit slammed into her with HD clarity. She didn't think it was possible, but her core pulsed yet again. She gasped from the stab of pleasure.

His fingertips left his mouth with a slight *pop*, then he was over her, staring down at her. Larger than life, the lethal alpha male surrounded her and had Alex struggling for her share of the oxygen in the room.

"Markus..." She panted. "The things you do to me." She

shook her head, trying to clear the buzz inside her skull.

"You're so damn gorgeous when you come." His voice oozed pure testosterone. It was the kind of sound that, if she hadn't already been naked beneath him, she would have been dropping her panties. "I could do that all night long." He skated a kiss across her lips. "Listen to you scream my name as your body trembles. So damn hot."

Alex moaned. "I want you," she whispered against his cheek, the stubble scratching her and sending chills in its wake. "Let me do the same for you." She clutched his shoulders, pressing him back.

The hard ridge against her thigh said he was more than ready for his own release, and Alex couldn't wait to be the one who got him there. She scooted out from under him, turning onto her side, and snagged the hem of his shirt. Markus covered her fist with his hand.

"Not tonight," he said, stopping her cold.

"But…" How could he not need this? Her mind went back to the previous time they'd been together and he'd helped to bring her to her first orgasm. He'd walked away then as well. "I want to," she said. She glanced down at the obvious and significant bulge in his pants. "You can't tell me you don't want it."

"Of course I do." He squeezed her hand. "But you've just recovered from a pretty bad stab wound. Let my blood do its job and rest tonight."

"I feel fine." She frowned. "I'm not that fragile."

"Yes, I know you're fine." He grinned, leaned in, and planted a kiss on her cheek. "Fine as hell." Withdrawing, he added, "This was about me pleasuring you." Before she could object again, he rolled from the bed and onto his feet. "Later."

He strode around the bed and toward the bathroom. "Rest, Alexandria," he called at the door. One arm came up, his hand capturing the doorjamb before crossing the threshold, but he didn't look back. "What I told you tonight — about my past — I want you to know I've never shared with another soul. Not even Arran." He closed the door.

Alex flipped over onto her stomach and buried her face in her pillow. Her mind whirled at the revelation. She'd actually glimpsed and touched the real Markus Santini. He'd opened up and allowed her to see the dark stains and scars on his soul.

There was good reason why Markus had so easily hardened and become Marguerite's lethal weapon. The seed had already been planted by his father. The man had forced him at a young age to become a killer. But he was capable of so much more than being the hand of death. Deep inside, she knew he possessed the ability to feel compassion for others.

For him, she'd let her guard down.

And oh my God, she'd enjoyed every minute of it. Mentally, she screamed into the thick padding of feathers. She hadn't been prepared for the pleasure he'd brought to her body. Worse, she hadn't been ready for the feelings constricting her heart like a fist when he'd closed the door.

Alex rolled onto her back and smoothed a palm over her sternum. Blowing the hair out of her eyes, she stared up at the ceiling. She refused to put a name on the cauldron of emotions feeding the tightness in her chest.

What the hell have I done?

Chapter Seventeen

Markus couldn't sleep.

He sat with his legs propped up in the spare chair, his eyes closed, but he was very much aware. The steady drum of the shower in the other room filled his ears, torturing him with images, fantasies, of what moved under the water's spray: Alexandria, naked, her skin glistening as water sluiced down her back.

Groaning, he repositioned, unable to shake the mental picture. His cock jerked, and he grunted from the relentless ache inside his balls, no matter how many times he jerked off.

After their encounter, he'd had to relieve some of the pressure when he'd bathed, but the reprieve had been only temporary. The moment he'd stepped back inside the bedroom, the scent of her arousal lingering in the small space, a wave of desire had hit him with hurricane force. He'd been a kite in a whirlwind of lust no longer able to control which direction he blew. And Alexandria was the eye of the storm. His calm center. However, if she knew the whole story about the monster in her bed, she'd send him crashing back down to earth.

Yet when she'd drawn him into the bed with her, there'd been no way he could resist touching, tasting, and pleasuring her. Watching her come with her flavor on his tongue had been intoxicating. No other drug on the planet could compare. One taste, and he was addicted. If he lived for the next millennium, bringing her to orgasm every night, it still wouldn't be enough. He would never get enough of Alexandria. But she was an addiction he had to escape.

Once this was all over and he knew she was safe, he had to let her go. That was why he refused to ever permit himself inside her. He couldn't allow things to ever go that far. If he ever spilled his seed within her, felt the tight walls of her pussy squeezing his cock—and he knew she'd be tight as hell—no one would ever take her from him.

He was a son of a bitch. A murdering bastard. He deserved every nasty name in the book. But he wasn't so much of a dick that he'd condemn a female he cared about to a life with him. *Fuck.* She'd done this to him. Gotten under his skin and forced his heart to open, to feel. But he didn't know how to do this. How to care so damn much without pulling her into his darkness.

The sound of the shower on the other side of the door slowed to a trickle, and the faucet released its familiar squeak having successfully cut off the flow. Alexandria shouldn't have been awake this early. Based on the lingering fatigue in his limbs, the sun hadn't fully set. But the last two days hadn't actually been typical.

Markus stilled his movement, staring at the nothingness behind his eyelids. With any luck, she'd climb back into bed and rest a little longer. Then once darkness fell, he had business to take care of.

Namely, hunting down Enrique.

Putting an end to the disastrous chapter of his life titled "Marguerite."

Alexandria didn't deserve to live with a target on her back because of his past. Markus coiled the sheet around his fingers. "I swear, Vixen, with every fiber of my being," he whispered into the shadows. "I'll set things right. I'll make sure any threat to your safety is eliminated—permanently."

It's what he did best. His father had made sure of it.

The bathroom door clicked and opened. Alexandria barely made a sound as she padded across the floor, then cool fingertips glided over his bare abs. His breath stalled, and her hand roamed south.

Oh fuck. What was she up to?

Her palm settled on his fly covering the swollen ridge of his cock, and his brain short-circuited.

"Alexandria…" he forced out through his clenched jaw. His eyelids popped open, and he captured her wrist. Although the voice inside his head roared for him to allow her access.

"I don't know why you didn't join me in bed this morning."

"You needed rest," he grumbled, her palm not budging from its resting place on his erection. "Not something more."

"Well, it's been hours, and I'm feeling much better." Her free hand traveled over the tats along his arm.

"The sun hasn't set yet. You shouldn't even be up."

"My dreams wouldn't let me sleep," she said. "My mind

kept replaying what happened last night." She lifted her leg and inserted it between his. Markus dropped his feet from the chair and pushed back, giving her more room between his thighs. "And what didn't happen last night," she added, a seductive smile playing on her mouth as she went down on her knees.

Ahh, hell. He shook his head. "Vixen, come on. You're not playing fair."

"I think I'm playing more than fair." She knocked his hold away from her wrist and proceeded to open the button to his jeans right before she lowered the zipper.

He should stop her.

A decent man would get his ass out of the chair.

Alexandria reached inside and delicate fingers wrapped around the end of his cock. She pulled it free, dragging a groan from his throat in the process.

But since when had he been a good and decent man?

Glancing up, she ran her hand up and down the shaft. He moaned.

"Damn, what am I going to do with all this?" A smile tugged at the corners of her mouth. Lips he knew felt like the delicate petals of an awakening rosebud. Dewy soft, waiting for that first kiss of sun and rain. "I can barely get my fist around you."

Opening wide, Alexandria sank her mouth over the flared head. Silky, wet heat engulfed him, and he seized the arm of the chair with his fists. The wood released a loud *pop* under the pressure.

"Shit…"

Lower and lower she traveled the length of him until the head of his cock bumped the back of her throat. *Holy fuck.*

His balls jerked, drawing tight. No way would he last with her. Not like this. He was too hot. Too hot for her, for too long. But damn, watching her go down on him…a fantasy come to life. An unreal moment in time.

She coughed and drew back, spiraling her hand back up his length. At the top, she glanced up from under her lashes and flattened her tongue along the back of his cock. Watching him, she slowly worked the sensitive underside in small circles.

"That's it," he hissed, and his head lolled. "Christ. You're killing me."

Up and down, she moved over his shaft, her palm gently squeezing his length as she tortured him with her tongue. Teasing him. Drawing him so damn close, then backing off.

His breathing reduced to harsh pants. Her tongue dipped into his slit, and Markus reared his head.

"You taste so damn good," she mouthed over him, her lips caressing the sensitive flesh.

Cum raced to the forefront of his cock, ready to blow. He growled and seized the base of his shaft with his fist, shutting down his orgasm. "Son of a bitch!" he gritted out, and kicked his chair back away from her.

Not like this! He wouldn't come like this with her.

"Markus!" she cried out from her position on the floor, her eyes wide with confusion. "I'm sorry. Did I do something wrong?"

"Fuck, no, baby," he said, his words guttural, and tugged her onto her feet. "I want you too damn much."

He claimed her mouth with his own, the taste of his pre-cum on her tongue. Her hands were on his back, nails biting into his flesh. Gripping her hips, he ground his erection against her, desperate for the feel of her.

Unable to take another second without being inside her, Markus broke away. "Need you."

"God, yes," she gasped.

Dizzy and frantic with need, Markus guided her around. Placing a palm between her shoulders, he bent her over the side of the bed. She'd dressed in the thin slip of a nightshirt he'd brought back for her, the hem stopping at midthigh. He grabbed it, yanked it up, and exposed her bare bottom. His cock throbbed at the gorgeous sight of her pussy, the folds swollen and glistening with arousal. For him. He cursed, barely able to draw enough oxygen into his lungs from the heavy burden of lust pulling him under.

"Dammit, Markus. Don't stop."

Grabbing the aching girth of his cock with one hand, his other braced on her hip, he moved in closer. The head of his shaft nudged her heated core, arcing another bolt of desire up his spine.

"Please," she muttered. "It's okay. I want you."

It's okay. Her simple two words of validation echoed inside his skull. *It's okay.*

But taking her wasn't okay. Gritting his teeth, he closed his eyes. *She's not yours to possess.* If Alexandria knew what he'd done to her, this would never be okay.

Summoning every thread of control, Markus stumbled back.

"Shit!" He swiped a hand down over his face and spun around. He had to get some air. Needed air that wasn't drenched in her scent. He bolted for the door to the upstairs and swung it open.

"Markus!" she called out. "Where are you going?"

Taking the steps two at a time, he charged for the surface. The only thought on his mind: escape. If he didn't, there was no way he wouldn't be buried to the hilt inside her.

On the first floor of the cabin, Markus targeted the front door. Footsteps pounded on the stairs behind him. He had to get out. Markus flipped the dead bolt and snatched the doorknob.

"Don't you dare cut out on me!"

Closing his eyes, he sighed. "Let me go, Vixen."

"Why?" she croaked. "I don't understand. What did I do wrong?" Her voice sounded strained. Hurt.

Fuck. The last thing he wanted to do was to hurt her even more. It was the one thing he'd tried to avoid. Rearing back an arm, Markus swung forward and slammed his fist into the wood. He slapped both palms onto the battered door and hung his head between his arms. "It's not you," he groaned.

"Isn't that what they all say?" she scoffed.

"I'm telling you the truth." Facing her, he pressed his back to the door.

"Then I don't get it." She shook her head, padding closer.

His pulse thrummed at her approach, still too high off her scent. He curled his fists, needing the strength.

"Your body tells me you want me." Her focus lowered to the hard evidence between his legs. "But you won't touch me." Her throat worked. "At least not in that way."

"I can't," he bit out. "End of story."

Alexandria's eyes flashed, and she bridged the gap between them. "The hell that's the end of it! You can't just do that to me and expect I'll walk away without questions. You have no idea what it cost for me to—"

"To what?"

"Never mind." She reversed course.

"No, you don't." Markus pushed away from the door and captured her before she could escape. "Tell me."

"I don't want to talk about it." She shook him off.

"Sorry." He grasped her shoulders and spun her back around. "You don't get a pass that easily, not after you had me spilling my guts last night."

"You just blew me off like I wasn't good enough for you to actually take to bed, and now you expect me to open up?" She slammed her palms into his chest, knocking him back, and stormed toward the basement stairs. "Go to hell."

"Dammit!" He descended the staircase after her.

"Leave me alone," she shouted the moment he crossed the threshold. "You wanted away from me so damn bad, get out!"

"You don't understand, Alexandria." He tried his best to be patient, which defied the core of his being, as he edged toward her. Except the vixen countered his every move. "Would you stand still for one minute while I try to talk to you?"

"Shoe's on the other foot now, asshole." She sneered. "How the hell does it feel?"

A spark of anger ignited, but he quickly snuffed it before it burned out of control and he said something he didn't mean. He needed to stay calm. Bracing his hands on his hips, he mentally started a countdown from ten. At least the momentary battle between them had quenched some of his lust, allowing his brain to function at a higher capacity than early caveman.

"Sucks, doesn't it?" she added, crossing her arms and

planting herself in one position. "Start talking."

"I've handled this wrong." Markus sighed. "I should have never allowed things to get this out of hand." He scrubbed a hand over his face. "It's just…" He raked her with his gaze. "Not touching you when…" Fuck. He couldn't get the words out right. Communication had never been his strong suit. For the majority of his life he'd been more of a man of action. Kill first. Ask questions later.

"A lot of words, Markus." Alexandria strode closer, putting them face-to-face. "But as usual, you haven't given me the real explanation. Why, when it comes down to you actually making love to me, do you try to escape my presence?"

Markus cupped her face, and his eyelids shuttered. "Don't you want to return to your beloved Enclave family?"

"What kind of question is that? Of course I do."

"Then I have to keep my hands off you, or more specifically, it's my other body part that has to keep its distance."

She frowned. "Are you saying that if you make love to me, you don't think…?"

"If I ever got inside you, Vixen," he gritted out with a shake of his head, "once would never be enough. And do you think your sister, or anyone else back at that mansion, would ever approve of you being in my bed?" He scoffed and turned away to drop his ass on the edge of the bed. "Once I've taken care of things, I have to let you go." His fingers curled into the denim encasing his thighs. "We have to stop before there's no going back."

Alexandria eased down onto the mattress beside him. Close, but far enough away there was no way they'd touch.

"What can I say?" he said. "I have a bit of a possessive streak. I tend to like to keep what's mine."

"What's yours, huh?" A short burst of a chuckle came from her, but he could tell from the sound the laugh hadn't originated from a place of humor. "Where have I heard those words before?"

"I'm going to fix this, Alexandria." He nodded even though he wasn't sure if she was watching him. "In my gut, I know Enrique was responsible for that ambush. I'm going to find him, and when I do, he'll wish he'd never come back here." The image of Alexandria lying on her back in a pool of blood flashed before his mind's eye. A burst of rage lashed through his veins. Markus lunged from the bed, snatched one of the chairs into his grip, and sent it flying into the rock wall. The wood shattered into a hailstorm of splinters. He watched as the broken bits and pieces fell to the floor, his chest heaving.

"Did that help?"

"For a millisecond," he said, panting, working on reining in his control.

He glanced over his shoulder. Alexandria sat there watching him in the long pale pink T-shirt he'd snagged for her before returning to the cabin. The sheer material did little to hide the dark nipples of her full breasts. *Shit.* His mouth watered. He'd never forget the way they'd tightened between his lips. The sweet and salty flavor of her soft flesh against his tongue. His cock swelled and bucked against the constraints of his zipper. Dammit. Why hadn't he thought to grab her thicker clothing? He cleared his throat, wishing he could clear his mind so easily.

"You going to talk to me now?" Markus snatched the T-shirt he'd hung on the back of the remaining chair and pulled it over his head. "I answered your question. Now tell me what's really going on with you, Vixen."

Alexandria drew her legs up, resting her heels on the bed's rail, and wrapped her arms around her knees. "You don't own the market on having an ugly past that you'd like to keep buried," she said, her attention falling to the dark red polish on her toenails.

He'd never asked her about the years before she'd stumbled onto his radar. Probably because he never wanted anyone picking around in his past, so he'd stayed out of hers. He liked who she was in the here and now. Liked what he'd seen in her. Why did it matter who she'd been before? Yet here they were, and whatever she'd gone through, like him, had left a scar. And the thought of it didn't sit well in his gut.

"Who hurt you?" The question clawed its way out of his throat. The veins on his forearm swelled with his restraint not to tear out of there the moment she revealed the answer so he could relieve some prick of his head. "Why did you feel as if it had cost you something to tell me that you wanted me?"

Alexandria didn't look up. She kept her head low, staring at the same place on her toes. Damn. He wanted to reach out, touch her, and hold her until she could tell him everything. But something told him if he did, she'd retreat even further.

"You were my first," she muttered, the words barely audible.

"*Uhm*...we didn't..." He shook his head. "The first what?"

"I didn't mean I was a virgin," she clarified. "I meant my first—you know..." She glanced in his direction, then back down. "Orgasm," she whispered.

His head whirled. She was beautiful, fiery, and passionate. "How is that possible?"

"God, Markus." She surged onto her feet, keeping her back to him. "Make me feel more like a freak, why don't you?"

Christ. He sucked at all this emotional shit. He stood and approached her, keeping enough distance so they didn't connect. "I'm just trying to understand. I mean, when we were together…"

"I know," she whispered. "That's never happened before now." She glanced at her fingers, her attention going to a chip in her index fingernail as if concentrating on something else allowed her to bring what she needed to the surface. Something she hadn't wanted to think about in a long time.

"Tell me what happened to you, baby," he said, more of a command this time than a question. He slid his hands inside his pockets. It was safer that way. Because he had a feeling he wasn't going to like what she told him.

"Since you were a part of the Enclave way back when Elle came to live there, you probably remember that she'd been on her own for a while," she said.

"I do."

"After she'd gotten on her feet, she helped me get out as well. But before I was old enough to leave, my mother went through some pretty bad 'relationships.' And I use the term loosely. The men who came through were more about keeping her in enough money to supply her drug habit than building any kind of lifelong commitment."

The thought of her growing up watching her mother self-destruct in front of her sickened him. "That had to be a nightmare."

"Definitely wasn't *The Andy Griffith Show*. Watching the door on my mother's bedroom revolve was nauseating." She nodded, then resumed her position on the bed and crossed her arms. He could have sworn a small tremor rocked her as if the room had suddenly turned cold. "Yet things got even worse when one night the door to my room opened, and I found out my mother's bed wasn't the only place her current boyfriend wanted to get his kicks."

Markus's gut boiled, a cauldron of rage bubbling, spilling over, blistering hot and ready to blow. "That bastard touched you," he bit out, fangs erupting.

She nodded, and her eyes squeezed shut. "Having him on me was vile enough, but it was the things he whispered in my ear every time he crawled on top of me that made me want to vomit." She shook her head as if she could dislodge the memory from her brain. "No matter how many years go by, some nights I swear I still hear his disgusting voice. Smell the beer on his breath." Her expression twisted, and she clutched her abdomen.

Keep it together, Santini. He clamped down on his molars, his jaw ticking like a damn pulse. He grabbed on to the bedpost for support, a reinforcement to stay put. She needed him present. Calm. Like she'd been there for him. But fuck, this wasn't him. His palms itched for action.

Inhaling deeply, Markus turned back around, searching inside himself for the right words to say. *Christ.* Words weren't exactly what he did best. But what he found there obliterated whatever he'd been about to say.

Tears streamed down her cheeks, the sight a blow to his heart. Had he ever witnessed her crying? She'd been a fighter from day one. Very little he'd ever said to Alexandria had appeared to intimidate her. Others would have shaken in their boots from his growl. But not her. Not his vixen.

From that first night, he could tell Alexandria possessed a fierce and determined spirit for life. She was a fighter. An atypical female who had balls enough to go toe-to-toe with a more-than-century-old vampire. A male who had held the power in the palm of his hand to snuff her existence from the planet.

She was perfectly exceptional.

At this moment, watching as her hard shell cracked from the pain of her past, his own damn heart shattered. He wanted to kill the bastard who'd done this to her. The sick son of a bitch had left a deep and permanent scar. Until recently, with him, she'd never fully allowed herself to enjoy her sexuality.

"You trusted me enough earlier to open up, show me your desires, and I shut you down," he said, the words almost choking him.

She looked over at him, and her throat worked up and down. "With other men, sex has been a chore. A task I felt like I had to go through to make them happy. But with you, it's different. Maybe I've changed. Or you've changed me. All I know was at that moment, I trusted you. And I wanted you."

I trusted you. A groan erupted inside his head, and it was all he could do not to grab her, take her in his arms, and show her how damn much he loved her.

He blinked and stared down at his boots. *Love?* Since when had that rotting muscle in his chest been capable of anything else besides hate and revenge? Being a complete asshole? Now that was more his speed.

"I hope you know that my reaction has nothing to do with you," he said.

"I do." She nodded and sniffed.

"You have no idea how much I fucking want you."

She smiled, but the effort didn't quite make it to her eyes. *You've got to make this right.*

"Oh God, I've made a fool of myself." She wiped the dampness away from her cheeks. "I don't do tears," she said in a husky voice.

"We've both opened up some old wounds, revealed a few things that nobody else needs to know about." Markus reached out and pulled her into his arms. To his relief, she didn't resist. "My lips are sealed, Vixen," he swore, and ran a palm down her dark tresses. He could live a dozen millennia, and he'd never tire of the feel of her hair in his palm, the feel of her body pressed against his.

She'd given him her trust. Was ready to give him all of her. But if he allowed that to happen and she didn't know the truth—all of it—he wasn't any better than the bastard who'd taken her against her will.

The lies needed to stop here.

If she never forgave him, he'd walk away knowing he'd at least given her the choice. After he returned her, though, he'd be hitting the door, anyway. In the Enclave's eyes, he would have betrayed them again by taking her in the first place. But he had to hold her one more time before letting her go. He brushed his hand down her back again, savoring the silky texture of her hair.

This was the right thing to do. He swallowed hard. So why the fuck did it feel like someone was carving his heart out piece by piece?

"Vixen," he said. She looked up from where her head rested on his chest. He stared down at her, and the moment he captured her gaze, Markus pushed inside. She flinched, but he held her tight while he sought out the part of her brain he'd shut down from her past. In seconds, he spotted the darkened cluster of neurons. It was as if they were waiting for him to return and patch the wires feeding the electrical impulses to that section of her brain.

Markus moved in, circling them, mentally gathering the broken pieces.

"Remember, Alexandria," he whispered.

Chapter Eighteen

"What the fuck is going on?" Enrique yelled into his cell phone's receiver at Christian, his blood pressure sledgehammering its way through his temples. "Why haven't you contacted me before now?"

"You expect me to pull out my damn phone at the kitchen counter and call you when Kenric and Guerin are whipping in and out like a bunch of damn pit bulls looking for someone to sink their teeth into?" Christian snarled. "Shit's gotten real around here since you and whoever the hell you're working with coordinated that ambush last night."

"Where the hell are you now?"

"I'm at the docks, hunting," Christian replied. "My babysitters, Arran and Elle, are a block away, doing the same."

"They allowed you to stray from their sides?" His spy sounded as if he was playing the game well. "You must be winning their trust."

"I guess." Christian grunted. "Not hard. They're nice

enough."

"Nice?" Enrique chuckled. "You're not there to find your BFF. You remember who your ass belongs to." He snarled. "Who made you."

"Like I could ever forget."

"I heard from one of the DEADs that things got pretty messy last night. Another one of the Enclave's warriors popped in and took out a few of them on his own, but not before one of the females got hit." Enrique perched on the edge of his desk. "Since I don't have Marguerite's daughter in my possession, please tell me Markus's bitch has at least been taken care of."

"I don't know if this is what you want to hear…" Christian sighed. "That was Markus who phased in and saved the day for Guerin and Eve. But we have no idea about Alex's status."

"What the hell does that mean?" Enrique straightened and shoved the chair out of his path.

"It means neither of them returned back to the mansion. Markus is gone, and no one knows where the hell he's taken Alex."

A smile stretched Enrique's face. "You're shitting me."

"Markus has disappeared, and the rest of the Enclave is freaking the hell out. Especially Elle. She is about to come unglued about her sister. I didn't think Arran was going to be able to convince her to come out tonight and feed. But somehow he got her out of the house."

"Well, don't you just sound so concerned." The stupid kid was getting under his skin. All he needed him to do was observe and report.

"I'm just saying," the male snapped.

"I hear what you're saying. You're sounding attached. You get attached, you become a liability. Everything is on the line here. We're too damn close for you to fuck this up."

"Nothing has changed," he rumbled. "I'm still with you. No one has any idea that you were involved with what happened last night. But based on the way Markus came tearing through the house when the shit started going down the other night, I'm sure he's suspicious as hell it was you who put it all in motion. He's going to be coming for you."

"I'm not worried about that sniveling SOB." Enrique turned and lifted the frog-shaped glass paperweight—he had an affinity for the amphibians—tossing the weight in his palm. "Unknowingly, he's done me quite a favor. There's one Enclave male out of the way of our real target. Plus, he's succeeded in distracting them for us." He laughed. "Markus was always too blinded by pussy."

"You mentioned before that Eve was going to be the answer to everything you ever wanted, but what do you plan to do with her?" Christian's voice held a nervous edge. "How is this supposed to work once you get your hands on her?"

"Let me worry about that," Enrique said. "And you keep me informed of everything you learn about her."

"You're going to kill her, aren't you?" Christian asked, his voice low and deep.

Oh for Christ's sake. Enrique bit back a groan, not wanting to alarm his guest. He rose and put his back to his European buyer, Dominic Diaz, and edged closer to the window, trying to place as much distance as possible between him and the male with his payday. "Don't tell me you're suddenly growing a conscience," Enrique muttered into the phone.

"My balls are on the line." Christian's words cut through

the receiver. "So is it too much to ask what the hell you're planning for her and whoever else gets blindsided by your plan?"

"I think someone has grown to like his new playmates a bit too much," Enrique sneered, his fangs glinting back at him from his reflection in the glass. "You fuck this up for me, Christian…" Enrique swore. "Hide as deep as you want behind their walls, but the Enclave will not keep me from making you wish you'd never slithered your way out of your mother's womb."

"Dial it back on the threats, will ya?" A heavy sigh made its way through the receiver. "What the hell? I never insinuated I wanted to stay here. This Goody Two-shoes shit they're preaching about protecting this town makes me sick to my damn stomach. I wanted to know what you were going to do with her? You know…after?"

"Whatever her buyer wants," Enrique said. Why not humor the son of bitch? Wasn't like he would be welcoming him back like a prodigal son, anyway. He shrugged at his reflection. "Once she's delivered. I'm paid." He glanced over his shoulder at Mr. Payday himself, who sat intently watching him with a smug look plastered on his face. "It's really not my concern."

"You mean, *we're* paid, correct?"

"Yeah. Yeah." He shook his head, rolling his eyes. "Of course that's what I meant."

"What's next?" Christian asked, his voice hushed.

"Keep me informed of Eve's movements," Enrique spat. "That's all you need to know." The less Christian knew of his plans, the better. His gut said Christian was still loyal, but he wasn't sure for how much longer. The cocksucker was born to serve, and there was nothing like the allure of a master vampire. Enrique should know. He'd spent more years than he'd like to recall on his knees servicing Marguerite, all for a sip of her ancient blood, another stroke of her hand, or her cunt around his cock. Both had been intoxicating and addicting.

"I said I would, and I will," Christian snapped. "I've got my ass sitting in the damn middle of this. I just wanted to know if you've got something else in motion?"

Enrique glanced over his shoulder. Dominic, wearing a suit that probably cost more than a year's rent on Enrique's apartment, sat with his legs crossed on one of the dinette's chairs. The arrogant bastard had brought in a few of his associates to help expedite their mission. "Everything is moving forward on this end," Enrique said. "Keep me informed the moment you know her next move."

"I got it, okay?"

"Christian," he said, his voice low, lethal.

"Yeah."

"I'm counting on you." Enrique tapped end call. He dropped the cell on his desk, and strode toward his guests. "Now where were we?" He grinned.

Chapter Nineteen

For the second time in as many nights, Alex needed a crane to lift her eyelids. Pressing the heel of her hands to her eye sockets, she attempted to rub away the lethargy. Her head throbbed as she rolled over in bed. Where was the damn bat that had used her skull for practice? Inhaling deeply, she tugged the cool sheet around her a little higher. That's when it hit her.

The smell.

Fresh and clean. Too clean. The only thing tingling her sinuses was a trace of furniture polish and window cleaner. She peeked under her eyelids, and the familiar scene of heavy oak furniture that decorated her bedroom in the Enclave mansion filled her vision.

"What?" Her pulse raced, and shoving against the thick mattress, she pushed up in bed. Glancing down, she noted the same pink T-shirt Markus had given her back at the cabin. "Markus," she whispered. When had he brought her back, and why the hell didn't she remember the trip? "Markus!" she called out, and swung her legs over the side of the bed.

"Alex?" Her sister rushed into the room. "Hey there." She stretched her hand out and offered up a washcloth from the bathroom. "I was just getting this for you, hoping it would help you come around. How are you feeling?"

"Confused," she said, accepting the cloth and pressing it to her face. The heat felt nice and refreshing against her skin. Alex glanced up. "When did I get here?"

"A few hours ago." Elle leaned against the tall, ornate bedpost. "Are you sure you feel okay?"

Physically, other than a being a bit foggy, she felt fine. She was completely healed from her knife wound. So why had she been unconscious? "Yeah. I think so. Did Markus tell you anything about why he returned with me? And more importantly, why the hell I was knocked out?"

"Uhm…" Elle toyed with the snaps to her blouse and smoothed the front of her capris. "Some of it."

What was going on? Elle was evading, which sent a tremor of panic down her spine.

"Some?" Alex stood, and a wave of dizziness coursed through her. She stumbled, but the back of her legs struck the bed, steadying her. Pressing a palm to the mattress, she gave herself a moment for the room to settle.

"Alex?" Elle was at her side. "I thought you said you were okay."

She swallowed and blinked. "I thought I was, too. I don't know where that came from." She glanced over at her sister. "What aren't you telling me?"

Deflecting her stare, Elle muttered, "What's the last thing you remember?"

"You mean while I was with Markus?"

She nodded.

"We'd been talking. Getting to know each other a little better." Alex eased onto the side of the bed. "I was actually pleasantly surprised, Elle. He was kind to me." She would never forget the way he'd touched her—in more ways than one. The tenderness he'd shown her when she'd talked about her childhood. "I saw another side of him I never knew existed." She chuckled. "A person I don't think anyone knew existed."

"Wow. I'm sure that was, *uhm*...quite enlightening." Elle faced her, yet for some reason, she wasn't looking at her.

"You're acting strange." She shook her head. "I know what he did wasn't right, and you had to be pissed off and worried."

"We were—I was. No one had a clue where he'd taken you." Elle shoved her long dark hair back behind her ears. "But that's something we can talk about at another time."

"Okay..." Alex nibbled her bottom lip. "What should we be talking about now?"

"About one of the reasons Markus brought you back to me—to us." Elle strode closer again and brushed her palm over Alex's hair. "He wanted you to be here, with me, when you remembered."

"When I remembered?" Alex looked up at her sister. "Come on, Elle. You're talking in riddles."

"He gave them back to you."

"Gave me what?" Alex stood, and Elle stepped back, her eyes wide, pupils dilated. Her sister was freaking her out. Gooseflesh lifted the hairs on Alex's arms, and her chest ached. "Tell me!"

"Your memories."

Elle's words were soft, yet they resonated through her like a shock wave. She couldn't move. Couldn't process what she was saying. All she could do was stand there and watch as tears welled in her sister's amber eyes.

"Think back." A lone tear escaped, leaving a glimmering damp trail down Elle's cheek. "He said your memories are all there now. All you need to do is wake them up."

Like a hard fist trying to block her next breath, nausea welled at the back of her throat. Alex clamped a hand on her neck and fought to hold on to her stomach contents.

He'd given them back.

Her suspicions had been right all along. She'd never believed that the cause of her partial amnesia had been related to psychological trauma. There had to be more to it than that. And now she had her confirmation. Markus had been the one to wipe her brain of her time with him and Marguerite.

Grabbing the headboard's post, Alex slumped onto the edge of the mattress.

"Alex?" Elle whispered. "Do you remember?"

Wake them up. That was all she needed to do to find her memories. But all she could see inside her head was Markus, half naked, his eyes glowing with passion and lust as he'd stared down at her between his knees. She could still taste the salty-sweetness of his rock-hard length on her tongue. She could see the beads of sweat on his forehead while he'd trembled in restraint as she'd taken him to the back of her throat. God, how she'd wanted him.

Markus had revealed things about himself—exposed details about his past he'd never confided to anyone before her.

Yet he hadn't told her about the weeks she'd spent as his prisoner.

I'm a monster. That he had admitted to her. More than once. Still, that same monster had given her more pleasure than she'd ever experienced with any mortal man.

So what had been so horrific or damning that he'd felt the need to hide from her? Dear God, for how long and how many times had she asked herself that same question? Fear wrapped its sharp talons around her stomach. Her breath hitched. Now that the moment she'd fought for was finally here, did she want to know?

"Alex," Elle called out to her. "Talk to me."

Unbidden, blurred images zoomed past her mind's eye. Distorted voices, as if they were being played on a turntable at the wrong speed, filled her head. Alex clutched her scalp. *No, no, no...* She panted, needing more air than the room provided. It was all coming too fast. The contents of her stomach roiled.

She darted for the room's exit.

"Alex!" her sister yelled and grabbed her from behind. Elle wrapped her arms around her. "It's going to be okay," she crooned.

Alex's legs buckled, and together, they crumpled to the floor. Pulling her in close, Elle cradled her against her chest. As if the events unfolding inside her mind had happened yesterday and not last year, Alex was there—in full living color—back inside Marguerite's lair.

I'm trying to escape when one of Marguerite's guards spots me. They drag me back inside the old mansion and upstairs into Marguerite's private room. Fighting and kicking every step of the way, I'm forced into the wicked bitch's parlor.

Surveying the room, my gaze finds Markus. My heart rate staggers at the sight of the dark alpha male.

Markus is a hard and controlled son of a bitch. Despite that unfortunate personality trait, my body responds to him, no matter how hard I fight against the chemistry. But the male glaring at me isn't the vampire who regularly visits my hellhole in the basement. As he approaches, his expression morphs into a stoic mask. The only glimmer of emotion is the frigid determination staring back at me from his gray irises.

"I don't like problems," Marguerite says. "Fix this one, Markus. If not, kill her. Or I will."

Dear God, what is he about to do to me? Run! *my mind screams. Except escape is impossible.*

He demands I come with him. Oh, fuck no. And I attempt to say as much. But before I can utter a defiant word, he's in my face; his large palms hold my head steady and force me to meet his gaze.

Something like a bolt of lightning pierces my skull. My brain jolts. I try to pull away from whatever Markus is doing to me, but my limbs refuse to respond to my will.

"What are you doing to me?" Terror floods my insides, hitting me like a rogue wave of screaming darkness, dragging me under, no matter how hard I paddle. Another arc of pain arrows through my head. I cry out, and my legs fail me, sending me into Markus's arms.

His voice slices through the pain, demanding my obedience. Every fiber in my being rages against his orders, but there is nothing I can do to resist him. He owns me. I am his to command. Helpless to deny his every whim.

A groan from some distant ache in her soul bubbled to the surface. The grip Elle had on her arms tightened, and a sob shook her sister's body.

How could the same man who'd held her while she'd cried, reliving the secrets from her past—the man who'd risked his life to save hers, and then given her such pleasure while denying his own—have done that to her? He had reached inside her mind, stolen her will. Manipulated her like an animated doll. The memory made her sick.

Stealing her humanity had been difficult enough to forgive him for, yet at some point she'd been able to do so. Shit, she'd nearly begged him to make love to her. Thank God some minute part of him had had the decency to restrain himself.

A flash of rage burned its way through her veins at the thought, and she shoved free of her sister's hold.

"Where is he?" Her pulse strumming in her temples, Alex stood.

Her eyes wide, Elle's mouth parted, her lips trembling. "I-I don't know." She shook her head.

"Dammit! I'll find him myself." Alex charged for the door. No way in hell would Markus get away with what he'd done to her. She couldn't reverse the fact that she'd been turned against her will. There was no going back. But God help her, when she was done making him pay for screwing with her mind, he'd curse the day they'd ever crossed paths.

"Wait!" Elle called out to her. "Alex, wait." She caught her arm, halting her before she could twist the knob on the door.

Alex whirled on her, ready to demand she let her go, when the expression on her sister's face grounded her. Worry for Alex's state of mind clouded her eyes, but there was more. Guilt ran like hidden rip currents through her whole demeanor. Others may not have noticed it, but she knew her sister, and Alex recognized the signs.

Suddenly, it all made sense. The way her sister had encouraged her to let it go when she'd confided in her about how crazy the blanks in her memory were making her. How she'd tried to convince her that not remembering what happened was in her best interest. Not to mention how odd Elle had been acting when she'd awakened.

"You knew, didn't you?" Like miniature grenades, the words dropped from her lips with their pins pulled, ready to blow their relationship to bits. "All this time." Her voice rose, and instinctively her hand went to her chest, attempting to contain her aching heart as it tried to beat its way through her breastbone. "You've known what he did to me, and you never said a word."

"I couldn't stand seeing you hurt more than you already were." Elle closed in, and reached out for Alex's arm.

"Don't!" Alex jerked back. The last thing she wanted or needed was her comfort. "Just don't." She closed her eyes and waved her sister off.

"You despised Markus," Elle began. "You hated him for turning you against your will, and after what you went through when I left you with our mother..."

Alex opened her eyes. Elle's face hid behind her palms, but Alex heard her quiet sobs.

"It killed me when I found out what had happened to you," Elle cried.

"I never blamed you," Alex said. "But don't go there. What you did has nothing to do with that."

Elle jerked her head up. "It has everything to do with that," she snapped. "I'm your big sister. I'm supposed to look out for you! But I didn't do that, did I? When I ran out, I left you without anyone to protect you."

Tears welled, clouding Alex's vision. Elle needed to stop. Learning the truth about Markus on top of reliving the pain of her past was too much to deal with right now.

"Elle, please," she begged.

"And when you went missing last year and ended up a victim of Marguerite and Markus's sick games, I'd failed you yet again." Her voice cracked.

"Would you stop!" Alex grasped her sister by her shoulders. "I'm pissed as hell that you kept me in the dark all these months when you knew the holes in my memory were driving me insane. I'm hurt." She tempered her voice. "But I've never felt that you failed me."

"How can you say that?" Elle sniffed and shook her head.

"Dammit, Elle. You saved my life. Don't you see that?" Alex smoothed her sister's hair back from her face. "The money you managed to send me helped me to finally get out of that situation at home. Then, when I was an idiot and got myself trapped in the basement of Wicked Ways, you were the one to drop everything and find me." Alex eased a few steps back. "You've *never* failed me." Placing her fingertips to her cheeks, Alex swiped away the damp trail of her own tears. "Now don't get me wrong, you've got some major sucking up to do to make up for keeping this secret."

Elle released a choked laugh. "I just thought if you didn't remember, you would be spared the pain." She frowned.

Her intentions had been good. Alex could see that. "I know you meant well," she said. "But I'm a grown woman. It wasn't yours or Markus's place to determine what I should and shouldn't know about my life, or what's been done to me." A renewed swell of anger crashed over her.

"I'm so sorry," Elle muttered. "I hope one day you can forgive me."

"Of course I'll forgive you." Alex nodded. "But it's going to take some time for me to come to terms with this."

"I understand," Elle whispered.

"Good." Alex nodded. "Then please, I need you to go."

"Are you sure?" Elle edged toward the door. "We could talk, or I could sit quietly and listen—whatever you want."

"No." Alex shook her head. "Believe me, I'm okay. Some peace and quiet is all I need."

"Okay." Elle pulled the door open, stepped through, and glanced over her shoulder. "I'm right down the hall," she said as if Alex had suddenly blanked on where they lived. "Please, call me if there's anything I can do."

"Don't worry," she said. "I'm going to be fine." And she would be, because for the first time in more months than she'd like to recall, all the darkened voids inside her head were beginning to fill.

The door clicked shut behind her sister, leaving Alex to her thoughts. Moving to the bed, she leaned in and sank her fingers into the cool sheets, needing the tactile sensation to ground her. Alex breathed deeply and closed her eyes, desperately trying to put a lid on the desire to tear through the mansion like a raving lunatic in search of Markus. Before she sought him out, she had to get her head together first. She needed to be smart, meditate on her new bundle of memories and gain some clarity. Then she and her sire would have a nice long chat.

Chapter Twenty

Markus opened the door to the mansion's study and a blurred right hook slammed into his jaw with teeth-rattling accuracy. Markus's head snapped to the side, testing the ability of his spinal column to keep his skull attached to his body.

Palming the throbbing lower half of his face, Markus cranked his head back around. Arran stood there, his upper lip curled back, fangs extended. The blond male hissed and reared his arm back, ready for round two. Markus seized the doorjamb and braced his legs. Shit, he guessed he deserved some payback for running off with what could be considered the guy's sister-in-law. Based on Elle's reaction when he'd returned with her sister, the entire Enclave had had their panties in a wad.

"That's enough," Kenric barked, and stepped into view from the shadows of the room. "For now. I want some of his face still intact so he can tell me what the *hell* he was thinking!" the commander bellowed. "Was I wrong to let you out of that cage?"

Markus made his way farther into the room. Of course they'd assumed the worst and thought he'd gone insane. Fuck. Who knows? Maybe they were right, and he was crazy for coming back?

Arran shoved the door closed behind him. Movement to his left caught his eye, and Markus noted Guerin, dressed in black leather, standing next to the fireplace, one hand wrapped around the edge of the granite mantel. So they were all here and primed to feed him his balls.

But last he checked, hell hadn't frozen over.

"You haven't answered me, Santini." Kenric closed in. "Was I wrong to have let you out?"

Markus surveyed the fanged warriors around him. "Looks like the answer to that question would be subjective."

"Dammit, Markus," Kenric chewed out. "What's going on inside that head of yours? You phased out of here the other night without permission. Then to make things worse, you took off with Alex. You kidnapped her!"

"I was protecting her," Markus snarled.

"By taking her away from those who had the resources to care for her? By taking her away from her family?"

"I don't have time for this shit." Markus backed away only to slam into Arran's hard chest.

"We're not done with you yet," Arran spat.

"You got your punch in," Markus muttered. "You're going to want to leave it at that." His fist curled.

"Markus!" The master vampire sighed. "Talk to me." His tone tempered, but Markus could tell the more-than-three-century-old creature of the night barely held the reins on his control. "There's got to be more going on here."

"That's why I came back." Markus glanced back over his shoulder at Kenric. "But what I walked into feels more like a lynching party, and I am the guest of honor. Doesn't seem like anyone here is ready for a chat."

"What did you expect?" Guerin chimed in. "Balloons and cake when you popped in?"

"You brought Alex back unharmed," Kenric said. "For that, we're all very pleased."

"I would never harm Alexandria!" The idea that they thought he would hurt her breathed oxygen onto the spark of anger simmering in his gut. "The only reason I stepped foot in this place was to return Alexandria to the care of her sister and to let you know I'm out of here."

"Out of here?" Kenric's questioning gaze darted to Guerin, his friend and second-in-command, before pinning Markus. "You're leaving the Enclave—permanently?"

"The Enclave?" Markus laughed. "I didn't realize I was a part of that gig anymore." He shook his head. "But yeah." He nodded. "I've got personal business to take care of with Enrique, so I'm moving on."

Alexandria's delicate, sleeping face flashed inside his mind, her long dark lashes casting shadows beneath her eyes as he'd laid her on her bed. He had no idea how long he'd stood there, memorizing her features, before Elle had rushed into the room. The thought of never seeing her again sent a pang of agony through his chest, threatening to double him over. Markus clamped down hard on his jaw, refusing to flinch. He had to do this. When she woke and took a good long walk through the memories he'd awakened, she would despise him.

The most merciful thing he could do for her now was to

remove himself from her sight. And her life.

"Enrique?" Kenric crossed his arms. "What business do you have with him?"

"The kind that involves a silver-plated dagger to his heart."

"Are you saying you think he was responsible somehow for the DEAD ambush the other night?" This time it was Guerin asking the question.

"I most certainly think that," Markus said.

"But how?" Kenric leaned his hips against one of the leather chairs. "What makes you think he has that kind of influence, especially since Marguerite is no longer in the picture?"

"I don't know *how* he's managed to make it happen," Markus said, the vein in his temple throbbing with his effort to remain civil. "But after the message he sent through Alexandria, then Christian showing up and bedding down with the Enclave..." The sharp points of his fangs dug into his lower lip. "Like I said before, it's too damn coincidental. I know him." Markus grunted. "Too fucking well. He wants payback—from the Enclave for Marguerite's demise, but especially from me. And he knows the best way to make that happen is through Alexandria."

"You sound like a male with a plan." Kenric laced his fingers and rested his hands across his lower abdomen.

"You're damn straight I am." Markus ran his fingers along the cherrywood shelving, absently scanning the spines of the books the Enclave's master had gathered over the many decades: Poe, Twain, Dickens.

"So how do you intend to find him?" Kenric asked. "And when you do, how do you intend to prove, without a shadow of a doubt, that he's the one who set the whole event in motion, before you kill him?"

"Locating the bastard won't be a problem. Eventually, someone who knows where the rat is holing up will point me to him." Markus faced the others in the room. "As far as proof, I don't need any hard evidence to know that attack had Enrique written all over it."

Like a bug under a magnifying glass, Kenric studied him before going on. "What happened between you and Marguerite's former commander that would have him seeking revenge against you?"

Spilling his guts to the males in that room about his history with Enrique would have about as much of a chance of happening as him becoming a Belieber. "Enrique and I had our differences when it came to leadership."

"That's putting it mildly," a voice murmured. All heads swiveled toward the library door and the uninvited male. Christian stepped fully into the room and pushed the door closed behind him.

"What the fuck are you doing here?" Markus snapped. The young vamp had some big-ass balls.

"You have something to say, Christian?" Kenric straightened from his spot against the chair.

"Yeah." Christian nodded, his attention nervously flickering among the warriors in the room. "Markus is right." He shrugged. "For the most part."

"What do you mean, for the most part?" Markus's pulse edged higher. Heat radiated from his chest, up his neck, and into his face. "Spit it out already." He charged the male, two-fisting the SOB's green hoodie, yanking the other guy up and into his face. "What the hell do you know about this?"

"Bloody hell, Markus!" Kenric appeared next to him.

"Give him a second to open his mouth."

Reluctantly, Markus exhaled and released the young vampire with a shove. Christian staggered, but quickly recovered, shrugging his shirt back into place on his shoulders.

"I'm listening," Markus chewed out.

"What I was trying to say…" Christian narrowed his green gaze at him, the tattooed black lines around his right eye adding an extra dose of menace to his expression. Markus had to choke back a laugh. It'd take more than this pip-squeak to rattle Markus's cage. Christian turned his attention to Kenric. "…is that what Markus said about Enrique wanting to dole out some revenge on his head is true, but Markus and Alex aren't his main target."

"What are you getting at?" Guerin asked, mirroring Markus's exact thought. The other two males in the room circled in closer.

Christian looked to Guerin, then back to Kenric and sighed. "Eve, sir."

Curling his fist, Markus raised his arm, and had to back-step a few paces to keep from carrying out the impulse to coldcock the traitorous asshole. "Son of a bitch!"

"You bastard!" Guerin roared and surged for the male, but Kenric grabbed him seconds before he made contact and shoved him back.

Markus pinned Kenric with his best *no one ever fucking listens to me* glare.

"I told you I didn't trust him the moment the bastard set foot in this house."

"You don't think Christian's been on my radar?" Kenric met him with one of his own *you think I'm stupid?* stares. "These are my walls, my people, my Enclave. I knew it was a risk letting him inside here, knowing Enrique had sired him. But that old saying is true about keeping your friends close and your enemies closer."

"So you knew he was a spy and you still brought him in?" Guerin closed the few steps separating him and the master vampire. "What the fuck?"

"I didn't say that." Kenric glanced over at the male in question. "I said I allowed Christian to move in to get a better idea if he was working for Enrique or not."

The redheaded vamp stared in the direction of the fireplace. The guilty asshole didn't have enough backbone to look them in the face.

"And if he was," Kenric continued, "what the hell was their agenda?"

"And you all wonder why I took Alexandria away to take care of her—to protect her." Markus flipped his hands up as if in surrender.

Kenric quirked his brow. "I suspected that if you knew about Eve, there was a chance Enrique would have known about her as well."

Dammit... He had a good point. Enrique had been with Marguerite longer than he had. Yet the way she'd handled Enrique indicated he'd never been more to her than an obedient tool and an occasional fuck. "But I never got the impression that she shared such secrets with him."

"She didn't," Christian said.

The warriors in the room turned back to the mole.

"He'd overheard Marguerite a couple of times talking about a daughter. Later, after she died, he found a picture of Eve in Marguerite's vanity. Then, when he spotted that same female with you, Guerin..." Christian shrugged. "He put all the pieces of the puzzle together, and sent me in for any additional information about her I could gather."

"I see," Guerin said and began pacing a slow circle around the male. Christian followed him with his gaze as far as he could, but seemed to instinctively realize, like a human who'd been pinned by a bear, that he shouldn't even dare to move a muscle. "What I don't understand is, why?"

"Why what, sir?" Christian muttered.

"You've gotten away with your deception this far, why come clean now?" Guerin came to a stop in front of the new vampire. "Don't you fear for your life?"

"You mean Enrique?" Christian looked up, meeting the larger vampire's stare.

"No. Me." Guerin snarled, then snagged the male by his neck, dragged him across the floor, and slammed the back of his head into the door with a loud *thud*.

"Do it," Christian wheezed out despite the tight hold Guerin had around his throat. "I'm sick of being somebody's puppet, their servant, or their Calyx." The other male's hand fell away from Guerin's fingers at his neck. "Kill me," Christian chewed out, and closed his eyes. "Just get it over with."

"What the hell…" Markus groaned. "You're not even going to give us the satisfaction of a good fight?" What was this world coming to?

"To hell with this." Guerin stepped back, allowing Christian to sag onto his knees. "I'm not going to kill you." The Enclave's second-in-command frowned. "Not that you don't deserve it, but because you still have information I want about Enrique."

"That, and the fact that he did come to us before things went too far," Kenric added.

Markus sauntered over to the male on the floor. "Get your ass up." Markus leaned over, grabbed a handful of his hoodie, and pulled him back up onto his feet. "You still haven't said why you came in here now and decided to essentially throw yourself at the mercy of the Enclave."

Christian's Adam's apple bobbed. "At first, I thought I could stomach what Enrique had planned. But after living here, seeing how things could be so different, getting to know Alex, Elle, and"—he glanced over at Guerin, then back to Kenric—"Eve, I couldn't keep up my cover any longer. Enrique gets fucking crazier every day." Christian wrapped his arms around his midsection. "I overheard what Markus said about his plans to go after Enrique, and I couldn't keep my mouth shut any longer. You deserve to know the whole truth." Christian looked to Markus. "If you still want to go after Enrique, I can help you."

• • •

Markus grunted, kicked the bedsheet off his legs and rolled onto his back. Keeping his eyes closed, he ran through the conversations with the other Enclave warriors, over and over, inside his head. Staying planted in his room and waiting for the moon to rise before acting on their plan was driving him insane. Worse, Alexandria was in her room, only a few feet away, and the last thing she wanted was for him to come anywhere near her. Yet not knowing how she was coping—what she was thinking—was eating him alive.

The delicate scent of vanilla mixed with honey tantalized his nostrils. His cock stirred, lifting the sheet covering his pelvis, his pulse a throbbing beat inside its head. Christ. His mind was playing tricks on him, tormenting him with her fragrance. He was fucking losing it. Markus squeezed his eyes shut, raised his arms, and settled the weight of his head on his palms. He had to let her go. If only he could force his mind to obey and give him some peace.

A slight stirring in the air was his only warning before the cool edge of a blade pressed to his throat and he felt the weight of another body straddling him.

Markus didn't twitch.

Didn't open his eyes. Sight wasn't necessary to figure out who the likely suspect was.

"Hello, Alexandria."

"Don't you dare speak my name," she said, pressing the serrated edge a little harder against his neck. The sharp points stung as they opened his flesh, and a warm trickle of his life essence pooled at the base of his throat. "You don't deserve to even feel the consonants on your tongue."

"You're right." He lifted his eyelids. Alexandria stared down at him, her hair falling around her face like a midnight veil. The warmth of her core seared his semihard cock through the thin fabric of the sheet. He curled his fists beneath his nape, willing himself to focus. If she hadn't been threatening to slit his throat right now, he'd be hot as hell. "I didn't deserve anything we ever shared." And he meant it.

"You make me sick." Her voice broke, and her body swayed on top of his.

"If nothing else, please believe me when I say how much I hated—"

"Don't!" She shook her head. "I don't want to hear your lies about how sorry you are or excuses about why you did that to me."

"I get that I can never make things right between us. I blew that chance a long time ago."

"That's one thing you've gotten right," she snapped. Her rapid breaths were the only other sound in the room.

"I also know you don't want to kill me," he said. She was pissed off. Understandable. But Alexandria wasn't a cold-blooded killer.

"You're so wrong." She reseated the dagger against his throat for emphasis.

The sharp edge of the blade dug into his flesh. Triggered by the pain, his fangs burst through his gums.

"Oh my God," she scoffed, leaned her head back, and tossed her hair over one shoulder. "Just yesterday, I almost cared about you. You sat there in that basement and let me open myself up to you like you were my friend. Like I meant something to you." Her voice trembled. "You listened while I cried about the man who'd molested me when I was a child, then held me, comforted me, and the whole time you sat there keeping your own dirty secret of how you messed with my mind." She drew closer, her cheek almost touching his, her breath warm on his ear. "You're a damn hypocrite," she whispered. "And I want you dead more than I've ever wanted anything in my life."

Markus closed his eyes. She hated his guts, and nothing he had to say, no excuse, would ever change that fact.

"Wait till sundown," he managed to utter despite the threat of her dagger. "After that, you'll more than likely get your wish without having to get your hands bloody in the process." It was the truth. According to Christian, Enrique had a partner with high stakes invested in acquiring Eve. Money meant resources. Power. None of them had a damn clue what kind of situation they'd be walking into. As a result, there was a good chance both he and Christian would end up dust. But not before he made sure Enrique went down with them.

"What are you talking about?" Alexandria lifted her head and glared down at him.

"As soon as the sun sets, I'm out of here," he said. "You won't have to worry about putting those pretty eyes of yours on me again." The moment the words exited his lips an arrow of pain arced through his gut. But he held it together. He had to. For her. Getting away from Alexandria was the best for everyone.

"Kenric's finally kicking you out?" A corner of her mouth lifted in challenge.

"Not exactly." The muscles in his arms began to cramp, and Markus eased his hands out from under his pillow.

"No you don't!" Alexandria drove her point home with a wiggle of her blade. "Keep your arms where they were."

Reluctantly, Markus shoved his hands back in place. Whatever she needed to feel in control.

"Kenric isn't forcing me to leave. I'm blowing this house to settle a debt with Enrique. He has to be stopped. We found out he's not only set his sights on you, but his primary target is Eve."

"Eve?" Her eyes widened. "How does he know about her?"

"Somehow he put two and two together after running into her with Guerin that night. Come to find out, that's why Christian is here."

"Dammit," she breathed, and her lashes lowered. "And Elle and I walked him right through the door." She opened her eyes. "Is Christian still alive?"

"Very much so. In fact, he says he's willing to get me a one-on-one with Enrique."

"Oh my God…and you believe this plan of yours could be a suicide mission." Keeping the blade in place, Alexandria leaned back. "I get it now," she said, her tone firm, determined. "It all makes sense why you allowed yourself to rot away in that cage in the basement. You would've rather died than have to face what you did with Marguerite—to me." She withdrew the dagger and slowly shook her head. "Death is too easy for you." She stared down at the weapon, the metal glinting from the low light filtering in from the hallway. "You're right." She glanced up. "I'm not going to kill you."

Alexandria maneuvered off him and stood. Markus rose up on his elbows as she backed away from the bed. Even in the shadows, she captivated him in her form-fitting black T-shirt and shorts. He would never stop loving her, craving her, with every ounce of what was left of his soul.

"I never thought you would," he said. "That's not who you are, Alexandria. Life's been hell on you, but through it all, you've managed to hang on to your compassion."

"Even now, you're so damn arrogant," she snapped. "Don't pretend like you know everything about me. Because you don't. You have no idea how close I came to following through with this." She palmed the hilt, pointing the blade toward her inner arm. "You hurt me," she said. "It took me a long time to come to terms with the fact that you stole my humanity, but this…" She shook her head. "You violated my mind. Not once, but twice when you stole my memories to hide the evidence. Then you played me. Pretended to care about me."

"That wasn't a game," he said, his voice hoarse. She could believe whatever she wanted about him and the reasons he'd had to do what he did to her. But when he'd shown her affection, told her he'd wanted her, his feelings had never been a lie.

"Bullshit!" She spun and headed toward the door, but stopped at the foot of the bed. "You can't do what you did to another person and then say you care about them. You can't have it both ways, Markus." She marched toward the door, grabbed the knob, and glanced over her shoulder. "Death is too good of an end for what you've done. You're going to live. I want you to face the choices you've made that can't be undone—night after agonizing night." She yanked the door open and stepped through. With one last glance, she added, "I'm going to make sure of it."

The door slammed closed behind her.

Markus grabbed the lamp from the nightstand, roared, and flung the delicate piece across the room. The glass and metal crashed into the tall chest of mahogany drawers with an ear-ringing shatter. "Just what the hell did you mean by that, Vixen?"

Chapter Twenty-One

The fourth shot of tequila scorched a path down Markus's throat, the heat no less intense than the first. Too bad the burn didn't accompany a buzz. One of the only side effects he didn't appreciate when it came to his vampire DNA.

From his spot on the covered patio, Markus faced the shadows of the alley across the street from the Twisted Nipple, a run-down dive bar on the banks of the river. Kicking his heels up on one of the vacant chairs, he slapped the bottom of the glass back onto the wrought iron tabletop. He'd picked the particular location for a reason: after sundown, most of the Nipple's patrons preferred the pool tables and the flat-screens inside, leaving him to drink in solitude.

"You ready to do this?" Christian straddled the seat beside him and plopped his cell on the table in front of them.

"Like yesterday," Markus said.

Christian tapped the numbers on the screen, then selected speaker. Time to see just how good an actor the former Calyx could be.

The number rang twice, then suddenly clicked. "This better be some news I want to hear, Christian, like Eve has resumed patrol tonight," Enrique said.

"I've got something even better," Christian said, giving Markus a lopsided grin.

"And how is anything other than what I initially said better?" Enrique snapped.

"What better male to bring in what you want than the one who's been living with the Enclave for the past year," Christian replied.

"What the hell are you talking about?"

Damn, Markus could almost hear the veins in Enrique's temple throb. The male sounded on edge, almost desperate. Perfect. Desperate men made foolish decisions.

"Markus," Christian said. "I'm talking about Markus."

"Markus?" Enrique scoffed. "How the hell is Markus supposed to bring me Eve?"

"Because last night, Markus walked out on the Enclave. And believe me, the parting wasn't nice to watch."

"You're shitting me!"

A grin tugged at the corners of Markus's mouth.

"Fascinating story," Enrique added. "But how is his departure supposed to help us?"

Christian leaned in over the phone, resting his forearms on the table. "As I said, Markus did not leave a happy male. Kenric was ready to lock the vampire in a silver cage in the mansion's basement after he ran off with Alex. She's back now, but the rest of the group wanted Markus's head for what he'd done. So, based on the guy's current mental state, he's ripe for the picking. Ready to dole out a little payback to the Enclave, you know." He glanced up at Markus as if seeking his approval of his performance.

Well, fuck. He had to admit, the redhead knew how to sell a story. Markus gave him a reluctant nod. But why was he surprised? The asshole had managed to maneuver himself inside the Enclave.

For a few moments, silence hung in the air like a thick, weighted fog, then finally, "I don't know." Enrique's voice sliced through the tension. "He's been with them for too long. He chose to return to them after Marguerite, so he's got some loyalty issues to them that he's never shaken."

"From what I've overheard, though," Christian added, "that wasn't how it went down. The dickhead has been in a silver cage for the past several months and has only recently been released."

"What the hell?" Enrique exclaimed. "Are you serious?"

"Dead serious," Christian said. "That's why I think this will work. Kenric hasn't even put him on rotation with the crew yet. Nobody fucking trusts him!"

Markus's gut clenched, and he quietly slid his boots from the chair. What Christian said was true, but it sucked bigger than shit listening to someone spin it like he wasn't listening to every word.

"I'll be damned," Enrique whispered, but Markus could hear the excitement in his voice. He knew the tone all too well. Enrique had bitten their hook. Now it was up to Markus to reel him in. "I take it that you know where our prodigal warrior has gone? You know how to find him?"

"Yup. I'm looking at him right now." Christian smiled. That much was definitely true. "He's sitting alone at a bar."

"Good. I'm thinking maybe it's time for a reunion

between me and my old friend. Text me your location, and I'll phase there in a few minutes. But if he moves, keep him in sight and me informed."

"Will do," Christian said, and tapped end call.

Markus wrapped his fingers around the next shot in line on the table and lifted it in salute to the young vampire. "Well done," he said.

Tipping up the screen on his smart phone, Markus checked the time. Ten past one in the morning. He leaned back and propped his boots on a vacant chair. It had been about an hour since Christian had made himself scarce after contacting Enrique.

Walking out the door of the Enclave, knowing it could very well be the last time he'd lay eyes on the place, had been tough. However, walking out without one last glimpse of Alexandria's face... Yeah. A taste of the fires of hell.

Better get used to that burn.

He reached for his next dose of tequila.

"Looks like someone could use a friend."

The hairs on Markus's arm lifted, and his gut roiled. Enrique's voice in the flesh, this close, unearthed memories he'd prefer to leave buried in their grave.

Markus quickly tossed the contents of the shot to the back of his throat, the drink making short work of the trip between his lips and his esophagus, and plopped the glass back onto the table. "I think someone needs to get their eyes examined," Markus replied, leaned back, draped his arms over his waist, and laced his fingers.

Enrique strolled onto the patio and into sight. "Ahh, come now," he said. "I'm just trying to be friendly."

"Friendly?" Markus barked a laugh and dropped his boots onto the concrete. "That's one word I'd never use to describe any kind of association between us."

"Well, perhaps it's time you and I change that unfortunate situation." A smooth smile spread across Enrique's face. The bastard thought he was so damn slick. The male yanked on one of the chairs, the legs making a loud scrape of metal against rock, and helped himself to a seat.

"I never said a damn thing about it being unfortunate." Markus shook his head.

"As with our previous…arrangement," Enrique began, reaching over to toy with Markus's empty shot glass, "you and I together may be more beneficial to your long-term goals than you sitting here drowning your bruised ego in cheap liquor."

Markus leaned forward, resting his forearms on the table while capturing Enrique's glare. "And what would you know about my goals?"

At that moment, Christian appeared behind Enrique's chair. "He knows that your time among the Enclave warriors has run out."

Feigning surprise, Markus shoved from his seat, the chair screeching against the floor. "What the fuck?" He glared at the young vampire, slamming him with his best *you're a dead man* expression. "I knew it," Markus snarled. "All this time, you've been Enrique's fucking spy." He charged around the table, knocking the damn thing off-kilter, and laid a right hook into the other male's jaw. Christian's head snapped to the side, blood slinging from his busted mouth and lip.

Markus had to make this look good. Before the redhead could catch his breath, Markus fisted him by the front of his shirt. Hauling him up onto his toes, he shoved his face into Christian's. "You're the one who fed this asshole info so he'd know when and where to go after Alexandria."

"Whoa, whoa," Enrique interjected, his tone laid-back as he turned in his seat. "Watch who you're calling an asshole. I'm not after your precious Alexandria."

"And I'm just supposed to take your word on that," Markus spat, still holding on to the new vamp.

"He's telling you the truth," Christian said, his lip already starting to swell. "Alexandria happened to be in the wrong place at the wrong time. She wasn't what that was all about."

Grumbling under his breath, Markus uncurled his fingers and released his hold on the other male's shirt. "But you're not denying it was you behind the ambush." Markus nailed Enrique with a hard stare.

Shrugging, Enrique added, "Maybe."

Markus groaned. "Stop pissing around and get to the point. Alexandria was injured during whatever kind of game it was you were playing. So I'd start talking if I were you, because I'd much rather snap your neck than look at your ugly mug."

"Damn, Markus." Enrique shook his head. "Ever thought about taking one of those…what do they call them…anger management courses?"

"You want me to talk about my anger?" Markus seethed, reached low, and pulled out the dagger stowed in the side of his boot. Before the male could twitch in response, he pressed the jagged edge against Enrique's throat. "Okay. Let's do that." Markus curled his upper lip, revealing his fangs. "Yeah. I'm pissed as hell. My blood boils at the mere sight of you. So let me make myself clear." He scraped the serrated edge against the other male's neck. "You even think of putting Alexandria in your sights, I will cut your eyeballs from your skull before I stab my blade into your heart."

Without a tremor, Enrique rolled his eyes up at him. "Draw blood with that dagger of yours and expect a great deal of your own to flow," the dark-skinned male stated.

Markus glanced over his shoulder and spotted Christian with a knife aimed at the back of Markus's neck. *Nice move.*

"You've got him well trained, Enrique." Markus flicked his weapon away from his target and painted on a smile for Christian. "Down, boy," he added.

"Cute." Christian grunted and turned away, sheathing his blade. "You're a real comedian."

"Thanks. That's nice to hear every once in a while," Markus said, facing the male. "I've always thought my sense of humor was unappreciated."

Christian flipped him a middle finger salute and brushed past Markus toward the unoccupied side of the table.

Markus sauntered toward the patio's wooden support pillar across from the crazy bastard and leaned against it. "You still haven't said why the hell you're here and in my face. And if Alexandria wasn't your target the other night, what the fuck are you after?"

"A little birdie told me that you've finally come to your senses, and you walked out on that sanctimonious bunch of"—Enrique held up two fingers from each hand and air-quoted—"warriors."

"By little birdie, you mean Christian." Markus cranked his head toward the quiet redhead. "So, what if I have?"

"From what I hear, Kenric hasn't been the most under-standing and sympathetic to your plight," the dark-haired male said, stood, and strolled toward Markus. "He'd love nothing more than to lock you back up in that silver cage for not agreeing with the drivel that comes from his mouth. Kenric knew Marguerite, but we understood her on an en-tirely different level." Enrique didn't stop his approach until he'd put himself directly in front of Markus. "None of them know you like I do, Markus. You and I have a history they couldn't possibly relate to." Enrique's mouth curled into a sly grin, as if he truly believed he'd gotten under Markus's skin. "I know what gets you off—what makes you *tick.*"

For that last comment alone, Markus would've loved nothing more than to rip the other male's heart from his chest. But he had to play it cool. Allow Enrique to think he'd begun to sway him toward his team. "Sounds like Christian's got a big fucking mouth," Markus snapped.

"*Mmm…*" Enrique cocked his head in the other male's direction. "Why, yes, he does." He smirked. "And it has served me well thus far."

The blatant innuendo had bile crawling up Markus's throat. "Don't make me vomit." He rolled his eyes and shouldered his way past Enrique.

After grabbing his glass from the tabletop, Markus made his way over to the side entrance to the club. At the thresh-old, he held up his empty shot glass, grabbing the brunette waitress's attention. She nodded and smiled, indicating she'd bring another round.

Markus turned back around. "Let's pretend you've suc-ceeded in acquiring my attention, Enrique. And at the risk of stating the obvious, you've been getting a blow-by-blow of what's been going down at the Enclave from your sub over here." He waved the dry glass in his hand at the young vampire on the other side of the table and settled himself in Enrique's vacant seat. With a one-two *thump*, Markus propped his booted heels up on the wrought iron table, crossing them at the ankle. "Yet you still haven't answered the million-dollar question." Markus *tsk*ed and shook his head. "Why? What do they have that you want so badly, and why do you need *me* to get your hands on it?"

At that moment, the server carrying his next dose of tequila reappeared on the patio. "Hey, boys," she said, flashing a smile and strutting over to him. Leaning over, she sat the shot glass on the table in front of him, making sure Markus got a good view of her cleavage. "Want to keep your tab going?" She straightened, placing her hands on her hips, her bar apron longer than the ragged edge of her denim shorts.

Markus nodded. "Keep it open."

"Can I get anyone else something from the bar?" The twentysomething female glanced from Christian to Enrique.

"We're good," Enrique answered for them both. "For now."

"Okay then." Her glossy red lips curved into a smile. "You know where to find me if you change your mind." She sashayed her way back inside, oblivious to the fact that she'd been in the presence of two of the most dangerous males on the planet.

Youth.

After Enrique's cool "for now", he worried about her life if she left the bar alone tonight. If so, he could end up blowing everything to hell by having to save her ass from becoming a late-night snack for the vampire and his DEADs.

Weird. A year ago, he wouldn't have given a damn if Enrique had wanted to turn her into a buffet. Yet now…it looked like he'd regrown a conscience. He cared about how Alexandria saw him. That was a large part of it. But perhaps most of all, he was so damn sick of treading water in this sea of darkness. Wasn't it about time he opened his eyes and swam toward the light?

Fisting his new shot, Markus made quick work of tossing it back, savoring the burn as it followed the path of the others down his esophagus. He lowered the empty glass back to the table with a hard *clunk* and rolled his head up to his former comrade. "You were saying…" He tossed the opening out there for Enrique to take a bite.

Enrique pushed away from the edge of the patio and strode over to where Markus sat. Bending over, he shoved Markus's feet to the floor, making way for him to plant his two wide palms on the table. Markus sat forward, trying his best not to chew a hole in his tongue so as not to tell the arrogant bastard to go fuck himself.

"Eve," Enrique finally said.

"Eve?" Markus shrugged, despite the fact he knew exactly why the female was of importance. "She's Guerin's mate. Who gives a shit?"

Enrique tilted his head and lifted a brow. "You don't do coy well, Santini. You know exactly who and what Eve is."

For what seemed like several minutes, Markus met the other male glare for glare before finally responding with, "You'll never get your hands on her."

A taunting chuckle bubbled up from Enrique. "Not alone, of course." He straightened and squared his shoulders. "That's why I've brought in reinforcements."

"Christ," Markus groaned. "Reinforcements? Why the hell do *you* want her?"

"Oh, I don't," Enrique sharply professed. "I couldn't give a shit about her. But others do, and they're willing to pay *very nicely* for a born vampire. One that I've heard can walk in daylight."

"Sounds like you've got this all planned out." Markus lifted his hands and dusted them off. "So why the fuck are you telling me about it? If I were you, I don't believe I'd have taken such a risk revealing your plan to a male who just walked out of the mansion you're so eager to get inside."

"I have no intention of ever going in there," Enrique said. "And I'm pretty damn sure you'd rather burn than set foot in the Enclave again."

Markus laughed. "Yeah. You got that shit right, at least."

"Good." Enrique nodded. "Then why don't I help you dole out some payback on the master of the Enclave?"

And there it was. The offer he'd been waiting on, right fucking there on the table. All Markus had to do was pick it up.

"And how do you figure you're going to do that?" Markus leaned back in his chair, narrowed his eyelids on the conniving bastard, and crossed his arms over his chest.

"What better way to draw her out than a prodigal warrior who wants to come home?" He grinned. "You're the bait. All you have to do is reel her in for me, Markus. And I'll do the rest. And you get the pleasure of sticking a virtual stake in your former commander's self-righteous heart." Enrique lifted his hands as if in worship of his own brilliance. "It's such a sweet-ass plan."

"There's just one problem," Markus interjected.

Enrique dropped his arms. "Tell me," he snapped.

"I haven't said yes."

"I know you, Markus," Enrique drawled. "I've witnessed what you're capable of when someone crosses you. You love being in control. This is too tempting for you to resist."

The soulless monster knew how to play him—how to stab at all the dark spots tainting his soul. Markus uncrossed his arms, leaned his elbows on the table, and crooked his finger at the other dark-haired male. Enrique replaced his palms in the spot near Markus, meeting him.

Markus curled his lip at the other vampire. "You're right."

Chapter Twenty-Two

The door to the Enclave's basement headquarters *snick*ed shut behind Alex as she tugged on her leather jacket. Everyone had gathered inside the massive room.

All except Markus, of course.

A week had passed since he'd walked out the mansion's door. According to the last report Elle had shared with her on his status, he'd successfully integrated himself into Enrique's inner circle. He'd done it. Gotten himself wrapped up in Enrique's madness. There'd been no doubt in her mind, though, that he would be able to lie his way through the front door. The male was a master when it came to deceit. She could attest to that.

But the news on Markus was seventy-two hours old. A lot could change in three days. Yet based on the buzz inside the room, something was going down—tonight.

Alex meandered over to where Elle stood talking with her mate. Both peered at a map of the docks along with Eve and Guerin. "What's the latest?" Alex checked out the four-square-block area Guerin had circled in red ink.

"Good news," Kenric called out. "We have some additional help coming in from Fairfield tonight." The Enclave's master dropped his cell onto the map and slapped his second-in-command on the back.

"Jean-Claude came through for us." Guerin nodded at this friend. "Looks like you still got it, old man."

"That's Fairfield, though," Elle said, her voice strained. "Are they going to make it here in time?"

"Got it covered," Kenric replied. "I expressed our need for a timely arrival, and Jean-Claude assured me the males he's sending have been to the area before. They'll be phasing to the locale, so travel time won't be an issue."

"That's good," Eve said. "One less thing we have to worry about."

"Out of what?" Christian walked over, his hands shoved into the pockets of his well-worn bomber jacket. His straight shoulder-length red hair covered most of his face and nearly all the tattoo swirling around his right eye. He stopped short of the group and propped himself on one of the leather chairs in the center of the room. "About two dozen damn scenarios that could go wrong tonight?"

"Is there something you're not telling us, Red?" Guerin edged around his mate, approaching the other male.

"Nope," he said, shaking his head. "I've told you everything I could get out of Enrique without raising his suspicion as to whose side I'm on."

"What about Markus?" The question came out of her mouth before she could pull it back.

"What about him?" Christian looked her way.

She'd gone this far. Why not ask and be done with it. "Have you seen him or talked to him since he went in?"

"Do you really care, Alex?" Elle wrapped her hand around her arm, drawing her attention. "I wouldn't think you'd give a shit about him after what he did to you." She frowned.

"I don't." Alex shrugged, loosening her sister's hold. "I'm just asking if Christian knew anything about his continued survival." *That's all it was. Right?* She only wanted him breathing so she could make sure he lived a long, miserable existence with the knowledge of what he'd done to the people he'd claimed to care about. So why did it feel like time had yawned? That someone had pushed pause, and her heart waited for Christian to fill her in on the smallest detail about Markus before it could resume beating?

"He's alive," Guerin replied instead.

"Good to know," she said, crossing her arms over her chest in a vain attempt to disguise the sudden, rapid beat of her heart from the preternatural creatures in the room.

"He better be, since Enrique is counting on Markus tonight to reel in his prize catch," Christian added.

"Wait…" Alex knew she probably had that deer in headlights look splashed on her face, but she couldn't help it. "Markus is supposed to personally deliver Eve to Enrique?"

"I received a call from him last night, saying he wanted to talk to me and Eve," Guerin said. "Enrique had to be listening, because Markus said he wanted another chance to come back to the Enclave. He said he thought if he spoke to us first, convinced me and Eve that he was sincere, perhaps Kenric would be more open to his second-in-command."

"But Christian confirmed that it's a ploy," Kenric said.

"He'll be there to capture Eve."

Her gaze darted between Kenric and Christian. "And you're actually going to put her out there? That's your plan? I thought Markus only wanted inside so he could take out Enrique?"

"Once we learned Enrique had brought in others and exposed Eve's existence to them, everything changed," Kenric said. "We have to bring down everyone involved in this, Alex. Put a cork in the information spread about my daughter." Kenric eased closer to Eve and palmed her arm. Despite the fact that they'd only met months ago, the expression on his face, the look in his eyes, spoke of the tremendous respect and love he possessed for Eve. "And it's going to take more than one male to make it happen," he continued, turning back to the others in the room. "It's imperative we snare every person involved, and unfortunately, the only way to make this happen is for Eve to draw them in close so we catch them in our net."

A gnarled vine of anxiety spread through Alex's chest. Outside of her sister, Eve was the closest thing she'd ever had to a friend. This plan was too dangerous. If anything ever happened to Eve, it would destroy not only Kenric, but Eve's mate as well. What those two had together didn't happen every day. Like Elle and Arran, Guerin and Eve were made for each other.

"You can't send Eve out there," Alex stated.

"Alex, you heard what Kenric said," Eve said. "I have to do this." As if by instinct, Eve palmed the hilt of the dagger at her thigh. "It means more to me than you know that you're worried about me. I've never had a friend before now who knew me well enough to care."

Guerin closed in behind his mate and rested his hands on her shoulders. "We both appreciate it," he said.

"What if I offer you an alternative?" Alex glanced at Kenric.

"What do you mean?" The Enclave's master edged around his second-in-command. His clear blue gaze captured hers, and with as little effort as breathing, they demanded she respond. "What kind of alternative, Alex?"

Steadying her resolve, she lifted her chin. "Me. You need Eve to lead you to them—to open the door, right? In the right disguise, I can do that for you. And by the time Enrique realizes he and his partner have been fooled, you'll have them."

• • •

The lazy and rhythmic licking of the water at the dock sent a calm, near serene, sense of innocence spilling into the night air.

Relax.

A bell rang out in the distance, its gentle melody driven by the sway of a boat.

Ding. Ding. Ding.

All is well.

Nothing to fear here.

Alex closed her eyes and inhaled, filling her lungs with the salt air. God, how she wished she could believe in its siren's call. Lifting her lashes, she looked up from under her hood at the dark warrior with his mouth pulled into a tight, grim line.

Nothing could be further from the truth.

"I still say you're crazy for doing this," Guerin whispered.

"Would you have rather had Eve out here, putting her life on the line?" She hooked her arm on his elbow, doing her best to paint the picture of a couple in love.

"I didn't say that."

She didn't have to look to know he'd chewed the words out through a clenched jaw. The tension in his biceps told her the male was strung tight.

"But I don't have to like the fact that it's you out here, either," he added. "I care about you, as well."

Warmth spread through her at his words. With anyone else other than Eve, Guerin was either the funny guy or the hard-as-hell second-in-command. He didn't do warm and fuzzy. So to have him express how he felt really meant something.

Alex gave his arm a slight squeeze in response. "Thank you," she uttered. Anything more would have probably made him uncomfortable.

"Let's go over this one more time," Guerin said. "What's the plan?"

They'd rehearsed the details before they'd left the mansion until her brain had felt numb from the repeated pounding over the details. She glanced up at him from under her hoodie, giving him her best *seriously?* look.

"For me," he drawled, pouring on the charm.

"Fine." She sighed. *Whatever. I'll go over it again. If for no reason other than to make the last leg of our trip pass quicker.*

"Markus is supposed to meet up with us in the next couple of blocks, believing his rendezvous is with you and Eve," she said.

"And you're allowing him to take you," he said, tightening his hold on her arm. "But we'll be hot on your trail. Remember... Don't drop your act. Keep your face covered for as long as possible, and let him bring you in. We need you to take us into the heart of the operation."

"I got it," she snapped, her nerves fraying around the edges. Inhaling deeply, she tried to find her calm center. Rehashing everything again was making her crazy. "I'm sorry," she breathed. "I'm just..."

"I know," Guerin rumbled. He pulled his arm free and placed a warm, comforting palm between her shoulder blades. "I know."

"I wasn't sure you two would actually show."

Her skin prickled at the sound of the familiar deep voice. A moment later, Markus appeared in front of them.

Reflex had her gulping hard, despite the fact that her throat was as dry as chalk dust. This was it. The urge to yank off her hood to get another look at the male who haunted her dreams—*who am I kidding?*—her every waking moment, rode her hard. But she kept her eyes cast downward and waited for Guerin's response.

"I said we'd be here," the Enclave's second-in-command grumbled. "Now spit out what you came to say. Not that anything that comes out of your mouth is going to change my mind about you. You're a loose cannon, Markus. Always were. Always will be."

Alex slid her palm to the hilt of her weapon wrapped around her thigh. Guerin was damn good. But they had no idea who and how many would be watching their interaction. Because one thing was for sure, Markus wouldn't be handling this alone. Enrique wasn't a complete idiot. He'd want Markus under surveillance, in case the former Enclave warrior decided to betray him.

"Well then," Markus said and sighed. "I never did give a flying fuck about your opinion of me." His right arm brushed back the loose flap of his dark leather trench coat, and before Alex could scream, Markus pulled a pistol.

A *pop* rent the air as a bright flame burst from the weapon's muzzle. Guerin cried out. Gripping his torso, the Enclave warrior doubled over a moment before his knees buckled. "Eve…" he groaned, the veins in his neck standing out in sharp relief.

"Guerin!" Alex cried out, and grappled for the crumbling large male. A single bullet shouldn't be capable of taking down a vampire as powerful as Guerin. Dear God, this wasn't supposed to be part the plan. She glanced up at the dark vampire holding the gun. "Markus…what have you done?"

Wide gray eyes stared back at her in recognition and disbelief.

Yes. It's me. Damn you. She screamed the words inside her skull.

Yet the muzzle of the gun continued to sway in her direction. Her heart stuttered. Was he actually going to kill her?

Another *pop* sounded amid a burst of light. A fleeting hot arrow of pain radiated through her arm. She gasped, and suddenly Markus's arms were around her.

"Scream," he commanded at her ear.

A wave of dizziness rushed through her head at the same time the heat inside her biceps began to fade.

"Trust me." He tightened his hold.

Apprehension sat like an anchor in her gut, weighing her down, pulling her under, but did she really have a choice other than to do exactly what he asked?

After that night in his cabin, she would have jumped into a murky abyss on his word alone. He'd gotten that deep under her skin. But that was before he'd ruptured the seal on her memories and shown her how deep the vein of darkness ran inside his soul. Before she'd watched him, without hesitating, shoot one of his own.

Yet the moment she'd taken Eve's place, hadn't she already put her trust in whatever he had planned? And after everything they'd been through, if he'd wanted her dead, wouldn't she have already been dust on his boots?

There had to be a good explanation for what he'd done to Guerin. Markus wouldn't turn on the Enclave again. Would he? He wouldn't do that to Kenric—to her.

Alex cried out and slumped in his arms.

Please don't hurt me again, she whispered inside her head. But she wasn't worried about the pain.

Once again, she found herself at his mercy. Her life in his hands. Except this time, her fear centered on her heart. Would it survive another break?

Chapter Twenty-Three

Fuck, fuck, fuck!

Markus swung his arm low and behind Alexandria's knees, lifted her up, and cradled her against his chest. She inhaled against his throat, and her body shuddered against his, causing his heart to clench.

What the hell had she been thinking? He surveyed the other male slumped on the sidewalk. Christ, Markus was so damn pissed. If he'd known Guerin had allowed Alexandria to switch places with Eve… He should have finished off the bastard instead of tagging him in his side where the silver would only hurt like a bitch. The cocktail of silver and a tranq in the bullet would only immobilize him, but knowing Guerin, he'd shake it off very soon. What the hell was he supposed to do now? How was he going to pass off Alexandria as Eve for long enough to take the others down before they both got killed?

"You're going to have to help me here," he whispered

with his mouth close to the dark blue hood covering her head. "When we get in there, you're going to need to pretend you're out cold. Keep your face hidden as long as you can, and listen for my cues."

A groan rumbled from her throat in confirmation. *Good girl.*

Closing his eyes, Markus pictured the front of the warehouse Enrique and Dominic had chosen for him to deliver Eve. Then he was falling, the world disappearing beneath his feet into a shimmering bottomless pit. A wave of momentary disorientation swamped him, and his gut rebelled. Markus tightened his grip on the precious cargo in his arms. Phasing any distance with someone other than himself expended more energy and was always a harsher trip.

But it was unavoidable.

He couldn't travel for nearly a mile with a body in his arms without drawing unnecessary attention from the human population.

The dim yellow glow of a streetlight shimmered into view. Markus blinked, clearing his vision as his boots resettled against concrete. His destination, a large, rusted metal warehouse, sat in front of him. A soft breeze blew loose strands of hair across his face and salt air into his nostrils. Inhaling, he steadied himself for what waited for them behind the large metal door. He had to get Alexandria out of this alive.

Fuck that.

Alexandria *would* make it out alive.

Christian and the Enclave had better come through. He'd modified his own plans against Enrique in favor of helping Kenric and Guerin bring down the son of bitch as well as the other vampires he'd brought in for this scheme. Yet somehow the only thing that had ever truly mattered to him had ended up in the middle of this—with her life on the line.

"Kenric, you'd better come through," he muttered.

Markus grabbed the latch on the metal door and yanked it open. Alexandria's head rested against his chest, her hood draped over her face. One of her arms fell free and swayed with each of his steps. He kicked the door closed and continued on, treading through the large dark space, aiming toward the beacon of light in the back of the building.

A few moments later, he rounded a series of crates and entered into what looked like a military triage setup. A metal surgical table sat near the back wall. Syringes, tubes, and an array of glass jars filled another nearby. Fucking hell. They were ready to dissect her. Except the "her" in his arms wasn't the female they were after.

We're so damn screwed.

"Anybody home?" Markus sauntered into the makeshift room. Out of the corner of his eye, he spotted movement.

"I knew you were the right person for the job." Enrique rounded the wall of crates to his left. With his lips spread into a wide smile, fluorescent lights glinting off his fangs, he eyed Alexandria's slumped form. "Finally." He sighed. "Dominic will be well pleased. As am I." He chuckled. "We're about to receive a glorious payday, my friend."

Markus laughed. "I think your glee has affected your brain. 'Friend' is pushing it."

"Who the hell cares?" Enrique threaded his fingers and cracked his knuckles, the sound of the snapping cartilage bouncing off the metal walls. "You have her. That's all that matters." The dark male edged closer as if prepared to inspect the package.

Shit.

Sidestepping the vampire, Markus made his way over to the empty metal table. "I assume this is for her?"

"That's correct," a new male voice said.

Dominic.

Gently, Markus deposited Alexandria onto the cool surface, making sure her covered head lolled away from the other males. Markus shrugged, adjusted his coat, and turned toward the others.

"Excellent work, Mr. Santini," Dominic said, one hand inside the pocket of his pin-striped trousers, while the fingers of his free hand worked a thin cigar. Behind him lurked two of his hired muscle, one on either side. Of course. At least two had tailed him during the retrieval.

"No skin off my neck," Markus replied. "What the hell has the Enclave ever done for me, except try to force their morals down my throat?" Markus reached down and pulled the dagger at his thigh free and twirled the hilt inside his palm. "If I'd wanted a spanking for my bad attitude, I could have found someone a hell of a lot prettier to deliver it."

Dominic smirked and another chuckle, coming from Enrique, echoed in the room.

"I like the way you speak your mind," Dominic said. "Once we're finished here, you and I should talk about your future plans."

"This was a...unique situation." Markus sauntered over to the table filled with an assortment of tubes and cylinders. Picking up one of the syringes, he examined the sharp point of the needle at the end. *Oh, hell no.* This madness must be stopped. "I do believe I've had my fill of reporting to a Master or Mistress." Markus's gaze roamed upward and to the hazy windows running along the perimeter of the room. *Where the hell are you, Kenric? I can't keep them distracted much longer.*

"Suit yourself," Dominic uttered behind him. "See to the female," he ordered his staff. "Strap her down and get her ready to be purged. We need to process her tissue and get her out of here as quickly as possible."

Panic seized Markus's chest, and he spun on his heels. "Wait," he called out, stopping the others in their tracks. "I'll handle her while you get whatever it is you need to set up."

"Fine," Dominic replied with a dismissive wave of his hand. "I don't give a shit who straps her down, as long as it gets done."

Markus sheathed his weapon and inserted himself between Alexandria and the other vampires in the room. Rolling her onto her back, Markus seized her wrists. Alexandria blinked up at him, her violet eyes darkened to a deep purple surrounded by a ring of fire. Her right hand edged closer to her thigh and Markus followed its path, watching as she wrapped her fingers around the hilt of her dagger. *Hell, yeah.* No one had checked if "Eve" had any weapons on her. He'd brought her in, so the others would have assumed he would have disarmed her in case she woke from the tranquilizer. That was his vixen. She wouldn't go down without a fight.

Giving her a quick nod of acknowledgment, he tightened the silver-laced restraint on her left wrist, leaving the other, nonvisible, hand unbound. A sizzle coming off her flesh met his ears, and a grimace rolled across her expression. An arrow of pain shot through his chest at the sight. *Fuck.* It killed him to hurt her.

Sorry. He mouthed the word, his spine rigid with constraint. It was all he could do not to roar, rip the bindings from her arm, and tear Enrique's heart from his chest with his bare hands.

"You guys weren't going to start without me, were you?" Christian appeared around the corner.

Air Markus had no idea he'd been holding made a mass exit from his lungs. The redhead's presence was a damn good sign. It meant the Enclave shouldn't be far behind. Markus's fists curled in anticipation.

"What the fuck are you doing here?" Enrique grabbed the other male's arm and jerked him forward, his upper lip curled back, baring his fangs.

"Why the hell would I hang around that mansion anymore? Tonight's the night we finally get our payoff. *We.* Remember?" Christian smirked.

"Whatever." Enrique grunted and dropped his hand. "Just stay out of the damn way." He turned his attention to Dominic. "Speaking of payoffs."

Dominic motioned to one of his bodyguards with a flick of his wrist. The large male grabbed a thick briefcase from the floor by his leg and hefted it onto one of the tables. "I've fulfilled my part of our bargain." Dominic lifted a finely arched brow. "And once I have everything I need from her, it's yours."

"Then by all means." Enrique nodded in the direction of Alexandria. "Proceed with all haste."

Dammit. He couldn't stall any longer. Where the hell was the Enclave?

"Take care of her," Dominic instructed his staff.

"Yes, sir," they responded in unison. One of the males finished gathering the supplies as the other approached Alexandria.

Stepping aside, Markus's jaw ticked and his palms itched with the need for violence. But they were outnumbered, and if he jumped in too soon things could unravel out of control—fast. And he refused to put Alexandria at even greater risk. Yet if the troops didn't make an entrance soon, he'd have no other choice.

The burly vamp-for-hire clamped onto Alexandria's hood and yanked it back before taking his blade to the sleeve covering the arm next to him.

Son of a bitch. His pulse pounded like a damn sledgehammer inside his head.

A wide lock of hair covered her face, but how long would it take before someone noticed it wasn't Eve? Before the large bastard rammed a needle into her arm?

"What the fuck!" In a flash of color, Enrique charged toward Alexandria.

Shit…meet fan.

Enrique shoved the bodyguard aside. The male staggered but regained his footing, confusion screwing up his face. A roar erupted from Enrique as he snagged a handful of Alexandria's hair, yanking her head up from the table. Alexandria gasped, her eyelids flickering open.

Markus wrapped his fingers around the hilt of his dagger. *Not yet. Not yet. Come on, Kenric.*

"You son of a bitch," Enrique growled, his head jerking toward Markus. "Did you really think substituting this cunt for Eve had a fuck's chance in hell of working?"

"What kind of trick is this?" Dominic shouted, closing in

on his partner in crime. "Seize him!"

The bodyguards charged toward Markus. Pulling his dagger, Markus backed up a few steps, maneuvering into his fighting stance. Clutching the hilt of his blade, he was more than ready for whatever the two overgrown dickheads wanted to throw at him.

"I'd control that temper of yours, Santini," Enrique called out. "If you want her throat to remain intact."

Flickering his gaze to where Enrique held Alexandria, his heart stalled in his chest. Alexandria stared back at him, fear etched in her pale expression. Enrique grinned, satisfaction gleaming in his black eyes as his blade pressed into her throat. Markus froze, allowing the hired muscle to slam into him, latching onto each of his arms.

"I still can't believe you'd put Eve's life above the female who only a year ago you would have done *anything* to save." Enrique shook his head.

"Let her go, Enrique," Markus commanded. "She's innocent in all this. It's me you want. Make me pay. Not her."

Enrique laughed, the sound manic, crazed. "So sorry, pretty boy. You've fucked me over once too often. And as delightful as it was, your cock's not going to save your whore this time."

Alexandria blinked at the reference, and her brow furrowed.

Dammit. Of course he'd bring up their past. Enrique would say and do whatever he needed to make the moment more agonizing for him. Markus's gut churned at the idea of what she had to be thinking of him. Because without a doubt, she had to remember now what he'd agreed to do with that sick son of a bitch.

Enrique nodded toward Dominic's guards. "You're going to want to restrain him with the silver-laced chains until I'm done with her."

"Before this night is over," Markus snarled, jerking hard on the male's grip, "I swear to you, Enrique, you'll feel the burn of my blade in your heart."

"Please," Enrique drawled, then laughed. "Don't make promises you know you can't keep." The dark vampire looked to Christian. "Grab the chain for the boys."

"He's not the only one who's going to pay for this mistake, Enrique," Dominic announced. "This is a major fuckup and I blame you." The tall, curly-headed vampire paced the room, mumbling what Markus could only assume were a plethora of curses in Spanish. "Dammit, Enrique. You know this is a setup. Kill them both so we can get the hell out of here."

"That's what I intend to do if you'll shut up!" Enrique spat. He yanked hard on Alexandria's hair, forcing her to cry out, her back arching.

Pain stabbed through Markus's own head at the sound of her distress. "You're mine, Enrique," Markus gritted out. "You only thought you knew misery with Marguerite."

"Hey, big guy!" Christian yelled, carrying a mass of chain in his gloved hand.

One of the guards holding Markus glanced Christian's way at the same moment the redhead tossed the thick metal toward him. Reflex had the burly vampire releasing Markus's arm to catch the flying silver-coated chain.

Yes! Who would have thought the young vampire possessed that much cunning?

Markus swung his forearm up and slammed it into the

vampire's massive skull. Out of the corner of his eye, Markus caught a blur of red flashing in Alexandria's direction.

Christian.

What the fuck was he trying to do?

Roaring, Markus whipped around and rammed a fist into the face of the other bodyguard. The tall hulk of a male staggered backward, blood spraying from his mouth. Markus jerked his attention back to the female who owned his soul, at the same time a venom-laced cry bounced off the metal walls, filling Markus's ears. Every neuron in his body screamed in helpless rage as Enrique stumbled away from Alexandria, his palm gripping his biceps. Christian's tall form lay sprawled on top of her, a crimson stream trailing off the table.

"Noooo!" Markus roared.

Chapter Twenty-Four

Markus's enraged bellow rang inside Alex's head.

Dammit. She couldn't move. Christian's dead weight had her pinned to the table. *Dead weight.* Dear God, had Enrique killed him? She'd never expected the young male to jump the crazy bastard. At the very moment she'd made a move for her weapon, Christian had come out of nowhere and dived for Enrique. The elder vampire had jerked the knife away from her throat and thrust it into the younger male, halting him in his tracks. She'd taken the split second of a distraction to launch her own attack on Enrique and sliced Enrique's arm with her silver-laced blade. But Christian had collapsed on top of her, dislodging her weapon from her hand before she'd been able to inflict much damage.

"Alexandria!" Markus called out, and the weight of Christian's body lifted from her chest. Alex groaned. "Fuck!" His wide eyes scanned her, and she could have sworn horror clouded his gaze at the sight of the blood covering her torso.

"It's not mine," she quickly explained. "It's Christian's."

A visible wave of relief washed over his expression. A corresponding warm and fuzzy rush filled the pit of her stomach. Her safety mattered—*she* mattered to him.

Markus glanced down at Christian's chest, and she followed his line of sight. A spray of crimson bloomed on the front of his white graphic tee, actively leaking his life's essence.

"He should make it," Markus muttered and lowered the other male's body to the floor.

Alex scrambled to work on the buckle to her restraint. She had to get free and help. *Shit.* She fumbled with the metal, her fingers not wanting to cooperate. This was taking too long.

"You're not going to get away with doing this to me!" Enrique yelled. Blood dripped from the open wound, and he fisted the thick hilt of a knife. Enrique charged back in their direction.

"Markus!" she cried out.

He spun, bringing his own blade up with him in a wide arc. He carved a path across Enrique's chest, opening a wide gash. The other male gasped and stumbled back.

But it wasn't over. Not by a long shot. Tossing the restraint from her wrist, Alex swung her legs over and shoved away from the table.

The guards were shaking off their blows, and the first one had already risen. Growling, the large male bared his fangs in Markus's direction. Alex grabbed the closest thing next to her, an aluminum IV pole, ready for his attack. It sucked, but it was better than nothing. She could at least give the bastard a damn good headache and slow him down. The powerful male pivoted, preparing to come after them, when another appeared.

With preternatural speed, the massive blond intruder collided with the guard. The impact lifted the hulk of a vampire from his feet, sending him flying into the metal wall on the opposite side of the room. His body slammed into the metal with a heavy *thud*, and he slid down the wall like a swatted fly into a heap of beefy arms and legs.

Turning toward her and Markus, the new guy grinned. "Miss me?" he asked.

Arran.

"Shit, yeah," Markus muttered. "About damn time."

A long sigh exited Alex's lungs. The Enclave had arrived.

At that moment, Kenric and Guerin appeared from the opposite side of the wall of crates. With his dark waves draped over his forehead and his eyes bloodshot, Guerin appeared barely recovered from whatever formula had been in the bullet.

"You sorry motherfucker..." Enrique cursed, and the *clang* of metal sliding against metal rang out in the open space. Alex's attention darted to the maniac's fist, where he'd exchanged his blade in favor of a large hacksaw from one of the carts. She didn't even want to imagine how they'd originally intended to use the tool. "This could have been a fresh new start." A perverted chuckle bubbled up from the battle-scarred male. A stream of garnet seeped from the wound in his chest, staining the ripped charcoal-colored shirt. A similar trail of blood covered his forearm. "But oh, hell no. You'd rather side with these pussies." He waved the saw at the others as he edged closer to Markus. Yet her warrior stood there in silence, his face a stoic mask.

Her warrior? At what point had she claimed him?

"I should have known better," Enrique scoffed. "Look how you screwed over Marguerite."

Something moved behind Alex, drawing her attention. The last guard, sensing he was outnumbered, made a run for the exit. Guerin zoomed in the direction of the escaping vampire, equipment in his path clattering to the floor.

This was her chance. A temporary diversion that would allow her to ease closer to Enrique. She scanned the various objects around her: vials, needles, jars. There had to be something better, smaller and heavier, she could use. The pole was too long and she might take out Markus in the process. She needed something blunt to knock the shit out of him and give Markus an advantage.

Dammit.

Nothing.

Well, except… Her lip curled. What the hell. If nothing else, this would be quite satisfying.

"You want a piece of me, Enrique?" Markus cocked his head and beckoned him with his free hand. "Come on. I'm dying for you to try," he said, his voice deep, his tone lethal.

Taking that as her cue, Alex inhaled deeply and, using all the supernatural force she could muster, charged the sadistic monster. She collided into Enrique, knocking the shocked vampire off his feet. Together, they hit the concrete, punching the air from her lungs. The hacksaw he'd been holding hit the floor with a loud *clank* and skidded out of sight.

"You bitch!" Enrique flipped, taking her to her back.

How the hell had he recovered so fast?

Straddling her, he held her in place with one arm and reared his other back, claws extended. "Going to rip you apart," he raged, fangs glistening in the fluorescent lights.

"Like hell," Markus snarled, and seized the furious vampire by the throat, lifting him off her with one arm.

Enrique's body left hers a second before Markus slammed the other male onto his back. Alex scrambled onto her knees, never allowing the two out of her sight. Enrique's hands clamped onto Markus's wrist, the warrior's knuckles white from his chokehold.

"That's the last time you'll ever put your hands on her," Markus avowed.

"Kill me," Enrique managed to squeak out. "But you'll never erase me from your mind."

"The past, Enrique," Markus said, "is where you're going to stay."

The chilling sound of bone crunching filled the space around Alex. Markus eased back onto his heels and retrieved his blade from the floor beside him. Lifting the weapon, he centered it over his target, then plunged the silver-coated dagger into Enrique's heart. Within seconds, the vampire's body began to crackle and pop. His torso distorted, swelling to twice its size before imploding into a pile of ash.

And just like that, he was gone. Forever.

Markus wiped the metal across his thigh, then slid it back into its sheath. Twisting around to face her, he straightened to his full height. Damn. He was a foreboding creature of the night with his swirling black and red tattoos wrapping both arms. His hair had come loose from its band and covered one side of his face, streaks of blood marring the other cheek. The male looked wild, untamed, and ready to strike.

His glare locked with hers and the effect should have sent shivers of intimidation down her spine. Yet gooseflesh raced across her arms, her nipples hardened to stiff peaks, and she realized she'd never wanted any man more in her life.

"What in the hell were you thinking?" Markus asked, breaking the connection.

"What?" Had he somehow read her mind? "What are you talking about?"

"Attacking Enrique like that?"

A spark of annoyance flashed over her, shoving her attraction to the side for the moment. "I was thinking of a way to help save your ass," she snapped.

"I had it under control," he bellowed. "He could have killed you."

"He didn't," she bit out. "I'm still here, and so are you." Silence blanketed the room, jarring her, and she did a quick survey of what was left around them. They were alone. "I guess we both got what we wanted," she muttered, doing her best not to look at him again. She couldn't. Because if she did, she wasn't sure if she could keep herself from diving into his arms and never letting go.

Madness.

"Shit! Where's Dominic?" Markus marched toward the exit.

"I don't know." She shook her head. "Guerin went after the guard, and then everything else happened so fast. I lost track of him."

A groan sounded from behind her, grabbing her attention.

"Oh God, Christian," she called out, pissed with herself for not checking on him sooner. She hurried to his side, shoved the exam table out of the way to make more room, and knelt. Alex jerked her hoodie from over her head, folded it, and pressed it to his wound.

"Hey there," she said, and with her free hand smoothed the hair away from his eyes. "Can you hear me?"

Christian cleared his throat, reached over, and covered her hand where she applied pressure to his chest. "Yeah," he croaked.

"That was very brave, jumping Enrique like you did," she whispered.

He blinked up at her as if trying to bring her into focus. "I don't know," he said, his voice raspy. "One little knife wound, and I'm out."

"Hey, getting stabbed is no walk in the park. It wasn't that long ago I was in your situation, and I was out for hours."

"But you're a woman," he said.

"Excuse me?" She snatched her hands free. "Don't tell me you're a male chauvinist pig?"

Christian grinned and started to laugh but the sound died a quick death as he wrapped his arms around his chest. "Oh, fuck." He grimaced. "Don't make me laugh."

"Then don't be a pig." She couldn't help but allow a small chuckle of her own to escape. "No. I'm sorry." Alex applied more pressure to his wound. "We need to get you out of here and fed."

"Markus!" Alex twisted and glanced over her shoulder. "Where is everyone?"

"We're here." Elle appeared, followed by Arran and Kenric. "Hey." Her sister darted to her side.

"I didn't know you were out there," Alex said. "I thought you were staying behind with Emily, making sure Eve stayed put?"

"No one was going to keep me home while you were

putting your life on the line," she said. "I was watching the exit and caught one of the bastards trying to get away."

"I'm glad you're here. We need to get Christian back to the mansion," Alex said, watching as the male's blood began to soak through the thick cotton. "He took a blade pretty deep to his chest."

"Hey there, tough guy." Elle smiled down at the redhead. "Didn't anyone teach you to duck?"

"Ha ha," he rasped. "How about teaching your sister to stay away from bad guys, and maybe I won't have to jump in front of a dagger next time." He coughed.

"Okay, okay," Alex said. "That's enough for now." She looked up and made a quick scan of the room, the absence of one warrior echoing inside her. "Where's Markus?"

About that time, Guerin and Markus appeared, both looking pretty satisfied with whatever they'd accomplished. "Jean-Claude's men report they've cleaned up the other males Enrique's buyer hired, and I took care of the one who tried to escape," Guerin reported.

Markus looked over at Kenric. "Did you stop Dominic?"

"If you're referring to the male dressed like he was ready for the red carpet? Yes." He nodded. "Elle spotted him slipping out and dropped him in his tracks before I got there. But she did give me the honor of dusting him off." Kenric smiled.

"Great," Alex said. "Since everyone is accounted for, how about we get Christian out of here before he requires a complete transfusion?"

"Good idea," Elle added as her mate closed in, and she took her place beside Alex.

Alex drew close to the fallen vampire, ready to move

Christian's upper body on to her lap in preparation of phasing him back to the mansion, when Markus tapped her shoulder. "I got him."

"That's okay," she said. "I can do this. It's the least I can do."

"Let me, Alexandria," he commanded. "*I* owe him this." His voice dipped low, the sincerity palpable in his tone.

Glancing over her shoulder, Alex met his unwavering gaze. "All right," she said, and rose.

Markus assumed her position near Christian's head.

"You don't owe me a damn thing," the redhead whispered.

"Shut up and drink." Markus lifted his wrist to his mouth, bit down, and then presented his arm to other male. Blood welled at the points where his fangs pierced the flesh. "You're going to need your strength for the trip."

"You know, you're really not my type," Christian muttered, looking up at Markus.

"You're so full of shit." Markus grunted. "And by the way, not in your wildest fucking dreams."

Christian snorted, then drew his upper lip back, exposing his fangs, and latched onto Markus's wrists. Mesmerized, Alex watched as the fierce male offered himself freely to his fallen comrade. Mere weeks ago, everyone would have laid odds that Markus would have walked away without giving a rat's ass if Christian had received help or not. But this Markus... Something inside her stomach fluttered at the sight of him on his knees feeding the injured male. This was the Markus she'd met in the basement of his cabin. The Markus who had made her care.

Too much.

. . .

At least a half hour had passed before Alex and the rest of
the Enclave arrived back at the mansion. Alex stood in the
center of the living room and watched as Kenric, Guerin,
and Michael assisted Christian up the stairs. That left her,
Markus, Arran, and Elle alone to stare at one another. And
every *thump* of boots ascending to the second floor seemed
to thicken the room's tension.

Arran was the first to clear his throat. "Let's go up, too,"
the blond warrior said to his mate. "There are a few more
hours before dawn."

"And what do you suggest we do with that time?" Elle
rewarded him with a smile that relayed she knew exactly
what he had in mind.

He sauntered over to her and slid an arm around her
shoulders. "I have a few ideas."

"I'm sure you do," Elle said, leaning into him as if she
were molding into a custom-made glove.

A pang of jealousy twisted Alex's midsection. She didn't
begrudge her sister's happiness. It wasn't that. The twinge inside stemmed from fear. She was so damn afraid of becoming that vulnerable. Because there was only one man who'd
ever fractured her facade. Only one man she'd ever wanted
to allow inside.

"Oh my God," Alex said and sighed. "Enough already.
Please take it upstairs."

Elle laughed, but her humor faded as her inspection
wandered from Alex to the other large male in the room.
Markus looked even more uncomfortable than she felt.

She shifted her attention back to Alex and asked, "Are you sure?"

Alex nodded. "Yeah. You two go ahead and enjoy your downtime." She gave her sister the best warm smile she could muster. "You deserve it."

Her sister cupped her face. "You were awesome tonight," she said.

"Yes, she was!" Eve appeared at the lower landing of the staircase. She brushed past Arran and Elle as they proceeded toward the second floor. "Guerin filled me in upstairs while they were working on Christian." She strode over to Alex. "I can't believe what you did for me. I'll never forget this." Eve shook her head, reached out, and clasped Alex's upper arms. "I've never had anyone in my life—a true friend—until I met you. Thank you, Alex." Eve pulled her in for a hug.

"I consider you more than a friend, Eve," Alex managed to get out past the thick lump in her throat. "You're very much like a sister to me. Like Elle, I'd do anything for you."

"Same here," Eve whispered. "You name it."

Alex stepped back, her heart swelling. She hadn't been sure if it would ever be possible, but she fit in here. This was her home and her family. The Enclave was where she belonged.

"You know what you can do for me?" Alex smiled up at her, blinking back the tears threatening to spill.

"What's that?" Eve released her and propped her hands on her hips.

"Don't ever change," she said. "Stay safe and happy with that mate of yours."

"Well, that I can easily and wholeheartedly agree to."

"Good." Alex crossed her arms.

"Eve," Kenric called, descending the staircase.

The tall blue-eyed female glanced over her shoulder at her father.

"Would you mind giving Guerin a hand upstairs?" Kenric stepped from the landing and faced them. "I need to talk to Markus."

The other male warrior turned his attention to the Enclave's master and sauntered closer.

"Sure." Eve nodded. "We'll talk more later," she said to Alex, then ambled toward the staircase.

"Excuse us," Kenric said and started for the door to the library. Markus glanced her way, but without a word, followed the commander into the other room.

What would he do now? Alex made her way to the kitchen in desperate need of a drink. Except alcohol wouldn't help to relieve her stress, so instead, she settled for coffee. Scanning the counter, she spotted a full carafe. Thank God, Michael had brewed a pot.

Would Markus stay with the Enclave? That is, if Kenric wanted him to remain with the team. Did she want him to stay? Alex grabbed a mug and poured a cup of the java, watching as the black liquid whirled inside the ceramic. The image was similar to the way her stomach felt at the thought of Markus walking away. She replaced the carafe onto the hot plate with a *clank* of glass to metal. Closing her eyes, she gripped the granite counter. Dammit. She couldn't stand the thought of never seeing him again.

Too much had happened tonight. Her emotions were all over the place. Maybe it was a post-traumatic thing from her close call with death and from what she'd recalled about Markus and Enrique's past.

She hadn't remembered that detail.

Not until tonight when Enrique had made his crude comment about their former sexual connection. Closing her eyes, she was mentally transported back to her small room inside Marguerite's lair. *Enrique is standing in the doorway, a coy smile on his face as he speaks with Markus. His insinuations are clear as to what he expects from the former warrior. And if Markus didn't fulfill his duties in every way, Enrique would go to Marguerite and inform their Mistress of Markus's desire for Alex.*

She and Markus would have both died in that hellhole if he hadn't gone along with Enrique's demands. Alex swallowed hard, pushing past the dry knot in her throat at the thought of what Markus had suffered. What he'd sacrificed for her. Yes, he'd turned her against her will and had manipulated her mind. But in a sense, wasn't that what Marguerite had done to him: taken what he believed was the last shred of his humanity? For months, the domineering female vampire had violated his mind and his body. And later, Enrique had done the same with his ultimatum. So in the end, who had been the one to actually suffer more under Marguerite's hand?

Opening her eyes, she gripped the cup and took a long swallow of the hot liquid.

She'd been so damn hurt and angry after he'd restored her memories. However, at the time, she'd refused to take a closer look at why her rage had burned so hot. Yes, she had every reason to be mad at him. He'd hidden what he'd done to her. But what she'd felt had been different.

Her feelings for him ran too deep. She'd been so furious with Markus because, despite the pain he'd caused her, she couldn't make herself stop loving him. The bottom of her mug hit the granite with a hard *clank*. The words repeated inside her head like a scratched vinyl record caught in a loop: *I love him*.

The decisions he'd made after he'd turned her had all been an attempt to keep her alive. He, too, had been a victim of Marguerite. He'd been lost to the power of her will.

Tightening her grip on her mug, Alex's decision became clear. She couldn't allow him to leave.

Not until they'd had a chance to talk.

And there was no time like the present.

Seconds later, she found herself outside the library door. Lifting her hand to knock, she noticed the door stood ajar, and Markus's deep voice carried through the opening.

"I can't stay here, Kenric."

"Why? The Enclave needs you, Markus."

"You know why," Markus snapped. "You have your mate at your side. You can touch her, hold her. Lie beside her through the day and inhale her scent until it drives you mad with lust. And you love every minute of it because you know she's all yours." She pressed her cheek against the doorjamb, needing the support. "But imagine trying to exist every night in the same house with the female who's marked your soul but you can't have her. Can't go anywhere near her."

"You're talking about Alex?"

"Yeah. Who else?"

A loud *bang* sounded as if he'd slammed his fist into a wall. She jumped.

"I'm so fucking in love with her." He groaned, and Alex had no idea how she still remained standing since she'd forgotten how to breathe. How to tell her heart to beat.

"Problem is," he continued, "I'm the one who took and then restored her memories, and now she hates my guts. But she deserved to know the truth. It was a risk I had to take. She had to know everything before I allowed her any closer."

A warm wet trail ran down Alex's cheeks, yet she didn't remember beginning to cry. He knew returning her memories would make her pull away from him, but he'd done it anyway.

Chapter Twenty-Five

Markus needed to stop the flow of self-pity pouring out of his mouth like a damn tidal wave. Since when had he become a male ruled by his emotions? Whoever had flipped the damn switch on his emo side needed to be castrated.

"But with time…" Kenric said. And there it was. A lame attempt at trying to make him feel better.

"It's not just that," Markus said. "There are other things. Information came to light tonight that I'd hoped she'd never recall. But Enrique ran his mouth and made sure she remembered."

"About what? Anything I can do to help?"

"Thanks. But no. I'd rather not get into it. I just know the info has added insult to injury between the two of us." Markus scrubbed his palms over the rough feel of his late-day stubble. "There's no alternative other than to get the hell away from here and out of her face. I'll be doing us both a favor."

"Okay. If you're sure there's no other way," Kenric said, leaning both hands onto the back of the thick leather love seat. "But I want you to know that during these last few days you've proven yourself not just to me, but to everyone else. It'll be a hard hit to the Enclave, personally and professionally, to lose you again."

Damn. This sucked bigger than hell. In more ways than one. But Alexandria had to despise him more than ever after what she'd heard, and then witnessed when he'd taken out Enrique. He was a killer. Dealing out death was what he'd been trained to do and what he did best. How could she even begin to get past it all and think of him as mate material?

"I'm sorry," Markus said. "But I'm—"

A knock sounded at the door, cutting off the rest of his sentence. The library's door eased open, and the last person he expected to see appeared.

"Hey there," Alexandria said. "Sorry for the interruption." She looked at Markus, then her gaze shifted to Kenric. "But would you mind giving me a few minutes alone with Markus? We really need to talk."

She still wore the simple white tank top and jeans from earlier, her hair cascading around her shoulders. Her clothing wasn't anything extraordinary, yet she stunned him. She was everything he wanted. But the last thing he could ever have.

"Sure, Alex." Kenric nodded and, looking at Markus, said, "We can finish later."

"Yeah," Markus said, unable to pull his attention away from Alexandria.

Kenric brushed past Alexandria, and the door clicked shut.

Running her hand along the back of one of the chairs, Alexandria edged closer. Unable to stand the tension choking him like a noose, Markus spoke first.

"I've got a damn good idea of what you're going to say."

She drew to a halt, leaving a few feet between them, her hand curling into a fist. "Is that so?"

"You want to be sure I know exactly how you feel. So go ahead. Get it out there. Draw your line as to how it's going to be around here." Markus crossed his arms over his chest. "But you can relax, I'm—"

Before he could finish, Alexandria was next to him, clasping his face, lacing her fingers into his hair, pulling his head toward hers. His mind whirled in an attempt to comprehend what the hell was happening. Her lips touched his, and his nerve endings sparked, sucking the breath from his lungs. But she was there, capturing his exhale. She moaned and deepened their connection, nearly short-circuiting his brain before breaking the seal on their kiss.

"There," she whispered against his lips. "That's much better."

His shaft went rock-hard. Markus groaned and reflex had him circling her arms with his hands and yanking her body next to him, sealing his mouth to hers once more.

Closer.

He rocked his hips into hers.

Dammit all to hell! He wanted her.

Here.

Now.

He needed to feel more of her. Markus released her biceps and roamed upward until he could thread his fingers into her hair. His cock bucked at the sensation. So damn soft, silky. *Shit.* He wanted to inhale the sweet scent he knew clung to the strands.

Breaking away from her lips, he breathed deeply and opened his eyes. Maybe it was the shot of cool air to his head that roused his conscience? Or maybe it was the expression on Alexandria's face? The one that resembled a woman who wanted to give herself to a man. More than likely, the latter had shocked his brain—the gray matter residing inside his skull, not his pants—back into reality.

"Wait!" he muttered.

But Alexandria wasn't listening. Her delicate hands were at work, attempting to shove the leather jacket off his shoulders.

This shouldn't be happening. "Vixen..." He clasped her hands and pushed them away. "Wait," he commanded, but he couldn't bring himself to let her go.

"Haven't we waited long enough?" Her eyes flashed.

Fuck... When she spoke like that it was all he could do not to tear her clothes off and take her like his body demanded. But he couldn't. Not until he knew for sure.

"It's just..." he started, searching for moisture in his parched throat. "I don't understand." He shook his head, confusion and desire leaving him dazed. "How could—? After everything you've seen and heard about me— How can you...?"

"Forgive you?" she whispered. Alexandria rested a gentle palm to his cheek. "We were both victims," she said. "I don't hold the trump card on pain. I understand. It took time...but I understand the why, Warrior."

Warrior. The title had once meant something until Marguerite had gotten inside his head and forced him to turn his back on the Enclave. Then she'd used the designation as a weapon to taunt him. As if what he'd once been had been a flaw in his character, a weakness. But coming from Alexandria, there was no shame associated with the word. What he felt seemed foreign, new. Yet he recognized the emotion: pride.

"Vixen," Markus growled, and captured her nape. "Make very sure this is what you want." He narrowed his eyelids, and there was no way in hell his irises weren't on fire, burning with need. Burning for her. "Because this time, I won't be able to stop from taking you—the way I need you right now." He lowered his head to hers, their foreheads brushing. "I want you." The three words were a carnal fact. "I want you against the wall. Then I want you flat on your back with my cock buried so deep in your pussy that I nearly go blind from the pleasure. Except no damn way would I miss watching you come."

Slowly, ever so slowly, he smoothed his hands down her arms. He had to take it slow. Unreel his leash one link at a time until she gave the command. She shivered, and the gooseflesh prickled his palms.

"After that," he continued. "I'll bend you over, take you from behind until I've filled you with every drop of my seed. You'll be marked so deep there'll be no question as to who you belong to." Markus bent a little closer, gliding his lips across her obsidian tresses. "You'll be mine. Not just for tonight, but for as long as I draw breath. Is that what you want?"

"I'd be lying"—her words came out breathless—"if I said it's not all I've thought about." Her hands landed on his chest, her nails biting through the cloth. "I can't deny it any longer. I care too damn much about you." She pulled back, and her gaze locked with his. "I'm yours, Markus," she breathed. "I've always been yours."

A sizzling bolt of heat arrowed through Markus's body and landed in his cock. His jaw clamped tight. He had to, or he'd lose his load. And there was no fucking way he'd allow his dick to blow until it was inside her.

Several loud *thud*s crashed around him. *Books.* Her back was against the library shelves, except damn, he didn't remember moving. All he knew was the driving need to have his skin next to hers. Her mouth on his. The soft feel of her breasts against his chest, and the sweet taste of her nipples on his tongue. "Mine," he rasped.

"Yes," she moaned. "All yours."

"Again," he demanded, mere inches from her perfect bow of a mouth.

"I'm yours," she said, her chest rapidly rising and falling against his.

Shit. His shaft pulsed against his zipper, demanding release.

"Yes." The word came out more animal than human.

"Show me," she ordered, her voice deepening to a purr. Then her hands were around his neck and she wrapped her legs around his hips. The heat of her core rode his erection. "Now, Markus," she cried out. "Make me yours."

Markus claimed her mouth. Hungry and hard. Fangs erupting and teeth clicking. The taste of their blood trickled over his taste buds, the flavor adding fuel to their fire.

"Fuck," he muttered against her. "I can't do easy, Vixen."

"To hell with easy."

He slid her bottom onto the massive mahogany desk on the far side of the room. With one swipe of his hand, he cleared the items from the wood in an eruption of glass and metal. Alexandria chuckled and lay back, her arms going over her head.

"Clothes off," he gruffly commanded, and he shed his jacket, shirt, boots, then started to work on his belt. But Alexandria rose and stopped his hands with her own.

"Mine." She lifted a brow, challenging him to claim otherwise. He may be a monster, but he wasn't a fool.

"Yours, Vixen," he pronounced without hesitation, and his swollen shaft jerked in agreement.

She tugged the leather strap free, and it clattered to the floor. The button and zipper came next. Cool air rushed over the head of his rod a brief second before the warmth of her palm surrounded the length. He hissed at the sensation, and his hands slapped the desk's surface for stability.

Markus watched, enthralled, a slave to her whim as she leaned over and the wet pink tip of her tongue flicked out. She scooped the bead of pre-cum from his slit, and his molars released a squeak.

"Fuck," he gruffed. "Killing me."

"I haven't forgotten the last time." She licked her lips and tightened her hold around his girth, staggering him. Not from pain. But from the sweet, sweet pleasure. "And damn. I want more."

A wicked smile curled her lips, and she bent closer again, ready to take him.

"Shit!" he hissed. "Hold up, baby." Markus twisted out of her grip, and Alexandria lifted her head, frowning. "Won't last. And I have to be inside you."

He seized her hips and scooted her farther back on the desk. She grinned and kicked her boots off. "No more waiting," she said, working the closure to her jeans.

Markus helped her make quick work of removing and discarding the denim.

"You don't need this," he said, regarding the black lace covering her folds. He slid his palms under her hips, nabbed the thin material, and tugged it free. "Or this," he added, targeting her tank top. He pulled it over her head and tossed the soft cotton over his shoulder.

Alexandria grasped her lower lip with her teeth as he planted his hands on either side of her. She released the closure to her bra and allowed the sheer fabric to fall to her sides.

And heaven had surely fallen from the stars because an angel lay beneath him.

Her thighs parted, and the smooth feel of her legs slid around his hips, snugging the head of his cock where it most wanted to be.

"Dammit, Vixen," he ground out, the thread on his control fraying.

"I'm yours, Markus Santini," she proclaimed. "No more sacrifices." Tears welled and fell from the corners of her eyes, twisting his heart.

"For you," he said, "I'd do it all again. If only for this moment."

Markus slid deep, burying his cock until he had nothing left to give. Her channel wrapped him, hot and tight, the sensation threatening to shatter the foundation of his sanity.

Alexandria cried out, and her nails dug into his biceps. "God…Markus." She gasped. "Don't stop."

"Hang on, baby." He drew back from her tight core, leaving only the head inside before rocking his hips and sliding back home. *Christ!*

"Yes!" Her back arched.

Fucking had never been like this before: a shattering of every mental wall. She made him feel raw, exposed.

And it was euphoric.

Sex with her wasn't a physical exercise to satisfy an itch. For once, he understood what it was to make love. It was transforming.

Over and over he pumped into her, his orgasm teetering on the brink with every thrust. *Not yet.* He needed more time.

Alexandria tossed her head back, cried out his name, and her core clamped down on his shaft. Her legs quaked around his hips. She was so damn beautiful.

"Oh, fuck!" He thrust deep, his sac tapping her bottom.

He didn't believe it possible, but his balls tightened even more. The cum inside rammed against the crumbling barrier inside his rod, demanding escape.

Markus gripped her hips and pulled her to him. "Wrap your arms around me," he commanded, and lifted her, his cock still buried deep. Alexandria did as instructed, clinging to him with her arms and legs. He turned on his heel and headed toward the center of the room, taking out one of the annoying dainty tables in the process. The fragile piece hit the floor behind him, showering the floor with shards of crystal.

He'd have to replace it later. The only thing that mattered at the moment was the woman in his arms. And they weren't nearly finished.

At an oversize brown leather chair, Markus eased Alexandria to her feet. His shaft slid free, and he wanted to curse at the absence. Alex groaned and trailed her nails down his bare chest.

He cupped her face. "Trust me," he said.

And despite the gnawing demand of his cock standing at full attention between them, he couldn't move until he had her answer. But he didn't have to wait long.

"I do," she replied, and those two simple words sent his heart soaring.

He captured her mouth with his, smothering the urge to howl with joy.

Dammit, he'd never get enough of her taste. He was starved. Couldn't hold back. She opened, and he drove his tongue inside. Exploring. Sucking. Straining to show her how much he desired every inch of her. He nibbled at her kiss-swollen lower lip, enjoying the sexy way she whimpered each time his fang caught the sensitive flesh.

"Turn around," he demanded, and Alexandria readily complied, giving him her back. Pressing his palm between her shoulder blades, he added, "Bend over, baby."

She lowered her torso over the back of the chair, her hair falling over one shoulder. In that position, Alexandria's bottom lifted, opened, giving him full access to her glistening folds.

"So fucking gorgeous," he groaned. He couldn't help but run his hands over the smooth curve of her ass, cupping the weight of her buttocks in his palm. She bucked back into his hold, beckoning him, and his cock jerked in response. The shaft throbbed and pre-cum beaded, covering the sensitized head. His cum churned inside his balls, eager to make its exit. But hell if he was rushing this.

Alexandria glanced back over her shoulder. "How long are you going to keep me waiting, Warrior?"

"Impatient?" Markus quirked a smile her way and bent over her, covering her back with his chest. The angle positioned the head of his cock at her opening. He rocked forward, parting her, teasing her with the tip. She gasped, and her head fell forward. "Like that, baby?"

"Yes." She moaned and pushed back, slipping more of his shaft inside.

Markus panted. "Earning that nickname, Vixen?"

He opened his palm and brought it down on her right butt cheek with a loud *smack*.

She cried out and looked back, hitting him with a wicked glare. "What was that for?"

"Be still," he ordered.

"Then don't torment me."

He cracked a laugh. "Living around you in a perpetual half-hard state for months? Now that's torment." Markus thrust forward, not stopping until he'd filled her with every last inch.

"God, yes! Markus!"

Her core quivered around his cock, shooting sparks of pleasure along his nerve endings. "Fuck, sweetheart." He couldn't help but groan as he withdrew before driving back inside. "So damn good."

"Harder," she cried out.

"My Vixen." Markus coiled his fist in her hair and pulled her head gently back, bowing her spine. With one arm wrapped around her waist, stabilizing them, he closed in on her throat. With the tip of his tongue, he traced her bounding pulse. "All mine," he added, circling his hips, grinding the head of his cock deeper into her core.

The familiar tingle along the base of his spine ramped in intensity. Christ, he was too damn close. He wouldn't be able to deny his release much longer.

A shiver raced over her body, and she bucked her hips.

Chapter Twenty-Six

A slow and steady heartbeat filled Alex's head. Lifting her eyelashes, a smile tugged at the corners of her mouth.

It hadn't been a dream.

The weight of Markus's large, calloused palm rested on her hip, and his chest warmed her cheek. Blinking, she assessed the shadowy figures of the furnishings around her. She'd been in Markus's room before, but only in her wildest dreams had she imagined they'd ever be here, together, like this.

Alex inhaled, savoring the sweet, familiar trace of his cinnamon and chocolate scent. Her mouth watered, and her fangs threatened to erupt. *Delicious*. Would she ever get enough of him to satisfy her hunger? She brushed her calf against his thigh, enjoying the way the light dusting of hair covering his leg tickled her flesh.

"Good morning." The deep bass of his voice rippled through the silence around them.

"Good morning," she said, even though it was actually the next evening, but morning for a vampire.

"I'm surprised you're already awake since I kept you quite busy through most of the day." He stroked her arm.

She grinned to herself at the memory of just how "busy" they'd been. "Did you get any sleep?" She ran her fingers over his breastbone and through the fine chest hair. The dark mass thickened between his pecs then merged to form a narrow trail that traveled down the center of his abs before disappearing beneath the sheet covering his hips.

"Some," he said.

Alex glanced up. "Did I bother you? Sleeping next to you, I mean." An empty pit of panic formed in her stomach, threatening to pull her inside. What if he'd realized having her in his bed was more than he'd asked for?

"Hell, no!" He moved so fast that she'd barely processed his reply before she was on her back with Markus's fiery glare staring down at her. "Never think that I don't want you here. I couldn't sleep because I was too damn afraid to close my eyes."

"Afraid?" Her head buzzed at the concept. "Why?"

"I was afraid that when I reopened them, you wouldn't be here. That you'd wake and realize what a huge damn mistake you've made, and you'd get as far away from me as fast as you could."

"Markus," she breathed, her heart splitting in two as she smoothed her palm over the stubble on his cheek.

"How the hell can I be expected to sleep when I could be looking at you?" He rocked into her, and the hard thick presence between his legs pressed into her thigh. Her stomach fluttered, and she captured her lower lip with her teeth.

"Who knew there was such a romantic buried underneath that hard exterior?"

"There wasn't," he said, and lowered his head, placing his mouth next to hers. "Until you."

He stole her lips with his own, tugging hers from the hold she had on it for a gentle kiss. "After everything…after what you remember, Vixen," he whispered next to her cheek, "you're here, with me. And it's so damn surreal."

"If you're referring to what Enrique alluded to last night, you did what you had to for *our* survival. It doesn't change who you are," she said. "In my mind, it only strengthened my opinion of who I know you to be: a male who would do anything for someone he cares about—no matter the cost."

Markus blinked as if he were trying to comprehend a foreign language. His mouth opened, and the most beautiful three words she'd ever heard fell from his lips. "I love you."

And she melted. Her brain misfired, and for a moment, she couldn't make her throat work.

"You weren't expecting that," he said, the tone declaring it as fact, not a question. He rolled onto his back.

"No," she sputtered. "I mean, yes!" She rolled to her side facing him. "That's not what I mean. *Gah!*" She was screwing this up royally. "What I'm trying to say, that my head isn't allowing me to express the way I want…is how could I *not* fall in love with you." Lightly scratching his chest, she curled her fingers. "I love you so much I don't know what to do with myself half the time." She swallowed hard, forcing back the lump of emotions attempting to choke her.

"Vixen," he breathed right before he grasped her arms and pulled her onto his chest. "My brain stays so damn rattled with need for you. I guess we're going to have to help each other get through this."

Straddling his waist, Alex leaned in and traced the full curve of his mouth with her thumb. "So, what is the best course of treatment for this 'condition'?"

A roguish smile played on his lips. "I think there's only one thing that can cure what ails us."

His cock flexed against her backside, and she couldn't help but grin. "Do tell."

"Exercise." A wicked gleam flashed in his eyes and he captured her nape. His fingers threaded into her hair. "Lots and lots of exercise."

Alex laughed. "I like that plan," she said, and his mouth claimed hers, stealing her breath.

She'd been beneath him, his body deep within hers, only hours before, but God...she craved him as if it had been years since she'd last tasted him, felt him thick and hard, pulsing inside her. Alex shivered at the thought. Her core tightened, moisture pooling. She broke the seal on their kiss with a gasp. "Need you," she whispered.

His nostrils flared, and he captured her lower lip with his fang, the sharp edge pricking the sensitive tissue. She jerked, yet the sting went straight to her clit, swelling her folds. Markus soothed the wound with his mouth, sucking gently, and her core clenched.

"Markus..." She sighed and rocked back, pressing her bottom against the hard presence of his erection.

"You can have me, baby," he murmured and his palms cupped the sides of her breasts. "Come here."

He tugged her up until her nipples brushed his chin, then his tongue appeared, and he dragged the wide surface across the hardened tip.

A rippling spasm seized her clit, nearly taking her to the edge. Alex cried out. "God, Markus…"

But he didn't stop there. He proceeded to perform the same maneuver to the other stiff peak.

"Christ," he said, his voice rough. "I love your breasts. The way they feel in my hands." He gently squeezed them. "The way your nipples grow even harder and tighter when I blow on them." A cool puff of air skated over the surface, sending another wave of arousal rushing from her sex.

"Damn." She moaned. "You love making me squirm, don't you?"

"Only when you're on my cock, baby." The sound of his voice, his words, rolled over her like a warm shot of whiskey: stimulating, intoxicating.

Alex groaned, and her head lolled. God, how she needed him. "Markus, please…"

"Take me," he demanded, and his hands fell away.

Rolling her head forward, Alex found Markus's arms above his head, his fingers wrapped round the headboard's spindles.

"All yours, Vixen," he said. "Use me." His gaze narrowed into a storm-filled fury. "Let me watch." He licked his lips as if the mental image had taken his hunger to a higher plane.

The idea of having his eyes on her as she rode him should have had her cowering with embarrassment. And in the past, that would have definitely been her. But this was Markus, and the way he looked at her made her feel…beautiful and confident. He trusted her.

Instead of awkward, she found herself aroused at the request. Hell, she was damn excited. Her nerve endings alive with anticipation.

"Your pleasure is mine, baby," he said.

She reached behind and tossed back the sheet covering his shaft. His erection flexed, then stood firm, eager and waiting for her touch. Alex wrapped her fingers around his rigid cock, the flesh hot, rock-hard, yet it glided so smoothly under her palm.

Markus reared his head back, the veins in his neck straining. A groan rumbled in his throat as if he were bracing himself to endure some great discomfort. But that wasn't the case. It was the exact opposite. Her heart raced, knowing that *her* touch made him crazy with desire.

Alex lifted, positioning the slick head of his erection at her entrance. Markus's eyelids shot open, and his gaze bored into hers. She pressed down, and his girth stretched her, sweetly burning her muscles. His cock slid deep, and she couldn't help but groan. The broad head bumped her cervix, filling her, completing her. Magical.

A hard tremor racked her body.

"Oh, God…" Alex planted her palms on his pecs, her hair falling around her face.

"Fuck." The rails inside his fists released a groan. "You've got to move, Vixen."

Slowly rising back up, the thick length of his cock dragged along her sensitive nerve endings. "God, you feel so good inside me," she muttered.

"So damn tight."

She slammed back down, sending his rod deep once more. Alex cried out from the blinding, sweet sensation, then rose, savoring her quickening need. Prolonging the inevitable.

"Vixen…" His eyes squeezed shut. "Got to—"

Markus bucked, forcing his cock back inside. Their bodies met with a slap of skin on skin. The sudden erotic impact arrowed a spark of pleasure so sharp, so sudden, she couldn't hold back the scream burning from her throat. Her fingertips curled, digging into his chest, needing the contact. Something to hold her down to earth, because she was flying.

More.

More of him.

Stroke for stroke, she matched him. Desire grew, coiled, and tightened inside her core. The world around her narrowed, converging on the constant thrust of his shaft. Every slide of his cock along the cluster of nerves inside. The pounding of her clit against his pelvis. The musky scent of their lovemaking, their mutual arousal, took her higher and higher.

Hunger and lust whirled into a tornado of need inside. Sweat beaded on her flesh and ran a cool trail down her spine. Her fangs throbbed. Her throat burned for the male beneath her, for the taste of his essence. Nothing else would do. No one else could compare.

Dear God, she was a storm on the verge of flying apart. "Markus," she moaned. "Oh, God. Need you."

"Take it, Vixen," he gritted out. "Now, dammit." He wrenched his head to the side, exposing the large pulsing vein at his neck.

His cock jerked inside her as if urging her on, and a spasm of ecstasy gripped her core. She gasped, squeezed her eyes shut, doing her best to make the moment last. But it was too good. Her orgasm couldn't be denied.

A ripple—no—a tsunami of pleasure rolled through her,

rocking her. Crying out, Alex struck, sinking her fangs into Markus.

A roar tore from her lover's throat and a wave of heat filled her core.

His essence flowed into her mouth, electrifying her taste buds. She swallowed, taking him into her bloodstream as his cock pulsed below, filling her with his orgasm. No narcotic came close to the rush, the sheer mind-altering bliss.

Being with Markus went beyond making love. He took her to a different plane: a place of color, light, and sensation where only they existed. And she never wanted to return.

Yet all too soon, she was falling, cascading back to reality. The tremors in her arms and legs eased. Inhaling deeply, she reluctantly removed her fangs from his flesh. With her tongue, she sealed his bite wounds and lifted her head.

"Hey, beautiful," he lazily drawled, his eyelids at half mast.

"Hey." She smiled.

"That was…" He shook his head. "You're amazing."

"You're pretty damn good yourself." She leaned in, brushed her lips over his, tugging on his lower one with her teeth.

Markus suddenly pulled back. "Stay right here."

He eased her onto her side. His shaft slipped free from her core, making her want to cry out in complaint from the loss of their connection.

"Where are you going?"

Unabashed, he padded away naked toward the bathroom. And damn if it wasn't a gorgeous show watching his firm ass disappear into the other room.

The sound of running water drifted into the bedroom.

"Are you taking a shower without me?" She rose onto the side of the bed, tugging the bedsheet up and over her front.

"Not exactly," he answered.

Not exactly?

A moment later, he appeared in the doorway, and Alex drank in the delicious sight of her warrior. His long black-as-sin hair hung loose over his shoulders, drawing her to the dark patch of hair on his chest. The pads of her fingertips tingled with the memory of how the fine strands felt against her skin. The exotic swirls and coils of the tats wrapping both his arms only added to his dangerous and sexy allure.

He strode toward her, and in spite of her best efforts to stay cool, her perusal fell south to the thick member swaying between his legs. Her midsection flip-flopped, and her mouth watered.

"You like what you see?" he asked, his tone taunting, daring her to deny that she was staring.

She flicked her lashes up, heat crawling up her neck and into her face. But she'd never been a damn shrinking violet. "Very much," she said.

A smug grin twitched the corner of his mouth. He strode closer, not stopping until he'd wedged himself between her legs and planted his palms beside her. "Good," he said. "Because I." He brushed his lips over hers, melting her with his touch. "Definitely." His mouth glided once more over hers. "Love what I see."

How had she existed before him?

Then his arms were around her, lifting her up, cradling her. The sudden movement drew a sharp inhale into her lungs.

"Where are you taking me?"

"Trust me." He placed a gentle kiss to her forehead.

"I do," she breathed. And she meant it. With everything inside her, she trusted him.

Glancing down at her, Markus's gray eyes darkened. "You're everything to me, Vixen."

"You make me feel it," she said, placing her hand over the heavy *thud* of his heart.

They crossed into the bathroom, and he continued over to the large jetted tub. Kneeling, he lowered her into the water. The warm bath enveloped her, and the delicate scent of jasmine and lavender bath salts filled her nostrils, her senses, relaxing her muscles.

He lifted the shower wand and turned on the spray. "You make me want to be more," he said and cupped her nape with his free hand. "Lean back onto the headrest."

She did as instructed. But inside, her mind buzzed with the idea of her big bad warrior on his knees bathing her. Alex's heart pounded, ready to burst from his tenderness. Not once in her life had any man ever cared for her in this way.

Warm water sluiced over her scalp and down her shoulders. Alex clasped his arm and opened her eyes. "You don't have to do this. I'm perfectly capable of washing myself."

"I know you are. You're more capable and stronger than any female I've ever known. But I want to." He broke free of her hold and snagged one of the bottles from the side of the tub. Squeezing a dollop of the gel into his palm, he added, "Let me take care of you."

Markus smoothed the shampoo over her hair, and it was as if his touch, his words, held the power to make her let go, to transport her. Unbidden, her eyelids lowered.

They'd come so far to get to this place. Surely two people had survived greater obstacles.

But she refused to look back anymore. Their past was over, sealed tight. Because she couldn't imagine a future without him.

His large, calloused fingers worked the thick lather through her strands, and the muscles in her arms and legs unwound with each stroke. "I love you." The three words rolled off her tongue. As natural as breathing.

Easy.

Real.

The massage to her scalp paused. "You know without a doubt, I'd die for you," he said. "But even more so than that, for you, I live."

Her lashes lifted, and Markus's gaze bored into her soul.

"My beautiful Vixen...I love you with all my being."

Chapter Twenty-Seven

Markus stretched out on his side along the edge of his bed and crossed his ankles, waiting for Alexandria to emerge from the bathroom after her shower. He wasn't about to miss this. For what seemed like an eternity, he'd dreamed of waking to this each evening, lying in his bed with the gorgeous woman on the other side of the wall performing the mundane daily activities such as showering and dressing for the night.

How so very ordinary.

Normal.

Fantastic.

Alexandria padded from the bathroom wrapped once more in one of the mansion's bath sheets. Her hair hung in a dark, wet, and glistening veil over her shoulders. She looked up, caught his stare, and smiled.

"I see you're already dressed," she said, and continued over to the dresser.

"Yup. Thought I'd wait here and enjoy the show."

"Voyeur, much?" She tossed him a wicked grin over her shoulder.

"Depends on who's on display."

"Oh, is that how it goes? I should feel very special to have your undivided attention then?" Her towel fell to the floor, unveiling the smooth, pale curve of her back and the most glorious ass that had ever graced the planet. Blood rushed to his cock, swelling his shaft. She leaned over to grab something from one of the drawers, giving him a view that truly deserved to be worshipped. That is—if he could've managed to move and drop to his knees with his dick so damn hard.

"No, baby," Markus said. "I'm the one who's feeling quite blessed."

She stepped into an undergarment, pulled it up, and a thin strap of black lace nestled between her cheeks. A groan rolled from his throat, and his cock throbbed. Fucking hell. How could one be envious of a single piece of cotton? He palmed the aching bulge pressed against his zipper.

"Are you on patrol tonight?" she asked, as if she were oblivious to his physical anguish. *Vixen.* She knew exactly what she was doing to him. Finishing her task of dressing, she tugged up a pair of tight leather pants, the cowhide conforming to her rear like a damn second skin.

Fuck this. She belonged to him. And it was about damn time he did something about it. He couldn't go another night without making her his. For eternity.

"Markus?"

"What?"

"I asked if you were on patrol tonight?" She smiled. "Where did you go?"

He swung his legs off the bed and stood. "I was thinking about you."

"Well." She shrugged, then quickly donned a shirt. "How can a girl be mad at that?" She slid a palm under her hair and pulled the damp strands free.

"No. I don't have to work tonight." Markus moved in and wrapped his arm around her shoulders, bringing her close. "We have someplace we need to be."

"We do?" she asked.

He phased, and the room around them shimmered into nothingness. The floor fell away, and they were in dizzying flight, weightless. Mere seconds later, they landed, coalescing in the basement of his mountain cabin.

"Whoa." Alexandria grabbed his arm, steadying herself. "You could warn a girl."

"No time." Markus tugged her around until her chest collided with his. "I needed this too badly."

He fused his mouth with hers, diving inside. She moaned, and he swallowed the sound. Her flavor sparked his already-simmering desire. So damn good.

Breaking away, Alexandria gasped. "Not that I'm not loving this," she said, patting his chest. "But why are we here?"

That was his vixen. Tenacious. She'd never been easily swayed from what she had on her mind. "I brought you here because I thought it was time we made what we have together permanent."

Her forehead wrinkled in disbelief and she took a step back. "Are you asking me to marry you?"

"I want more than that, baby." He closed the distance between them, unable to stand another moment without her touch. "Something deeper. Unbreakable." He pressed his body to hers, loving the way he could sense her every inhale. "Mate with me, Vixen." It wasn't a question. Hell, no. He was bastard enough to put it out there like a command, because the idea of her rejection wasn't compatible with his existence.

"You're serious…" She maneuvered out of his arms and turned away.

And his heart crashed against his breastbone.

"Yeah," he muttered. "I'm damn serious." He clasped her wrist, needing to make sure she didn't make a run for it. "You don't want this?"

She glanced over her shoulder, and he could have sworn moisture welled in her eyes. Looking up at him from under her lashes, she croaked, "You jerk." She shoved at him, knocking him backward. "Of course I want this…more than anything. You caught me off guard." She shook her head. "I just needed a moment to catch my breath."

"Damn, Vixen." Markus smoothed a hand over his chest.

"I'm not normally a fan of surprises." She crossed her arms under her breasts, pushing them up until they swelled in the vee of her sleeveless black leather tank top.

"That makes two of us," he grumbled, finding it hard to think straight with her cleavage making his fingers itch.

"But for you, and for this occasion, I'm happy to make an exception." She smiled, and with a sway of her hips, moved within reach.

"Well, aren't I the lucky vampire tonight?" He gave her his best arrogant smirk.

"Yes, you are," she said. "And I'm the most fortunate female on earth." She licked her lips, forcing a growl from his throat at the sight.

"That's right." His voice went primal. "You're mine." He fisted her hair and tugged her head back. A sharp exhale escaped her, but her eyes flashed with arousal.

Fuck. His shaft bucked against the restraint of his zipper. He wanted her so damn bad. Right there. Bent over the bed rails. Her legs bare. Thighs spread wide. Her pussy wet, glistening, yearning for his cock.

But that would have to wait. Markus uncurled his fist from her hair. He had to do this right.

"So how do we do this?" She ran her fingers beneath his shirt, her nails scratching over his abs. And he couldn't help but imagine them running over the head of his dick. He groaned.

"First, you're going to have to stop what you're doing," he said. "If not, I'm going to be inside you, and we'll never get around to mating."

"Well, we wouldn't want that," she drawled, and pulled her hand away. "I do enjoy teasing you, though, and getting you all hot and bothered." Smiling, she tugged his shirt back in place.

"Don't worry, Vixen," he said. "You'll get your chance."

Markus maneuvered around her and over to the night-stand, where a few days before he'd placed a pouch containing what they would need. Mating her had never been a question. Alexandria had been his from the first moment he'd seen her. He'd only been waiting for the perfect moment.

"This is for you." He handed over the dark blue velvet bag and began undressing.

"What's inside?"

"Pull the gloves out and put those on first." He tossed his shirt onto the chair behind him and worked on shedding his boots and jeans. "The bindings inside contain silver."

"Oh…" Alexandria opened the drawstring to the soft material and proceeded as instructed. "I take it I'm going to be tying you to the bed with these?" she asked, straps in hand.

"That's right." Naked, Markus climbed onto the bed and stretched out onto his back. Still rigid, his cock settled onto his abs.

Smirking, she stared down at him. "Well, you seem mighty comfortable with the idea that I'm supposed to bind you with silver." She shook her head. "This is going to hurt like a bitch."

"Does it appear like I care?" He wagged his eyebrows, more than ready to proceed.

She stared back at him, scrutinizing his expression. "Not in the least."

"Then don't worry about me," he said, making damn sure she could see how much he needed her. "I want this, Vixen."

"So do I." Her tone was gentle, yet her expression had never been more serious.

"Do it," he commanded, and placed his arms over his head. "I have to submit to you, then you drain me."

"All of you?" Alexandria placed one binding around his wrist, and his flesh sizzled against the toxic metal.

Hissing, he bit down with his molars.

"Damn," she spat. "I'm sorry."

"I'm good," he gritted out. "And yeah. All of me," he

added. "Once you finish, my soul will seek yours out, and then you'll need to feed me. Bring me back. When I leave, I'll take a portion of you with me. Once I return and wake, it's over. We'll be blended." He inhaled deeply, bracing himself for the next wrist strap. She was so damn worth it.

"I can't wait for you to be a part of me," she said, and pulled the last binding tight.

Another sizzle filled his ears and the burn arrowed up his arm. He closed his eyes, dug his nails into his palms, and held on as the initial heat wave passed.

"From what I know that Elle's shared with me, we'll be able to communicate telepathically," she said. "Imagine how intimate that's going to feel."

"Fucking intense." His cock jerked. "I'll be able hear your thoughts, sense what you feel when I'm buried inside you," he said, his voice hoarse with growing lust.

Alexandria strolled around the foot of the bed, pulled her tank over her head, and allowed it to fall to the floor. Christ, she was a midnight seductress with her coal-black hair streaming in waves down her back.

She undid the hook to her bra. The lace tumbled down her arms, and her full breasts swung free. His mouth watered at the sight, fangs bursting from his gums. Holy hell, his cock pulsed, ached with need.

"Don't make me wait." Markus yanked on his bindings, rocking the bed.

"Never, my love." A sultry glow emanated from her violet gaze. Inserting her thumbs at the waistband of her pants, she shimmied out of the leather and the barely-there piece of cotton and lace covering her sex.

"Gorgeous," he rasped. "Come here, baby."

Like a succubus stalking her victim, Alexandria crawled onto the mattress and straddled his legs. Lowering her head to his cock, she looked up from under her lashes. "Submit to me, warrior," she commanded, her breath teasing his flesh.

"Yours." He groaned, and his shaft twitched with anticipation. No way in hell could he ever deny her. If she desired, he'd find a way to give her the moon.

Her tongue flicked out and she dragged the flat tip along the back of his cock from root to tip. A hard shudder seized his body.

"Fuck…" He grunted. "Again."

She gripped his rod with a tight fist, and his spine arched. "Who's in command here?"

"Shit." He sucked in a calming breath. "You are."

"That's better." She pulled his erection toward her mouth once more, and the head disappeared inside her lips.

Air punched free from his lungs. Sweet torture.

Slowly, her tongue followed the sensitive rim, exquisitely exploring every inch of him. His molars ached from the tension on his jaw. He had to hold back. No matter how badly his body screamed for release.

"Vixen…" He shook his head, squeezing his eyelids shut. "Can't… Fuck. Too good."

Suddenly, her warm, wet core enveloped his cock. His eyes sprang open as she sank over him, taking him balls-deep. He roared. The desire to grab her hips and drive into her over and over took him to the edge.

Her head lolled, and her thick midnight locks brushed his thighs. Nails biting into his legs, she slid up and down on his stiff shaft. Drenched with her arousal, his erection leisurely disappeared in and out of her pussy. The visual was maddening, destroying him.

"Goddammit," he bit out. "Fuck me." He panted.

She groaned, taking him, riding him. "Feels so good." She came forward, planting her palms onto his chest. "Never want this to end." The white tips of her fangs glinted in the pale room light.

"We never will, baby," he rumbled and twisted his head to the side, giving her access to his throat. And it was all the encouragement she needed. His love dived in, driving the sharp points into his vein.

"Alexandria!" he bellowed, his lungs burning as his orgasm burst from the head of his cock.

A gasp sounded at his neck, and she shuddered. "Markus…" she cried out, and her pussy clamped down on him. Her core pulsed around his shaft, drawing every drop of his cum from his balls.

"Christ!" he gritted out. "Love you."

She pulled at his vein, drinking him as she continued to rock up and down on him.

"That's it, baby," he murmured. "All of me." The room dimmed, and unbidden, his eyelids lowered. "Yours," the word fell from his lips, heavy, thick.

"Markus?" Her voice called to him from some distant plane. He needed to be there. But she was so damn far away.

"Vixen?" he yelled, but it was as if her name rang out only inside his head.

"Come to me, my love," Alexandria ordered.

And he had to obey. She was where he was meant to be.

Breaking free from his earthly body with ethereal fingers, he sought out his mate. Like a red-hot target for his icy form, a fiery glow surrounded his mate. He sank into her.

So warm. So very warm. A prism of color exploded before him, red, blue, and yellow, a welcoming firestorm.

"My love," her voice enveloped him. *"My God, Markus,"* she whispered inside his head.

"Alexandria…" She was glorious inside and out. Her spirit moved through him, danced in perfect time with his. They were made for each other. Destined to be one.

"You have to come back," she said. *"I need you here with me."*

Something tugged at him. It was as if some unseen force had seized the fibers of his otherworldly body and begun to reel him in. A part of him wanted to cry out at the injustice of having to leave a place so pure and divine. However, his other half knew there was more, a purpose he'd yet to fulfill.

"Drink, Markus," she shouted. "Come on, you stubborn bastard. You have to take more than that."

A tearing sensation resonated inside his head, yet there was no pain. Bright light flashed, and his world went mute. He was falling, spiraling toward some magnetic point. Yet there was no fear. Somehow he knew exactly where he'd land.

Sound exploded in his ears a split second before his gut cramped. Hunger, sharp and fierce, seized his mind.

"Alexandria?" he muttered and blinked, his surroundings hazy. That's when it hit him, like a switch had been flipped to *awake* on his taste buds. He groaned, and his cock surged to life. Alexandria's essence trickled down his throat.

"More, Vixen." He snarled and struck.

"Take from me, my mate."

"I hear you," he said, drawing more and more from her vein into his body. *"You did it, baby."*

"We did it," she replied, and there was no way to miss the smile in her words, even inside his head.

Satisfied for the moment, Markus withdrew his fangs and closed the wound to her wrist. Alexandria slid from his hips and onto her side.

"Having you in here"—Alexandria patted her chest—"I've never felt so whole and content in my life."

He closed his eyes, savoring the stirring of her spirit. Her mind hummed with life, yet somehow it wasn't annoying. The sensation felt right. "I know exactly what you mean."

"It feels like I've been waiting on you ever since the day I was born," she said, rising onto her elbow. "Even though our beginning was rocky, to say the least, you never surrendered. You pushed me, kicking and screaming, until you made me trust again." She grinned. "And I'm so glad I stopped fighting my feelings for you."

His heart swelling and hammering against his sternum, Markus cupped her face. "You were the one who never gave up on me. You brought me back to life, baby, and made me want to stay." He brushed his lips over hers. "You are my reason. My next breath. You've been a beacon shining through the dark." Threading his fingers through her soft strands, Markus tugged her closer. "I never want to lose your light."

"It's yours," she said, splaying her hand over his heart. "I'm yours. Forever."

Epilogue

"Have you talked to him?" Markus took another swig of the dark brew from his mug and lowered it to the granite. Kenric worked his fingers into his leather gloves.

"Not yet," the master of the Enclave said. "When Christian comes down, we'll learn together if this is what he wants."

"So it's happening this evening?" Arran brushed past Markus with his own cup.

"I believe it's time," Kenric said, and glanced over at his mate, who'd come up beside him. "Michael's prepared everything for us below." He wrapped a possessive arm around her, pulling her close. "In fact," he went on to say, "as I discussed earlier with Emily, this will be the perfect time for a renewal of sorts."

"A renewal?" Alexandria entered the kitchen and slipped her arms around Markus's waist. Her presence sent a tingling warmth up Markus's spine, comforting, yet stimulating at the same time. He swallowed a pleasure-filled groan. Having her in his life, as his mate, fulfilled him in more ways than he'd ever imagined.

Six millennia could have gone by and he would have never believed *his* life could be this good.

"Yes," Kenric replied. "A renewal for some and a new beginning for others."

Rumblings from the staircase telegraphed the arrival of Guerin with his mate. The pair headed over to join them.

"Did you stop by Christian's room and inform him we need to speak?" Kenric asked his second-in-command.

Guerin nodded. "Yeah. I told him you wanted to talk to him down in the command center. He said he'd be down in just a few."

"Good," the commander said. "And our ink guy?"

"On the way," Guerin added.

"Excellent." Kenric nodded. "I hope he's bringing a hell of a lot of black and red." He smirked. "Everyone," the elder vampire called out. "Please join us downstairs."

It'd been years since Markus had been part of an Enclave commitment ceremony. The last had been for Arran, his partner. They'd both been very different males back then, empty, withdrawn. Then Marguerite had come along, and emotionally, Markus had died inside.

Alexandria threaded her hand in his, her touch enticing him back to the present. He glanced down at her violet eyes, the love he found there drawing him in, fueling the next beat of his heart. His vixen. The moment she'd entered his world, she'd reawakened his soul.

"You ready?"

"You bet." Together they followed the others to the lower level.

Inside, the overhead lights were off, and the conference table glowed with what appeared to be a dozen fat red candles blazing down its center.

"Gather around," Kenric instructed.

The chairs had been removed, allowing each of them to take a place around the edge. Kenric stood at the head, Emily to his right, followed by Guerin, Eve, Alexandria, and Markus. Before each of them, a single silver-plated dagger lay flat, the blade pointing toward the center. The opposite side of the wood contained the same arrangement in front of Arran and Elle. An empty place remained for Christian. That is, if he chose to join them.

As if Markus had conjured the male with a thought, the basement door slid open and the redhead appeared.

The young vampire stepped into the room, his attention landing on the candlelit table surrounded by the warriors and their mates. "Wow!" he said. "I'm touched. And it isn't even my birthday."

"Get over here, you cocky SOB," Markus spat.

Dressed in a pair of well-worn jeans and a dark blue shirt with the top two buttons open, Christian sauntered over.

"What's going on?" He came to a stop at the end opposite the Enclave's master.

"It's time we make this official," Kenric stated, his arms crossed over his chest. "Christian Quinn, I hereby offer you a place among us as a warrior of the Enclave." Leaning forward, his fingers splayed, the master braced himself on the table's surface, locking his gaze with the vampire subject. "Do you accept this role to become a protector of humanity against those of our kind who are lost to Death Euphoria? Are you willing to lay down your life, if needed, to protect our species and to save those who cannot defend themselves?"

His expression stoic, Christian met the gaze of each male and female, as if evaluating his acceptance among them. Finally, he settled back on the commander. "I accept."

"Well done," Kenric said and with a wave of his hand indicated a spot for him next to Elle. Christian moved into his designated position.

"There's not a member of this house who hasn't put their life on the line at one point or another," Kenric said, addressing his team. "The Enclave isn't strictly a male group anymore. We've become a community. One that is made stronger by the females at our sides."

He turned his attention to Emily and tapped his mate with a nod. "Starting with you, my love, it's time I make this right. Emily Ross, I hereby offer you a place among us as a warrior of the Enclave."

The auburn-haired female's brows lifted, and Markus noticed her sharp inhale of surprise. *Nice work.*

Markus had to agree. The master's mate deserved an official spot among them. More than once in the past couple of years, she'd put herself out there without hesitation for the team. Not to mention the hell she'd endured and had overcome because of him. She was a worthy female.

After repeating the same declaration as he had with Christian, Kenric and the team waited for her reply.

With her shoulders squared and her chin high, Emily surveyed the others. When her attention fell to Elle, the other female met her with a smile and a nod. Moments later, Emily looked at Alexandria, who also gave her an approving subtle nod. Then it was Markus's turn. Except this time when he faced Emily the experience didn't resemble anything like their previous matchups. Her stare possessed no glaring challenge, no judgment. Instead, what he saw he could only define as…respect.

Damn.

It wasn't physically possible, but Markus could swear that under her inspection he grew an inch or two taller. He nodded, and the corners of her mouth lifted before she moved on and returned her attention to her mate.

"Absolutely," she replied.

The commander beamed, but quickly smoothed his expression for the remaining serious business at hand.

Next, he made the same proposal to the remaining females in the room: Eve, Elle, and Alexandria. Markus had to fight his own stupid grin as his vixen eagerly accepted Kenric's offer to join them.

"Last, but most definitely not least, I'd like to address Markus Santini," Kenric called out, capturing his full attention.

What the hell?

"Yes, sir?" Markus replied.

"I know you already bear the Enclave symbol on your shoulder, but as we all know, a lot has gone down between us since then," Kenric began. "Some things we'd all rather not remember. Others, we never want to forget." The elder vampire looked to his mate as if he needed a moment to gather his thoughts, savor a couple of memories. Then he continued. "One of those 'things' I'm pleased to recall is how, in the end, you pulled through. You came back to us, made it right, and you found yourself again. As far as I'm concerned, I never doubted there was a place inside you that never left us. That said, I'd like to formally offer you an opportunity to renew your vow to serve humanity. To reestablish your commitment here to your fellow Enclave warriors." Kenric fixed his attention on him, and for the first time in his life, Markus was floored.

Son of a flaming bitch.

A lump threatened to form in his chest. *Oh hell no.* What had falling in love done to him?

Rein it in, Santini.

It was the surprise element. That had to be it. He hadn't seen this coming.

And he hated surprises.

Kenric had mentioned a renewal, but Markus had thought in the informal sense. Not calling him out in front of the group and getting all sentimental and shit. The mushy stuff between him and his mate behind doors...that was different. Private. For her, he willingly exposed that side of himself. But not in front of the Enclave.

However, fuck it...he wouldn't trade this moment for any damn thing. This motley squad was his family. And he'd tolerate whatever they wanted to put him through. They'd ridden through hell and back with him, and after all was said and done, his fellow warriors had accepted his baggage. No matter how heavy it was.

"What do you say?" Kenric asked, jerking him back to the moment.

"I say...what are we waiting for?"

A cheer went up around the table.

"My sentiments precisely," Kenric said.

The commander stepped toward the rectangular oak cabinet along the wall. There, he collected a small hammered copper bowl and returned to the table. After placing it in front of him, Kenric gathered his dagger in his right hand.

"Sacrifice." The master vampire raised his wrist and placed the blade over his pulse. "Honor." He slid the serrated edge over his flesh, releasing a trail of crimson. "Loyalty." The flow trickled over the edge and into the glimmering copper beneath his arm. "These are the values of the Enclave. And through our blood we bind ourselves to the code. To one another."

The current warriors moved to the bowl and followed suit with their daggers. One by one, their essence mingled with the master's.

"Now, each new member," Kenric ordered, and Emily stepped up with her blade. She dragged the serrated edge over her wrist and allowed her blood to flow into the bowl. Her mate stood by her side, watching, and no one could miss the expression of pride on his face.

Eve came next, then Elle, Christian, and lastly, Alexandria. Without a moment's hesitation, she made her incision. She'd worked hard for this honor, and he, too, was damn proud of his mate.

Sealing her wound, Alexandria stepped away and Markus moved into place. The flickering candlelight gleamed off the garnet fluid inside the copper as he fisted the hilt of his dagger.

Unreal.

Over the last several months, Markus would have bet that he'd be dead before being offered a spot back inside the Enclave. He glanced over at Alexandria, who stood by his side.

This moment.

This female.

Proof that even for bastards like him miracles still occurred and dreams could come true.

Markus's blade bit into his flesh, sharp, burning, but the pain was irrelevant, trivial compared to what it symbolized: a family bond. One that he'd die for before he ever allowed anything or anyone to try to sever those ties again.

With Markus's life's essence added and his vein sealed, Kenric collected the receptacle. Raising it up above his head, the master vampire addressed his Enclave. "Unity in our blood and our mind-set. Defend humanity. Protect our existence." Bringing the vessel to his mouth, he added, "Drink, Enclave." He sipped from the bowl, then offered it to his second-in-command.

Guerin accepted, drank, and passed it to Arran. Around the table the vessel moved, each vampire sipping from the dark mixture. Blending a portion of each warrior within themselves.

The bowl made its way to Markus, and he cupped the round container between his hands, the metal warming his palms. His pulse thumped inside his ears as the heady cocktail rocking inside the copper tantalized his senses. He brought the vessel to his lips, his mouth watering, and tipped the contents onto his tongue. The powerful mixture electrified his taste buds and ignited his esophagus. He groaned as it merged into his being. His veins sizzled.

Damn, what a rush.

A low rumble grew around him, every male and female joining in.

"Enclave!" a shout rang out, each warrior fisting their weapon, lifting them, hilts pointed upward and toward the center of the table. "Enclave!" again they bellowed.

His heart pounded from the sound, from the mingling of their essences inside him. He needed his female. Now more than ever, he needed to be inside his mate. He wanted her inside his mind as she flowed through his veins, their hearts beating in time.

The revelry mellowed to adrenaline-laced chatter, and he bent his head to her ear. "Let's get out of here."

"Are you sure?" she whispered back. "Kenric will be okay if we leave?"

"The ceremony's over," Markus said. "He'll be fine if we head out."

"What about my tattoo? My Enclave symbol?" She grinned.

Markus wrapped his arm around her. "I'll make sure you're back in time to get yours, Vixen," he rumbled in her ear. Her palm clasped his cheek in sensual response.

Reluctantly he tugged himself free. "Hey, you guys," Markus called out and all heads turned his way. "If you'll excuse us, Alexandria and I have something we need to take care of."

"You have to leave now? We're about to celebrate," Arran said. "And lay down some ink."

"This can't wait," Markus said, giving Alexandria a gentle squeeze to her shoulder.

Kenric nodded as if he somehow understood the urgent need for their exit. "Enjoy," he said. "We can take care of Alex's symbol once you return."

"Thanks," Markus said. "Catch you all later." He slid his arm around her waist, drawing her near. Leaning in, he lowered his voice for her ears only. "We have a celebration of our own to attend."

Acknowledgments

To the best critique partner a writer could ever hope for, Naima Simone, you are a true blessing from God. Best of all, I get to call you my friend. I can't imagine doing this without you. Love you, girl!

To my editor Erin Molta, thank you for sticking with me throughout this series! Your insight and patience have been truly appreciated. I look forward to working with you on many more titles and series to come!

About the Author

Jessica Lee is an EPIC eBook Award winner and international best-selling author of paranormal romance. She lives in the southeastern United States with her husband and son. In her former life, Jessica was a science geek and spent more than twenty-five years as a nurse. But after the birth of her son, she left her medical career behind and discovered her passion for writing romance. And she's never looked back! Jessica Lee is currently published with Entangled Publishing and Resplendence Publishing, plus several self-published titles.

Enjoy Jessica Lee's titles? You're invited to join Jessica and Naima's Saints and Sinners street team.

To sign up for Jessica's FREE Newsletter go to: http://eepurl.com/b_Lcf

For all her latest information, please visit www.jessicaleenovels.com